THE ACCIDENTAL FAIRY

THE ACCIDENTALS

BOOK 14

DAKOTA CASSIDY

ABOUT THIS BOOK

Did you ever think you'd meet a bigger, foul-tempered potty mouth than Nina? Well, folks, meet Primrose Dunham.

It's Christmas and as the OOPs gang prepares for the holidays another "accident" finds its way to their doorstep. That accident turns out to be angry, foul-mouthed, rude and, well...

Just like Nina.

Primrose Dunham has been accidentally turned into a fairy. As if she wasn't already angry enough with the world, now she has sporadic powers she can't control, pointy ears, and a weird hump on her back that everyone keeps calling a "wing."

If that's not enough of a shock, a vampire, a were-wolf and a halfsie come to her "rescue"...whether she wants them to help or not.

Oh, and the man she's been trying to avoid—the literal boy next door and her one-time bestie, Rafferty Monroe—gets turned as well, thanks to Primrose!

It'll take more than a Christmas miracle to thaw Prim's frosty attitude, protect her from her sinister stepfather, and figure out why there's a price on her head in the fairy world. But it's nothing the OOPs ladies—along with assorted paranormal friends and framily—can't handle. Right?

COPYRIGHT

The Accidental Fairy

 The Accidentals

 Book 14

 Editor Kelli Collins

 Cover Art Katie Wood

 Published 2023 by Dakota Cassidy

 Copyright © 2023, Dakota Cassidy

 All rights reserved.

This book is a work of fiction. Any similarity to actual persons, living or dead, locales, or events is wholly coincidental. The names, characters, dialogue, and events in this book are from the author's imagination and should not be construed as real.

DEDICATION

My ever-faithful darlings,

I almost can't believe we're embarking on yet another accidental adventure, but we meet again! Thank you for showing up. I don't know what keeps you coming back, but I'm sure glad you do!

As to this edition, please note, I've played fast and loose with fae folklore and the stories surrounding them to suit my own selfish needs—as in, I took bits and pieces from each country's legends about fairies and mixed 'em all up to make my own batter. Any and all mistakes/tweaking of ancient mythology are mine and mine alone.

Huge thanks to my youngest son, he himself a software engineer, for explaining the correct lingo for Prim's profession. I love you, buddy. You'll always be my little Antichrist.

Also, eternal thanks to my amazing Facebook folks for helping pick the heroine's name. Y'all are the best!

I'll see you next year with two more Accidentals. Until then, if you celebrate the holidays, no matter what you celebrate, stay safe, stay warm, and my fondest wish for you...I hope it's spent with the people you love. Much prosperity to you and yours for the coming year!

Love,

Dakota XXOO

ONE

"What the ever-lovin' fuckity-fuck is this?" groused a beautiful Amazonian-ish woman with hair like ribbons of ebony silk falling down her back, nearly reaching her waist.

She held Primrose Dunham between her slender fingers with a sour expression of absolute distaste. Lifting her high, this stunningly pale creature examined her under the blinding light of an unfamiliar kitchen.

You said it, sister. What the ever-lovin' fuckity-fuck?

As Prim looked around at this beautiful kitchen with its shiny appliances, Christmas lights strung from every corner, baskets big and small filled with shiny ornaments and decorative balls on the counter and the floor by a big dining room table, she realized everything looked *enormous*.

As if she'd been shrunk...

Had she been drugged? How could this be real?

Two more ladies came to stand by the beautiful woman, their eyes squinting, brows furrowed. One blonde and pretty with flawless makeup, sapphire-blue eyes, and bouncy, beach-waved curls brushing the length of her spine. The other with chestnut-brown hair, upswept and shiny, her makeup tasteful and elegant, her eyes soft and kind.

"Well, I'll be dipped," the blonde muttered with a cluck of her tongue. "Where in all the world did you find something like *this*, Mistress of the Dark?"

"Oh, fuck you, Ass-Sniffer, I didn't *find* it. It found me. It came flying at me outside like some drunk toddler when I was with Carl and Charlie, building a fucking snowman. Buzzed me in the head, so I snatched the fucker up in my hand."

Yeah, she had.

Like some kind of blurred fucking ninja.

It had been an accident, of course. She'd zapped the pale lady in the face because she had no idea what she was doing, and with the speed of light, this alleged Mistress of the Dark had reached up and caught Primrose midair, effectively stopping her *wings* from moving.

Because how the fuck was she supposed to know how to make goddamn wings work? She knew they were wings because she'd felt them fluttering behind her.

But the bigger question still remained, how did she get wings to begin with?

Jesus and shit.

"Why are you catching bugs, Nina?" Ass-Sniffer asked as she made a face. "Could you be any weirder than you already are?"

Nina shoved Primrose in Ass-Sniffer's face. "Eat a bag of dicks, Marty. I'm not catching bugs. Look at the fucking thing."

"Is that a firefly? How curious that a firefly survived the snow and colder temperatures," the elegant lady said, her voice soft as she hugged a young boy of maybe three or four—with skin that had a green cast to it—on her hip. "I thought they died off after the summer."

The dark-haired goddess made a face and even though it was an unattractive one, she still managed to be supermodel flawless.

"It's not a fucking firefly, Wanda. Use those half-werewolf, half-vampire eyes and look at the GD thing." Now she jammed Primrose in the pretty lady's face, forcing a squeal from her mouth when she pinched her wings too tight.

Her wings. How, in all of the fucked up of fucked up, did she get wings?

"Fucking firefly! You're so funny, Auntie Nina," the little green child repeated with a giggle.

Nina leaned over and dropped a kiss on the small boy's head with a grin so stunning, it might have taken Primrose's breath away if she weren't already breathless, because, you know, she had wings...

"You're gonna get Auntie Nina grounded." She took him from Wanda with one arm and gave him an affectionate squeeze when he wrapped his arms around her neck.

"I love you, Auntie Nina," he cooed, burying his face in her cascade of hair.

"I love you, too, Green Bean. Now quit sayin' the stuff I say, because it's bad and it's gonna get you time in the thinking corner and we all know how much you love the thinking corner. Get on outta here, little man, and go find Carl and Grampa Arch and see what they're up to." Nina dropped another kiss on his dark head before setting him on the floor with a pat to his backside.

The lady named Wanda sighed with a happy smile as she watched him scurry off to find the people Nina was talking about.

"He's getting so big, isn't he?" Then she shook an authoritative finger at the pale woman, her lips pursing. "And if you don't stop using that foul language around my son, I'm going to borrow some of the duct-tape you use on Carl and tape your potty mouth shut, Vampire."

Um, duct-tape? Who was Carl and why did they use duct-tape on him? What kind of freaky-deaky double-Dutch shit was that?

"Shut the fuck up, Wanda, and look at this thing, would ya?"

Nina jammed Primrose back under Wanda's nose, her tiny legs dangling perilously as she wobbled in her steel grip. The very pretty lady named Wanda's eyes widened and she blinked before pressing a hand to her mouth. "It's...a...little person? Holy mackerel... What is it?"

Apparently, Wanda had used her half-werewolf-half-vampire eyes. *Half-werewolf, half-vampire? Like, what?* What was happening?

Primrose, for all her shock and dismay, finally managed to speak up. Trust that for someone as fond of confrontation as she was, to have been rendered incapable of speaking might be considered a miracle by some of the people she'd tongue-lashed.

"I'm not an *it*, lady! I'm a fucking *she*! Now let go of me, or I'll blast your sorry ass into next year!"

Now the blonde lady, Marty, peered at her as though she was some science project to be examined under a microscope.

She gasped, too. "It's a person, Nina! A cute little person with...wings! She has wings, and they're so pretty! Give her to me this instant before you hurt her!"

The blonde lady, her bracelets jangling in the quiet of the kitchen, tried to snatch Primrose away from the woman named Nina, but she batted her hand away and held her higher still.

"Get the fuck outta here, Marty. Whatever the fuck it is, I'd bet my ass it's a shitty problem we don't need just before Christmas. I have plans for the holiday and I'm not gonna let them get trashed. *It's* going back outside where it came from."

Primrose winced. But...but... Her wings had just begun to de-ice. It was damn cold outside. Ask her. She knew. She'd only flown what felt like a zillion miles to get here.

"Plans?" Marty scoffed, crossing her arms over her winter-white, knee-length sweater, blocking the taller woman's exit from the kitchen. "To do what, exactly, Nina? Bake cookies you can't eat? String popcorn? Go door to door caroling and make every male cat in the neighborhood line up outside my house because they think you're in heat and your singing sounds like a boy band member's being skinned alive? *Please.* Who are you kidding? You don't have plans because *we* don't have plans. We do everything together, especially the holidays, and you know it."

Nina stuck her neck out, jamming her face in Marty's. "Maybe I *am* gonna make cookies. Maybe I'm goin' rogue this year for Christmas. How about that, Ass-Sniffer? You don't fucking know."

Hold that thought. Forget everything else. Forget the tone of dismissal in Marty's voice and Nina's defensive but feeble denial. Forget the bit about vampires and werewolves. Forget that she'd admitted she had wings.

This incredibly beautiful woman couldn't eat cookies?

Blasphemy!

Why couldn't she eat cookies? Who can't eat cookies? Though, maybe that was why her skin was so flawless and eerily pore-free.

Nina held her up again, swishing her back and forth like a supper bell under Marty's nose. "So *no*. No can do, Marty. I'm not gonna get stuck with whatever the fuck this is."

"Hey!" Primrose yelped. "Stop manhandling the goods, lady!"

Wanda's eyes flew open wide. "Did you hear that? The tiny person talks!"

Tiny person. Hah. She was almost six feet on a good day, thank you very much.

Nina frowned. "I didn't hear a fucking thing. Open the door, Wanda, because it's goin' the fuck outside!"

Wanda's eyes narrowed, her beautiful orbs glittering. "If I heard it, you heard it, Nina. I'm not the only one with vampire hearing. Give it to me, now!" She held out a hand with a stern look the nuns from Prim's old Catholic school would bow down before, but Nina shook her head.

Vampire hearing?

Vam-pire-hear-ing, Primrose. You heard her.

"Nope. Not today, Wanda. I'm not gettin' caught up in some shit because you can't mind your own business and not bake cookies for every fucking stray that crosses our path. Now, leave well enough alone. *It* goes back outside."

"Give it to me, Vampire, or I'm going to kick your scrawny ass!" Marty yelped.

If this were an ordinary day in the life of Primrose Dunham, she'd applaud Marty's threat. She wasn't afraid to throw hands either—to the great dismay of her therapist.

But this wasn't a normal day in her life. This was stupid crazy.

When Nina refused to hand Primrose over, Marty tilted her chin upward, her eyes aglow.

There was a low growl, a snarl that for as long as Primrose Dunham lived, she'd never forget. And then there was hair. Big, bushy tufts of it sailing across the room. So much hair and teeth.

Lord, those teeth...

"Marty! No!" Wanda yelled, lunging for the beast who'd simply appeared before her very eyes, this thing that looked as though it was straight out of a movie set.

But slow that roll. Had Wanda just called the beast *Marty*? How had that gorgeous, blue-eyed blonde turned into...*that?*

There was no time to ponder more as Marty rushed Nina, crashing into her long torso, Primrose got a bird's-eye view of the pointy teeth that shot out of Nina's gums before she was launched across the room.

Primrose went sailing across the kitchen, cabinets and shiny appliances whizzing by before she slammed into a hard surface.

Dizzy, she slid down the cupboard door and slumped against the lower cabinet, vaguely noting the ball of hair rolling toward her looked like the size of a killer bunny.

"Ladies!" a short blue man with a tuft of equally blue hair, dressed in a pristine black suit covered by an apron that read "Kiss the Cook", shouted and stomped his foot. "Have I not warned you this behavior is unacceptable in a household I run? I will not have this sort of discord around the children! This isn't WrestleMania, this is our home—act like it! If you wish to come to fisticuffs, you will take it outside!" Then he whipped off his apron, covering his eyes and holding it out into the room. "Mistress Marty, you will put this on your person this instant!"

Primrose scrunched her eyes shut, trying not only to block out the pain in her back and the throb of her skull, but the scene that had just played out before her.

Because it was mad nuts. Absolute insanity.

So much so, Primrose fought to process it even as her body lurched forward.

Bending at the waist, her limbs jerked and shook, and her heart thrashed about in her chest as though it were fighting its way out from under her skin.

She groaned at the searing pain in her back, rolling to her side to note there was something hanging off her big toe. She stared at it long and hard before coming to a strange conclusion.

It was a tiny hiking boot.

Her boot?

Wiggling her fingers and toes, Prim blinked then shot forward in surprise. She ran her hands over her limbs, checking every part of her person.

Holy shit! She was back to normal! Scrambling to her feet, she forgot about the tiny hiking boot—and that, likely, everything else she'd had on when this whole fiasco started was the same Barbie-doll size as her shoe—and tried to bolt.

Until everyone gasped, so loud and so sharp, it made her ears ring. She looked at all of them and their surprised expressions.

"What?"

The short blue man cleared his throat, his eyebrows raised. "Madame, might I offer you something to cover yourself? A robe, perhaps?"

She looked down the length of her body and gulped. Well, fuck.

With a wince, she looked around the homey kitchen, desperately trying to hide her nakedness.

Yanking a kitchen towel from the wall oven handle, she shook it out and lamely made an attempt to press it to her breasts while placing a hand over her southerly regions.

Everyone stood stock still. Marty, her hair a ruffled mess of various shades of blonde, wore nothing but an apron. Nina, the dark beauty, her elongated teeth gleaming in the overhead kitchen lights. And lastly Wanda, her upswept hair now disheveled, one low-heeled shoe lost in the melee.

Every last one of them gaping at her like she was some sideshow freak.

That was when her unfiltered big mouth took over.

Prim straightened and glared back at them in indignant defiance. "Excuse the fuck out of me, but after what I just saw, who the fuck do you think you are, staring at *me*?"

Quite suddenly, the very pale Nina tipped her head back and began to laugh—or maybe it was cackle.

Primrose tilted her head and cocked her ear.

Yeah, that was definitely a cackle.

CHAPTER TWO

Wanda was the first to move toward her, her palms facing forward in a gesture of peace, but Primrose was having none of it.

She eyeballed a crock filled with cooking utensils on the sleek white counter beside her and grabbed the first thing she could plant her hand on to use as a weapon.

Maybe a spaghetti serving spoon wasn't terribly threatening, but it was better than nothing.

Until she realized she'd removed her hand from the apex of her thighs. But whatever. This was kill or be killed. A little pubis mons reveal wasn't going to stop her.

Prim held the spoon out in front of her and waved it at them. "Stay the fuck away from me or I'll beat your asses black and blue!" she hissed, using the spoon like she was a saber-fighting Jedi.

The Nina woman snorted and cackled again. "Chill the fuck out. We're not gonna hurt you. Unless you keep waving that shit at me," she groused, snatching the spoon clean out of her hand. "Better be careful, or I'm gonna go get the fly swatter."

Show no fear. She'd dealt with her share of bullies in her time. Being as tall and thin as she was since the fifth grade, there'd been plenty of fat-mouthed boys who'd had something to say about it, and she'd whipped every one of their snarky asses.

Primrose straightened until she was eyeball to eyeball with this flawless goddess. "Fuck you! Stay the hell away from me."

Nina smiled, a maniacal grin full of devilish amusement that revealed very white, very straight teeth. "Yeah. Right. Or you'll beat us with your scary spaghetti spoon in a naked fight to the fucking death? Try me."

"Nina! Don't frighten the poor thing," Wanda ordered, cracking her neck and running a hand along her silky rose-colored shirt.

For the first time, Primrose noticed Nina's T-shirt beneath her black hoodie. It read: "I Eat Children."

She gulped harder. Judging from Nina's whole persona, that probably wasn't a total lie, but it didn't explain her affection for the little boy. Still, why take chances?

"Just let me get the hell out of here and I'll be out of your hair."

Marty smoothed said hair, using the window on the wall oven to see her reflection, and wrinkled her nose. "And how will you do that? It's twenty degrees out, you've shredded your tiny clothes like the Hulk, you're naked as a blue jay, and we're miles from town. How about you just let us help you instead—because it looks like you're going to need help. Or is turning into a bug with wings something you do on the reg?"

"We can help," Wanda backed Marty's statement.

Help her? After what she'd just witnessed? After all that hair and teeth and talk of vampires and were-wolves? Wasn't that akin to inviting the devil for a sleepover?

No thanks. She didn't need any help. Well, maybe a coat or something. Possibly a pair of shoes. Okay, maybe a ride back to her place.

Fine. She needed help. But it wasn't anything she couldn't get from an Uber and a trip to the local Target.

She'd had a lot of therapy to help deal with her hot head and her anger issues. She'd learned lots of techniques she was tossing to the curb in favor of her favorite pastime. Lashing out.

And where does being angry get you, Primrose? What will you achieve? Will it get you what you want, or will it simply satisfy your lust for destruction and then you'll suffer the consequences? She heard Dr. Shay's gentle, soothing voice ask those all-too-familiar questions in her head.

But she'd been talking about people like her boss, and that stupid bitch of a Karen in HR who was always complaining about dress codes and her hiking boots. She hadn't given her rules for managing her anger with people who grew hair and teeth.

However, she had seen results with Dr. Shay's methodology.

Deciding to take a kinder road to a pending exit from this madness, Primrose shook her head, twisting her mother's ring around her pinky finger—a coping mechanism Dr. Shay had taught her to keep her anger in check.

Think about your mother, she'd said. *Think about how she would handle this situation and how proud of you she'd be if she saw you deal with this in a courteous, respectful manner—even if you don't think the situation warrants your respect.*

Thus, Prim responded. "No, thank you. I'm fine. I don't need help. I'll just be on my way," she said woodenly, because even after a year of therapy, it was still uncomfortable for her to express anything but angry outrage when in a sticky situation.

And this was sticky. Or maybe it was defensive. Either way, it wasn't good, and all she wanted to do was go home to her dog and cat and climb in bed and forget everything she'd seen in the last few days.

Christ, the shit she'd seen. Toadstools the size of her living room furniture. Colorful lights on umbrella-like trees. And a dungeon...

Nina clucked her tongue. "You learn that shitty speech in therapy?"

Primrose tilted her head, and snapped, "Sound familiar?"

Before Nina could get to her and wrap her hands around her throat, Wanda was between them, holding out a fuzzy bathrobe the blue man had given her, wearing a disapproving scowl. "Why don't you put this on and we'll talk, yes? It's obvious something is happening and you need help. So let's start with who you are. Okay?"

Give her captors her name? No, ma'am. Not today. No matter how amicable and pleasant these nutjobs were.

As Wanda waited for her to speak, Marty pulled her shredded sweater over her head and smiled warmly. "I'm Marty Flaherty. This is Wanda Jefferson, and the mouthy broad is Nina Statleon. It's nice to meet you."

She eyed the woman's hand, her nails painted a soft blue, shiny rings on her fingers, and mentally shook her head. Nope.

Rather than take Marty's hand, Prim lifted her chin and refused to tell them her name. "You don't need to know my name, but thanks for the threads."

She snatched the bathrobe from Marty and held it in front of her, realizing there was no way to put it on unless she dropped the towel.

Nina rolled her eyes and spat, "Close your fuckin' eyes so Nameless can put her robe on."

Prim licked her lips and muttered, "Thank you." Again, her response was wooden and stilted, but it was the courteous thing to say. According to her therapist, anyway.

She had to start saying the right things and stop exploding or she was going to end up doing jail time. If it hadn't been for Rafferty and a really nice, animal-loving cop, she'd already be in the clink for assault and battery over a dog. But in fairness, the asshole had deserved it.

Even while he'd been carrying on about his *injuries*, he'd threatened her. Right before they'd stuffed her into a patrol car, he said they'd see each other again and she'd be sorry.

Prim would have flipped him off if she wasn't in handcuffs. Instead, she'd made things worse by telling him to eat a bag of crusty dicks.

Still, whether the asshole deserved it or not, that wasn't the way to handle her anger. She'd been lucky to get away with court-ordered therapy sessions and probation.

Prim didn't know if these women would call the police, but she wasn't going to stick around to find out —because she didn't want to do probation again.

As everyone closed their eyes and she shrugged on the robe, Prim squared her shoulders and took a deep breath, heading for the door.

"Hold up," Nina demanded. "How the fuck do you plan to go anywhere with no shoes and a bathrobe? Sit the fuck down and stop being a dipshit." She pointed to a round table in the kitchen made of wood, meant to seat an enormous amount of people.

You know, she was really putting an effort into the mantras Dr. Shay had taught her, but this woman? This beautiful monster with pointy teeth and pale skin was testing her ability to maintain her new cool.

"I said, *I'm going now*. Thank you for the robe. If you'll tell me where the fuc— Where I am, I'd be happy to send it back to you through UPS."

Wanda's soft voice intervened. "Nina, kindly shut it. *Please*. You weren't exactly welcoming. How else would you expect this poor woman to feel after you threatened to throw her back out into the freezing cold? Now, let Marty and I handle this. You sit quietly and *do not* interfere or I'm going to make you regret it."

Prim wanted to stick her tongue out at Nina, but she figured riling her up might trigger something as whacked as what Marty had done earlier, and she wasn't sure she was ever going to sleep again at night as it was. So she refrained.

Instead, Prim locked eyes with the softer, quieter Wanda. "I appreciate the offer, but I don't need any help. I'm leaving now."

As she attempted to make her way toward the door, which she could see from across the large expanse of the open-concept space, Marty stepped in front of her, her blue eyes warm and sympathetic.

"Do you really think that's a good idea, considering..."

"Considering?"

Marty reached around and plucked at the back of Prim's neck where something was poking her skin, something she'd opted to ignore in order to beat feet the hell out of here. "Your wings, silly. Or wing, I guess. Right now, you have only one and it's beautiful. But won't it be hard to catch an Uber with your bare feet, a bathrobe, and a wing poking out of your collar?"

Making an attempt at fearless, Prim looked over her shoulder at her reflection in the row of windows overlooking the farm sink.

An iridescent, sparkly tip of gossamer pink and blue winked at her.

Listen, she'd been in plenty of pickles in her twenty-nine years. Most of them because she didn't know how to keep her mouth shut and she liked a good verbal spar. But this time? This time she hadn't done anything. Nothing.

One minute she'd been sound asleep next to her dog, Freddy Mercury, and her cat, Katy Purry; the next, she was in some weird room that looked like it came from medieval times, stuck in a damn jar.

And now she had a wing. She couldn't take the hit for this one.

Prim blinked. "I..."

Wanda took her hand, her soft skin warm and soothing when she clasped Prim's. "You don't understand, but we do. Please tell us your name so we can help you—because we *can* help."

Prim licked her dry lips and found herself being led to the kitchen table, where a Christmas tree shaped plate of freshly baked snickerdoodles sat, along with a steaming mug of coffee.

The blue man with the blue hair (she couldn't believe she was witnessing this) appeared out of nowhere and smiled at her, his eyes gentle as he sat her in the chair. "I do so hope you like coffee, Mistress...?"

"Primrose...uh, Dunham. Or Prim is fine." He'd asked so nicely, she found herself doing the exact opposite of her original plan, which was to keep her stupid, flappy mouth shut.

He winked and chucked her under the chin. "Prim 'tis, then. I'm Archibald, or Grampa Arch, as the children call me. Is coffee acceptable or would you prefer tea?"

Prim thought about asking for a stiff drink, but decided against dulling her senses—not yet, anyway. When she got home, she was going to bathe in a bottle of vodka.

Nodding, she looked at him and tried to remember her manners. "Coffee's fine. Oh, and...um, thank you."

Marty and Wanda both sat down and waited as

she sipped her coffee, pushing the plate of cookies in front of her.

That's when she wondered if they were drugged. Maybe these people had something to do with what had happened to her in the first place, and this was all some ruse to fool her—to woo her into a state of submission?

Like Hansel and Gretel, when the witch fattens the children up with treats before lobbing their asses into the oven.

Prim stopped mid-sip and set the mug down, despite the enticement of rich hazelnut, folding her hands in her lap.

Nina leaned over the table and eyeballed her, her dark eyes like pools of chocolate. "Drink the fucking coffee, Primrose. Nobody's drugging you, you moron. If we wanted you dead, you'd be dead. Trust and believe."

"Nina! What did I just say? Shut your face," Wanda ordered before turning to Prim and scooping up her mug to take a sip. Then she bit into the soft cookie and nibbled the bite. "See? No drugs. Please, have something to warm you up, Primrose. You must be frozen after being outside with so little on. Plus, Arch will be offended if you don't at least have one."

Shit, those cookies looked good, and if Prim were honest, she'd admit she was chilled to the bone. That skimpy albeit shiny leotard and frilly tutu she'd been zapped into weren't exactly made for this kind of weather.

Yet, wherever she'd been while in that glass jar, before she'd escaped, had been warm. How she'd ended up in that cuckoo outfit to begin with was yet another facet to this nightmare she wasn't ready to delve into.

But she couldn't resist the cookie. She had a sweet tooth that wouldn't be denied and she couldn't remember the last time she'd eaten.

Prim took a bite and sat in silence as they looked her over, sending messages to one another with their eyes.

She was no good at the girly shit every other woman on the planet seemed to excel at, so she didn't try to figure out what they were saying. Prim Dunham was a straight shooter.

Her next words made that clear. "Why are you all fucking looking at me like I'm the one who's weird? That's not my damn hair rolling around the floor like a tumbleweed." She pointed at the huge tuft blowing past her bare feet.

Marty laughed, a tinkling sound not unpleasant to Prim's ears. "Fair enough. We're not staring to be rude. We're trying to figure out what you are and how you came to be. So why don't you tell us how this happened."

She didn't have an answer. "I don't know. One minute I was in my bed with my dog and my cat, getting ready to crash because I had a shitty day, the next I was..."

Wanda cocked her head as she nibbled delicately on a cookie, her eyes wide with anticipation. "You were...?"

Fucked. Well and truly fucked.

THREE

When she didn't answer, Nina ever so kindly filled in the blanks. "You were somewhere you didn't fucking recognize."

Fucking bingo. Prim gave a slow nod, swallowing her bite of delicious cookie. "Yes."

"And where was that, Prim?" Marty asked, letting her chin drop to the palm of her hand, her eyes filled with interest.

"A glass jar in a dungeon." That was the best way to describe what she'd witnessed. A dungeon. She didn't remember a lot about it, but she did remember the feeling deep in her gut that she needed to escape.

Nina tucked her hair behind her ears. "A fucking *dungeon*? Define dungeon. BDSM? Whips, chains, ball gag, Mistress Naughty Pants, dungeon?"

Prim blinked, tucking the bathrobe around her neck, suddenly chilled. "*What?!* No. A *dungeon*,

dungeon. You know, like medieval-castle, Disney dungeon. Heavy wood door with a barricade on it. Candles lit all along the concrete walls, a rack with chains and handcuffs...and not like police-issued handcuffs, either."

Ask her, she knew all about police-issued handcuffs.

Wanda hid her skeptical surprise, but not well enough that Prim didn't catch a glimpse of it before she covered it with a vague smile. "Then a dungeon it is. How long were you there? *Who* was there with you? How did you get out of the dungeon?"

She bit the inside of her cheek. It was all kinda vague and hazy. "I don't remember a lot about actually being in the dungeon, and I have zero damn idea how I got there. I remember waking up and seeing all that kooky shit from the inside of what I later discovered was a fucking jar. Like a Mason jar, ya know?"

Marty's mouth fell open. "So someone stole you from your bed, turned you into...whatever they turned you into with wings and put you in a jar in a dungeon."

Well, now that she heard it out loud, it sounded absolutely fucking crackers. But yeah. That's what happened.

"I know it sounds like I'm making shit up, but that's what happened. I swear it."

Why she wanted to convince these women she

was telling the truth made no sense. Why did she care if they believed her?

Maybe because no one else is ever going to believe you? Or maybe it's because you'd give anything for someone to...

Prim mentally shook her head at that inner voice of hers that just wouldn't shut up. She didn't *need* anyone to believe anything. The end.

Wanda waved a hand with a smile. "Hah!" she chirped. "Believe me when I tell you, this doesn't even come close to the things we've heard in our time as paranormal professionals. We believe you."

What the shit was a paranormal professional and how did she get as far away from these people as possible? What had they seen that was batshit crazier than what she'd just told them?

Little voice inside your head again with a tiny reminder. You did just see a woman transform into a beast right before your very eyes. How could your story be any crazier? You ask, I answer.

True.

Marty reached a hand out and touched hers, making her jump and snatch it away. "Listen, I see your skepticism. I feel it in my bones. We were all once where you are. But if you'll let me explain who we are and how we got here, maybe you'll have a better understanding about our reasons for believing you."

When Prim didn't deny them the opportunity to tell their story, Wanda took the wheel.

When they were done, Prim was left feeling like it

might have been better if they'd let Jesus take the wheel.

She sat quietly, incapable of processing everything she'd heard. Horrified these people believed they were paranormal creatures.

"Primrose?" Wanda asked softly. "Are you okay?"

Her backbone quite suddenly made an appearance and she sat up straight, the haze of confusion parting. "I'm pretty fucking sure I'm not the one you should be checking in with. Your mental health is wishy-washy at best. I'd call a damn professional and make a group therapy appointment."

"Said the chick with fucking wings," Nina snarked, flicking the protrusion on her back.

The touch of her fingers jolted Primrose. Okay. That was fair. She had a wing. But maybe that had been done to her when she was in the jar?

Like, maybe that dungeon was run by some organ traffickers or something and they'd implanted this thing on her back because...

Because what, dipshit? Because in return for a kidney, they thanked you by giving you a wing? Use your critical thinking skills, you idiot.

Well, it made more sense than vampires and werewolves and accidents in alleyways. Didn't it?

Does it, Prim?

Or maybe, she theorized, maybe this was like a body modification gone wrong. Sort of the way some kids had their canines filed to resemble vampire teeth, or plastic surgery to make them look like Barbie.

Maybe she'd been someone's guinea pig in a lab in a dungeon.

Yeah, Prim. And they housed you in a Mason jar while they fashioned you a wing. Let's not skip the part about how you, an almost six-foot, one-hundred and sixty-pound grown woman, actually fit in a Mason jar. Or are you forgetting that part?

Optical illusion? Drugs that had altered her perception of reality? There could be a million explanations for what was happening.

And she said those very thoughts out loud as she narrowed her eyes in Nina's direction. "Is a wing the same fucking thing as telling people you're a werewolf? Or a vampire? Worse, believing that shit? I really think you people believe you're supernatural beings, and that's fine by me. You can be whatever the hell you want to be. You do you, boo. As for me, I'm out because I don't want to be a werewolf or a vampire or any of the bullshit stories you just fed me."

"Fairy!" a gruff voice with a slight southern accent called. "I smell a fairy, Boss. What gives?"

An enormous man with high-tops, a football jersey, heavy chains around his neck, a knit hat, and hands the size of slabs of beef entered the room, his grin cheerful as he leaned down and dropped a kiss on each of the ladies' cheeks.

"Fairy!" Wanda proclaimed as she hopped up from

her seat and hugged the large man. "Of course! It all makes sense now. I don't know why we didn't think of that."

Nina slapped the man on his broad back. "How goes it, dude? Where ya been?"

He winked and grinned wider, a cheerful smile that somehow, even in all the madness, made Prim feel warm inside. A feeling she wasn't used to and didn't welcome despite how nice it felt.

"I been deckin' the halls a lil' bit. Thought I'd take a break from my holiday shoppin' and drop by to see if the kids wanna go tubin' with ol' Uncle Darnell."

Marty wrapped her arms around the generous middle of ol' Uncle Darnell and inhaled. "You're the best, D. We're in the middle of something, and it won't be long before they'll be in the middle of it, too, if they don't have a distraction. You're the perfect distraction."

He dropped a kiss on the top of her blonde head. "What are y'all into now and why do I smell fairy? Seelie, I think...if I'm sniffin' right anyways."

Smell fairy? Sweet Caroline. This was too bizarre for her and she didn't care how Darnell or all this huggy-fuzzy friendship crap made her feel. If this guy was claiming he could smell fairies, she wanted off the ride.

As she was about to rise and hit the bricks, he stopped her cold when he stuck out his hand and said, "I'm Darnell. Good to meet ya."

Prim looked at his hand and hesitated for only a second before his earnest presence and gentle demeanor found her placing her hand in his big paw. "Primrose Dunham."

He pulled her into a hug—a hug she loathed to admit she didn't hate. "A fairy. So cool! Dang, never thought I'd meet one up close and personal. Sho' good to meet ya. So what brings ya to our neck'a the woods?"

Wanda tapped him on the shoulder. "She doesn't know why she's in our neck of the woods, Darnell. She doesn't even know she's a fairy and neither did we until you told us. I thought baby dragon, personally. Fairy never crossed my mind."

"A fuckin' fairy? Tooth or godmother?" Nina joked, but Wanda shut her down with that stern look.

Darnell eased back, his round face full of surprise. "Aw, shoot, Boss. I didn't realize y'all was here doin' the introduction to the paranormal. Sorry to interrupt."

The introduction to the paranormal? Was this a cult? Shit, shit, shit. She had to get out of here. Her brain was about to explode with an overload of too much psychosis.

Backing away, Prim looked over her shoulder to see if she had a clear path, her chin hitting the top of whatever was on her back, but even that wasn't going to stop her.

Head down, Prim spun and barreled toward the

heavy wooden front door with a gorgeous cedar wreath covered in lights and red and white velvet ribbon.

Oddly, in the middle of her escape, she remembered Christmas wasn't far off and she needed to get a tree to at least make an attempt at celebrating a holiday she'd once loved.

For her mother. Because it had been her favorite holiday.

Flinging the door open, Prim almost landed on her ass when the velocity of the wind hit her square in the face. It whooshed through the door, snowflakes slapping at her skin in cold pricks.

Yet, she didn't stop to think about her bare feet or her lack of clothing beneath the bathrobe. The only thing she could think about was getting the fuck away from these crazy people.

She didn't bother to try to organize her thoughts or make sense of what she'd actually witnessed. There had to be a rational explanation for what was going on —for what she'd seen Marty do.

She'd worry about it when she got home because regardless of what was happening to her, she needed to get to her pets. Katy and Freddy hadn't eaten since fuck knew when because she had no idea how long she'd been gone.

But she was going to find out. As soon as she ran through the vast expanse of snow in her bare feet, half naked.

Jesus, it was colder than the Arctic Circle. As she pushed her way through the harsh wind, her fingers already like icicles, she began to rethink her choice to flee.

"Hold the fuck up, dingbat!" she heard Nina's unmistakable husky voice call out, seconds before she was right in front of her.

Prim might have crashed into her had it not been for Nina putting her hands up to stop her from running farther, before she gripped Prim's shoulders.

"I said, hold the fuck up." Nina's pale face fairly shimmered in the moonlight as the wind tore at her long hair. "Listen, if you're determined to skip the hell outta here, at least let us give you a ride to wherever the fuck you're going before you freeze your stupid ass to death."

Instantly, Prim was on guard again. "I think I'm gonna pass. I got it from here."

But Nina curled her fingers into the top of the robe and snarled at her. "Listen, nitwit, and listen fuckin' well because I'm only gonna say it once. I don't give a shit if you're the fucking tooth fairy. You don't have to listen to us or believe us about what-the-fuck-ever. I'd just as soon you take your scrawny ass home and stay there. Deal with whatever happens all by your lone-some—because believe me, some bad shit's gonna happen. Bad shit always hap—"

"Happen? What's going to happen?" she asked, her heart thumping wildly in her chest.

Nina tightened her grip and hauled her closer, the snowflakes landing on her perfect nose. "I said *listen*. I don't know what's going to happen, but it's gonna be somethin' that rocks your little world.

"But guess what? I don't care if *you* don't care— and you obviously don't give a shit. Know what I *do* care about? My friends in there who'll sit up all night while they braid each other's hair and worry about your dumb ass. So at the very least, let us take you home so they can make sure you're okay and then you're on your own. But you're a straight-up fool if you think you're getting home looking like this." She pointed to her beet-red feet, mostly covered in snow.

But how did she know they were going to take her home? How did she know they weren't the people who snatched her from her damn bed and put her in a jar so they could perform ungodly experiments on her in the first place?

"They ain't gonna hurt ya, Primrose," Darnell said, coming to stand with Nina. "I promise. Nobody wants to hurt ya. We just wanna help."

What was it about this guy that she couldn't resist? Why was he so appealing? Why did he come off so non-threatening? If anything, she should be afraid of him. He'd claimed to smell fairy. Who said stuff like that out loud?

But she was, in fact, inexplicably drawn to his big frame and his easygoing tone.

Still, that little voice inside her head, the one that

tried to reason with her, the one she was always at war with, was also a skeptic. What if they were offering her a ride home because they wanted to know where she lived so they could come back and snatch her up after they'd lulled her into a sense of security?

"For fuck's sake. Enough of this bullshit. I don't know what's goin' on in that empty head of yours, but we're taking you the fuck home."

Without another word, without the chance to have one more misgiving, Nina did indeed snatch her up, tucked Prim's long, lanky form under her armpit and stomped toward the garage door of this palatial farmhouse, lit up with exquisite Christmas lights and an inflatable Santa on the lawn.

"Heeyyy!" Prim protested.

"Start the fucking SUV, Darnell!" she belted out. "If I don't get this bitch outta my face, she's gonna be the first human I drain dry until she's nothing but a GD husk of skin and bones!"

Drain...

Wait, did she mean drain her of her blood?

Holy bloodletting.

CHAPTER

FOUR

B ut did the idea of being drained dry stop her
from opening her big mouth? Did any dire
situation, where imminent harm might come
to her person *because* of her big mouth, ever stop her?

No.

Because she could never let anyone have the last
word.

"Put me the fuck down!" Prim hollered, bouncing
and struggling against Nina's side as she held her like
a piece of luggage being carried from the airport.

But Nina continued to ignore her protests, her grip
on Primrose that of a steel band as she yanked open
the door to a black SUV and yeeted her inside with a
grunt, slamming her shoulder against the far door.

"Don't fucking move," she threatened as she
climbed in beside her, her expression dark and obviously aggravated. "Where the fuck do you live? Tell me

now, or I'm gonna rattle your fucking cage like it's never been rattled before."

Prim was so stunned by this woman's strength, by her quick movements through the snow, she blurted it out before she could stop herself.

Darnell jumped in the driver's seat and started the car, backing out in efficient silence.

She didn't live far from here, but it was far enough that it wasn't a leisurely stroll. As the trees and big patches of land covered in snow and little else sped past her, Prim noted they were going in the right direction.

Under most circumstances, she'd be mortified for anyone new to see where she lived, but tonight, she just wanted to get back to her pets and a stiff drink. She'd have to set aside her pride and forget that she lived in a shithole she'd inherited in favor of ensuring her furbabies were all right.

Fifteen minutes later, just as she was finally warming up, they pulled up beside her dark, dilapidated two-story Victorian house. Prim sighed with relief that no one was going to take her hostage and kill her after they experimented on her body, even as her new appendage boinked her in the back of her neck.

She didn't look at Nina or Darnell when she gripped the handle of the door to jump out as fast as possible, but Nina stopped her by grabbing her robe-covered arm. "*This* is your fucking place? It looks like an abandoned flop house."

Darnell scratched his head as he peeked over his broad shoulder. "You sho' this is your house? You don't hafta lie to us, Prim. Boss was right when she said we'd take ya home. We really don't mean any harm. We just want you safe."

Humiliation be thy name.

Okay, look. It was a dump. She knew it, and compared to all the other houses in her quaint but older neighborhood, hers was an eyesore with its crumbling steps and sagging windows, but she'd just moved back in after being gone for as many years as she could stay away.

She'd been in an apartment for almost seven years, and hadn't considered buying a home till somewhere down the road.

And then, one day, she'd been contacted by a lawyer who said she now owned the home of her youth. It was paid for, and who couldn't use a few extra bucks every month if they didn't have to pay rent?

So Prim had reluctantly come back. She almost regretted it, but for the fact that she was saving nearly three grand a month in rent on a one bedroom. Except she *still* only had one bedroom, because the other three in this ramshackle house were unlivable.

But that money she saved every month was going

to go toward fixing up the place—if she didn't die of exposure first.

This was Buffalo in the wintertime and the heat wasn't exactly in working order—or even the electricity, on the whole. It was sporadic at best, and probably a fire hazard.

But it was hers, and she had big plans to restore it to its former glory. Something she hoped her mother would be proud of if she were still alive.

As she caught a glimpse of the Christmas lights along the street, she remembered how much her mother had loved them and that sharp sting in her chest returned.

Nina tugged a lock of Prim's hair. "I asked, is this really your fucking place? Answer the damn question."

Prim swallowed hard, forcing herself to focus on Nina's question and not allow her melancholy for the time of year to take over.

"Yep. This is my fucking place. Thanks for the ride. Appreciate everything. The show, the manhandling, all of it. Bye."

Prim hopped out of the shiny, ultra-deluxe SUV and sprinted through the cold snow toward her crumbling steps to the wide front porch, where she prayed her front door, which was temperamental because it was so warped, had decided not to latch properly and she could jiggle her way in.

She'd done it before, fingers crossed she could do it again because she didn't have her key.

When she tried the doorknob, in the typical fashion this entire day had taken, it didn't budge.

Well, fuck.

But she heard Freddy Mercury howl long and loud when she tried to get in—it was his "I'm shriveling away, feed me or I'll die" howl.

Screw it, she'd bust into the window.

Marching toward one of the only two not-boarded-up, floor-to-ceiling windows on the wide-planked, rotting porch, her feet like blocks of ice, she plucked at the ripped screen and tried to open the window, all while Freddy barked like he was on fire and Katy Purry meowed as though she'd been dipped in acid.

Prim tried to push the window up, but to no avail. It was stuck from years and years of globbed-on paint.

Fuck, fuck, fuck. So much fuck.

"Trouble?" she heard Nina say from behind her, her husky voice right near Prim's ear..

Prim whipped around, embarrassed that she had to break into her own house. "Are you still here? Don't you have a bloodletting to attend?"

Nina rolled her eyes. "All good paranormals know that shit doesn't go down till after midnight and my phone says it's only nine. Now, do you fucking need help or is this really not your house? You squatting? And don't bullshit me. I'll know if you're lying."

Prim huffed as she eyeballed her with the harshest glare she could summon—the one that made people uncomfortable, according to Darleen in HR. "No, I'm not squatting. This is my damn house. I have a job. I make good money as a software engineer. I don't need to squat."

But Prim had underestimated her glare in comparison to Nina's, because she glared right back, making Prim fight an outward cringe. "Move," she ordered with a pointed finger.

There wasn't much choice in the matter, mostly because her feet were frozen and about to fall off. So Prim did as she was told.

Nina grunted before she used one finger and lifted the hazy glass of the window with ease.

Lord love a duck. There had to be an explanation for what this woman was capable of other than being paranormal, but Prim didn't have time to come up with one.

She'd made a promise to Freddy when she rescued him from that bag of crusty dicks that he'd never be without a warm bed and food.

She'd kind of defaulted on her promise.

Katy, instantly aware the window had been opened, jumped up onto the cracked sill and began climbing out, but Nina, as quick as a blurry flash of limbs and hair, scooped her up, preventing her from jumping.

She scratched Katy's white, fluffy ears and cuddled her close. "And who are you, Fluffy? Oh, my goodness! Who's so pretty?" she cooed in baby talk at her as Katy instantly settled in her arms. Nina looked at the tag on her rhinestone-studded purple collar. "Katy Purry? Mommy's a funny fucking lady, huh, sweet baby?"

Katy responded by rubbing the top of her head against Nina's chin.

If hearing this rough and tumble woman talk to Katy so tenderly wasn't enough shock to make her keel right over, she then called to Freddy Mercury, "Hey, buddy! Chill out. Mommy's comin'."

And he *did* chill out. Freddy instantly stopped howling.

Gripping the crooked blue shutter, Prim had to fight to hold herself up, hearing the tone in Nina's voice and the fact that Freddy Mercury had actually listened and stopped barking.

He almost *never* listened to her—not even after extensive training with a whistle and an airhorn and anything she could get her hands on to keep him quiet so her apartment neighbors wouldn't complain.

Nina glared at her again, her eyes glittering under the glow of the shaft of light the streetlamp gave off. "You goin' the fuck in or are you gonna stand around out here in the snow until we gotta hack your feet off because you were stupid enough to run the fuck around like a chicken with her head cut off with no shoes and get hypothermia?"

Prim didn't think twice, she pushed her way inside her house, her legs stiff as she climbed through the window and immediately tried to turn on the light.

Of course, like everything else in her rundown shithole, they didn't turn on.

Nina followed behind her, Katy still in her arms, and planted her feet in the middle of her box-filled shambles of a living room. "I'm startin' to think you're bullshittin' us and you don't really live here. It's so cold in here, I can see your damn breath."

Prim tried the switch again. She'd had some success a couple of times before simply flicking it on and off. "Well, I can't remember the last time I brushed my teeth. Maybe it's I-haven't-brushed-my-teeth-in-forever breath," she answered as she aggressively flicked the switch on and off.

Finally, the lights blazed on with a buzz and a hum, leaving the sad state of her living room bathed in a disturbing glow.

Prim instantly repeated the silent apology in her head, the one she always used when she was faced with seeing the hellhole her childhood home had become.

I'm sorry, Mom. I'm so miserably sorry.

God, this place was a mess. Crooked bookshelves bracketed the wall with a fireplace, some of the shelves cracked and falling down, held up by a wing and a prayer.

The mantel hung on precariously by a thread, and the furniture was old and dusty but for the kiwi-green velvet couch she'd brought with her from her apartment.

Boxes she hadn't gotten around to unpacking were stacked in a corner on the peeling linoleum floor, an ugly orangey-brown that had been all the rage back in the day but now looked dull and yellowed in areas.

While the room was what in this day and age considered open concept, opening to the kitchen, the ceiling between sagged and, Prim feared, might collapse given a stiff breeze.

And the kitchen. Jesus Christ and a death trap, the kitchen was a hellhole. The appliances were covered in baked-on grease, the white stove's surface rusty and chipped. The fridge was likely better off housing bio-hazardous material than a tuna sandwich.

It was the one appliance she'd ordered two minutes after she'd moved back in, due to be delivered at the end of the week.

The oak cabinets that had once been in fine shape and held all her favorite treats, now fell off the wall. Some were entirely removed. The countertops were peeling and there was a fissure the size of the Grand Canyon along the one by the old, rusted porcelain sink.

But that sink, once sleek and white, had been one of her favorite places to hang out with her mom. After dinner, when they did the dishes together and they'd share their days. Prim on a stepstool, dishtowel in hand, and her mother rinsing dinner plates and giving them to her to dry.

If she gave the state of her house too much

thought, if she let herself get wrapped up in what was instead of the here and now, she'd become overwhelmed by everything that needed doing.

She'd remember how she'd failed her mother...

Nina looked around, her beautiful eyes filled with shock. "Jesus and fuck. This place is a GD garbage dump," she muttered as the once-howling Freddy Mercury now cowered behind Prim's favorite armchair. The one her mother used to sit in to read her bedtime stories when she was little.

Prim rolled her eyes and headed to the thermostat in the hopes she could get the heat going as successfully as she'd done the lights, because it was damn cold. "I just moved back...er, I just moved in. It's a fixer-upper. Shit like this takes time."

"It's gonna take a fucking bulldozer," Nina snarked, closing the window before gently setting Katy on the couch. Kneeling on the floor, she tapped the spot in front of her. "And what's your name, little dude? Come see Auntie Nina. Come on, now."

Lo and behold, her once-abused, dumped-on-a-deserted-back-road, frightened part Dachshund, part Jack Russell terrier wiggled his way out from behind Prim's chair and sat in front of Nina. His ears, long and spotted auburn and white with a splash of black, twitched as he contemplated befriending this stranger.

"Be careful. He's a little skittish." She figured it was

only fair to warn her that Freddy could be a little nippy when he was fearful.

"And why is this little goober skittish? Huh, sweet baby? Tell Auntie Nina."

"The guy who had him before me dumped him. Broke his leg so bad, it's going to be twisted and crooked forever. I caught the prick dumping him on my way home from the store. I landed in jail because of that heartless piece of shit—" Prim stopped short. That was more than this volatile woman needed to know. "All I'm saying is be—"

"Yeah, yeah," she mumbled, not waiting for Freddy to approach her. She scooped up his sausage-like body and tucked his head under her chin, stroking his sleek back as she read his tag.

And Freddy pressed his nose to her jaw with a sigh of blissful happiness.

Nina cradled him, dropping kisses on his smooth head. "Freddy Mercury, huh? Somebody likes Queen." He shivered against her, his long body trembling as she examined Freddy's crooked leg. "What kinda fuck-pants did this to you? Do you want Auntie Nina to eat his legs off, sweet boy?"

Prim gulped. Could she eat someone's legs off? "He's okay," she reassured, her heart clenching when she thought what could have happened to Freddy if she hadn't come along. "I mean, his leg doesn't hurt him. He gets around pretty good..."

Nina grunted and promptly ignored her. "That's

not what I asked, is it, Goober? I asked if you want me to fuck up the asshole who did this to you?"

"I did punch him in the face," Prim confessed.

"You shoulda ripped his fucking cowardly throat out."

"Well, in the interest of an actual prison sentence..."

Nina ignored her again and focused on a shivering Freddy. "You cold, buddy? Tell your mother to pay the damn electric bill. Until then, let's text Uncle Darnell and tell him to build us a fire in that big, ugly fireplace. How's that?" she cooed, using her free hand to pull her phone from her pocket and text.

Prim was dumbfounded. The only person Freddy allowed to pick him up was her, but to look at him now, you'd think Nina was made of NY strip and bacon —two of his favorite treats in the world.

Before Prim could protest, Darnell's big frame stood in the window. He opened it as easily as Nina had and hiked his meaty leg over the sill and climbed in, a frown on his previously cheerful face. "Dang cold in here. Lemme see what I can do."

Without another word, Darnell set about digging through the firewood she'd had delivered just last week, but hadn't used because she didn't have a clue how to make a fire in her old fireplace.

But she remembered sitting by it all those years ago, Christmas carols playing, her mother laughing... until things went horribly wrong.

Shaking off her memories of what her house had once been, Prim decided these people couldn't be so bad.

Her dog, who was afraid of everyone and everything, appeared almost in love with Nina, and by the looks of Katy and the way she'd forgotten all about food in favor of rubbing up against Darnell's leg as he loaded logs into the fireplace, the cat didn't think they were so bad either.

She hated to admit it, but it was nice to see the house filled with people other than herself—even if they were absolute bonkers.

Everyone appeared to be getting on just fine without her, so Prim took that opportunity to run to the back bedroom and find some socks for her positively chapped feet and some clothes so she could feed Freddy and Katy.

Making her way through the kitchen, she pushed past more boxes and dove for her dresser, digging out a favorite worn pair of jeans and some thick, wooly socks.

As she shrugged out of the bathrobe and pulled on the thickest sweatshirt she had, Prim tried not to look at the thing on her back in the mirror on her dresser.

But her eyes refused to look away and she found herself mesmerized by the shimmering rainbow colors under the dim light of the small lamp on her nightstand.

It partially pushed out of her shoulder blade, the

curved tip brazenly sticking upward and touching the back of her neck, just grazing the bottom of her pixie haircut.

Prim quickly turned around and pulled her sweat-shirt down over her breasts. Grabbing a brush, she swiped at her hair with its multi-colored streaks of blue and pink, with a little yellow thrown in for good measure.

Feeling a little more like herself, she ignored the lump poking out of her shoulder and stomped out of the room, heading toward the kitchen to grab some food for her furkids, only to find Nina had handled that.

Freddy and Katy sat at her feet, snarfing down their very late dinner, while she spoke softly to them and Darnell stoked a fire that could almost be considered roaring.

That it wasn't filling the room up with smoke was to his credit.

As she watched her animals betray her by consorting with the enemy, she allowed herself to enjoy the warmth of the room and reminded herself a thank you was in order.

"Thanks, Darnell. I don't know the first damn thing about starting a fire in that mess of crumbling stones and grate. Appreciate it."

He rose from his place on the hearth and winked. "No sweat. You feel better now?" He pointed to her change of clothes with a grin.

"I'm warmer." She rubbed her arms to emphasize how much warmer.

"Give the fucking guy an inch, would you?" Nina groused. "We could have just left you to freeze to death."

That was fair. Or they could have stolen her kidneys. She should definitely be grateful she still had all her organs.

Instead of arguing, she gave an inch—a grateful one. "You're right. Thank you for starting a fire and not letting me freeze to death. Also, thank you for not stealing my kidneys."

Darnell laughed, and Nina clucked her tongue with a smile. "If I wanted your fucking kidneys, I'd have 'em right now—like spread on a damn cracker."

Prim nodded. "Good to know. Anyway, I have shit to do, like check in with work, seeing as I don't even know what day it is and I'm not sure if I'm gonna get banged for a personal day. Thanks for the ride and the fire. Take care."

She needed some alone time to figure out what was going on with her back, and maybe it was foolish of her to send them away, but she needed a doctor, not a bunch of women who claimed to be things that didn't even exist except for on a movie set.

Oh, Primrose Dunham. Already have you forgotten all that hair and teeth?

As Nina opened her mouth to protest, likely to inform her she was an idiot for not letting them "help" her, Marty and Wanda arrived in a cloud of perfume and rolling bags of luggage. They'd somehow managed to yank the door open. Freddy started barking and Katy howled.

Prim opened her mouth to stop the chaos, but Wanda pressed her finger to Prim's lips to quiet her. It smelled of a floral moisturizer and what she was pretty sure were gummi bears.

She was about to protest, but Wanda, in her classy winter coat and elegant high heels, flashed a warning with her eyes.

"Listen to me, Primrose Dunham," she said in a tone that rivaled Sister Felicia Margaret Cabrini, the most feared of all nuns from Our Lady of the Sacrament. "I have news. News you're not going to like, but news nonetheless. Now, you *will* sit down, you *will* listen to what I have to tell you before someone gets hurt, namely you, and we'll make a plan. Are we clear?"

Nina leaned over and whispered n her ear, "Take my advice and say 'clear' or prepare to get your fucking scrawny ass whooped like it's never been whooped before. You don't want quiet Wanda to eat your face off, because believe me, it's always the quiet ones who do the most damage. It ain't pretty."

Prim's heart pounded in her chest as Wanda glared at her and pointed to the couch, her lips a thin line of irritation and, worse, disappointment.

Ugh. She hated disappointment.

Yet, it wasn't only her tone of voice that frightened Prim, and she wasn't frightened by much—it was her eyes. They were so fierce, so intense; it almost made her cringe.

Wanda pushed Nina out of the way, her chest rising and falling, her eyes flashing colors. "I asked, *are we clear, Primrose Agnes Dunham*?"

Aw, man. She'd used her middle name. How had she found out her middle name?

Shit.

Prim gulped and silently nodded. "*Clear.*"

CHAPTER
FIVE

W as this some kind of joke? Like a prank orchestrated by the people in HR who all hated her guts?

What the shit was a Seelie? The only Sealy she knew about had to do with a Posturepedic mattress, something she was likely going to need if this damn thing sticking out of her back didn't go away.

Prim clung to Freddy, who'd vacated his place on Nina's lap and come to comfort his mistress in her time of absolute panic by quietly sitting on her lap, not moving a muscle.

"Prim? Are you all right?" Marty asked in her sweet, soothing tone as she reached over and placed a hand on her shoulder. A hand obviously lent in comfort but only serving to incite.

She shrugged Marty's hand away, angry at the

outlandish tale she'd just sat through. "You fuckers are absolute crackers, you know that? You expect me to believe that I'm a fairy because someone goofed? Like, *what*? Who *makes* fairies, cuckoo bird? That's just insane. You can't make a damn fair unless you're Walt Disney!"

Wanda, who'd been all piss and vinegar a moment ago, was suddenly softer, gentler, her face slathered in a sympathetic expression. "I know this doesn't make sense, Prim. It never does at first, but you absolutely must believe me when I tell you, you're in danger. There've been rumblings about you in our world. There are people looking for you who want what you have."

Prim rolled her eyes, clutching Freddy to her chest. "Right. The dark forces of the Unseelie, who want my power."

"Exactly," Wanda confirmed, taking a dainty sip of the tea Marty had somehow managed to conjure in Prim's crumbling kitchen.

Prim gaped at them, her jaw unhinging as she set Freddy on the floor and hopped up off the couch. "I don't know who the fuck is behind this, but if it's that smarmy, nosey bitch Darleen from HR, she's gonna have to work a whole lot harder to get rid of me! You tell her I said her whiny, pissant of a son can eat shit. I earned my position fair and square because I'm better at my job than he is."

She needed to find her cell phone and call her boss.

There was funny and then there was too fucked up for words.

Darleen wanted her head on a pike and had ever since Prim had begun working at Teeson Tech. She'd tried all manner of stunts to get her fired, because Prim had taken a job Darleen thought was a shoe-in for her son, Lance.

She'd balked at her clothes, the colors she dyed her hair, her shoes, her potty mouth, the days she'd requested for sick leave—but it didn't change facts.

Lance couldn't code the way Prim could, and she'd smoked him when she'd earned the position of senior software engineer three years ago.

She'd worked her ass off to get the gig after slogging away, head down, long hours, coding like it was gonna save her life for two endless years before she'd nabbed the position.

And it would be just like Darleen to hire actors to fuck with her head in order to oust her from TT. Had she created this whole stunt as revenge to get her fired?

Extreme? Maybe.

But Lance was a mama's boy, and he was Darleen's pride and joy. When he'd lost the job to her, there'd been a whole lot of chatter from not only her coworkers, but the people who thought Darleen walked on water. She'd made Prim's life miserable ever since.

Nina grabbed her by the arm and sat her back down in the chair. "Did you hear what my fucking friend just told you? Your ass is in danger, and it ain't from whoever the fuck Darleen is. Now sit there and shut it and listen to what we're saying."

Darnell stepped in then, his gentle tone and easy-going demeanor instantly soothing her. "Prim, please listen. I can show you stuff like you never seen before. I can take you places you gonna wish you'd never been, if it's proof ya want. But if these ladies say you're in danger, you're in danger, and it don't have nothin' to do with somebody named Darleen.

"Whoever took you from your bed the other night did something they shouldn't've done. I don't know why they did it. I don't know how, but they did it and now you have power you don't know how to handle. That ain't never good. That has to be figured out."

For some reason, she didn't want to hurt Darnell's feelings. He came off like a real teddy bear, which could all be part of the act these whacks put on, but she couldn't help but like him.

"Because the Seelies want my super-special secret power, right?" she replied, stiff-lipped.

"No. The *Unseelies* want your power. Er, I think..." Wanda mumbled with a frown, sipping more of her tea.

Prim's unsettled stomach rolled and her pulse quickened. "You *think*? Shouldn't you know? You came in here, guns fucking blazing, telling me the craziest story I've ever heard about how you heard a rumor from your werewolf aunt's mother's best friend who

knows a fairy in her quilting group who says some
lunatic snatched me up outta my bed, took me to
fairyland, gave me some powers I wasn't supposed to
have—and those powers are all powerful, of course—
but you don't know what those powers are, specifi-
cally—and after all that, you don't even know if it's
true?"

Yep. That's the story they'd fed her. She was
kidnapped by good fairies, kept in a jar, given powers
that were some kind of big deal, powers everybody
wanted, including the bad fairies, and someone from
the bad fairy camp was going to try to kill her and take
her powers for the bad fairy team.

Sure, they were.

Marty made a face, puckering her lips. "It wasn't
my werewolf aunt. It was my husband's werewolf
cousin's best friend who heard the rumor in a *pottery*
class."

Prim scoffed, pushing up the sleeves of her sweatshirt. "Forgive me for fucking up the particulars. She
heard this rumor in a *pottery* class."

"She did," Marty defended. "And Anna's a reliable
source. I mean, sure, she's the Pack gossip, but she's
almost always spot on."

She lifted her chin and fought laughing directly in
Marty's pretty face. "The Pack? As in werewolf pack,
right?"

Now Marty rolled her eyes. "Look, now that I
hear it out loud, I realize it sounds ridiculous. I get

that. But yes. My *werewolf pack*. I'm a werewolf, and I'm not sure what more I can do to prove it to you than what I've already done. Regardless, you're in danger of them coming back. It was *you* in a glass jar, wasn't it, Prim? Wasn't it you who flew into Nina's face? Wasn't it you the size of a cockroach on my kitchen floor just hours ago? You can't deny that happened."

She'd had a little time to come to a theory about that on the ride over... "The fuck I can't. I think someone drugged me and I was hallucinating."

Nina yanked on the thing poking out of her back, making her yelp. "Like that? Are you hallucinating that, fucknuts?"

Enough. She'd had enough of this bullshit. Pushing her way past Nina, she pointed to the door. "I don't know what the explanation for that is. You people hacked me up, augmented me, did some kind of weird experiment on me. I don't fucking know. I only know, you gotta go. Get the hell out of my house and shut up about fairies and powers and—"

It was then everyone gasped—even Nina.

Prim looked at all of them, their mouths hanging open, their eyes wide, and if she hadn't already lost her cool, she exploded.

"*Whaaat*? What the fuck is wrong with all of you? What about get the hell out of my house don't you understand?" she hollered, scaring Freddy, who ran to Nina and begged to be picked up.

Darnell was the first to recover. He spoke quietly, his words measured. "You got a mirror, Prim?"

"Yeah!" she barked defensively, jamming her hands into her jean pockets. "So?"

"You might wanna look in it."

"If it'll make you fruitcakes get out, I'll go look." Without another word, she stomped off to her bedroom toward the mirror above her dresser.

Then her mouth fell open, too.

No.

This wasn't happening.

How could this be happening?

But when she lifted a hand and saw nothing but her sweatshirt rise and fall with the movement, Prim realized it had to be true.

She was invisible.

"WHO THE FUCK ARE YOU?" a very tall woman, a stunningly beautiful woman, greeted Rafferty outside Prim's dilapidated door.

"Um, maybe the question here is, who are *you*?" he asked, keeping his tone pleasant.

She held up a finger under his nose, her gorgeous dark eyes narrowing to slits of suspicion in her head. "I'm asking the questions, and I asked, who the fuck are you?"

Jesus, she reminded him of Prim. Mouthy, rude, unfiltered, beautiful. Just the way he liked 'em.

He stuck out a hand and smiled at the growling, eerily pale creature who stood guard at Prim's door like an angry soldier. "I'm Rafferty Monroe." He waited a moment and when she didn't return the same courteous introduction, he said, "Polite society dictates it's your turn for introductions. So, who are you?"

She lifted her chin, but she didn't take his hand. "That your girlfriend in there?"

He rocked back on his heels and drove his hands into the pockets of his jeans, burrowing into his down jacket while this woman wore nothing more than a hoodie when it was maybe twenty degrees out.

"Depends on who's in there. Do you mean the cute woman who's almost six feet tall, with the short multicolored hair and a mouth to rival a sailor?"

She eyed him back, a glare so intense her dark eyes swallowed him whole, and not in a good way. "Yeah. That's who I fucking mean."

Rafferty smiled. "Oh, then no. She's not my girlfriend." Not for lack of trying, though. He'd been head over heels for Primrose Dunham since the fifth grade. "She's my new neighbor...and friend." He tacked on the last words, but he wasn't sure if it was to reassure himself or this woman.

The woman edged nearer Prim's warped door, keeping herself between it and him. "How delightful, but unless you got a welcome-to-the-neighborhood casserole, go away."

Ouch. She was as tough a nut to crack as Prim, but who the hell was this stranger to tell him to go away, and why was she here?

However, unlike Prim, he believed in catching flies with honey—not the word "fuck" and the imminent threat of death.

He held up his hands in surrender. "No casserole, but I've been trying to call her for two days and she hasn't answered. Not even so much as a text. If you don't mind, I'd like to check on her and see that she's okay."

With a finger, the woman jabbed him in the chest so hard, it felt like she was going to bore a hole through his flesh. "She's busy and can't take your call right now. So go the fuck away. I'll give her the message."

He found himself a little annoyed. No—he was a lot annoyed. Who was this woman, and why was he hearing other voices he didn't recognize coming from behind Prim's door? She didn't have friends. She hated everyone.

Was this some kind of weird take on a home invasion?

So he sighed. "'Fraid I can't do that. I need to see that Prim's all right. I'm not leaving until I do."

"Maybe you misunderstood what the fuck I just said. I *said*, she's busy. That means, you say thanks and turn your ass around, walk down those shitty steps, hope you don't break a leg while you do it, and go back to wherever the fuck you came from." She paused a moment before leaning into his face with hers. "Go!" she shouted so loud, it made the hair poking out from his beneath his knit hat shoot upward.

Suddenly, the door popped open and Prim stuck her head out. Her beautiful green eyes glaring at him, she barked, "Rafferty? What the hell are you doing here?"

He grinned at her over the head of the mean woman. "Hey, pretty lady. Good to see you again, too."

"What are you doing here, Raff?" Prim demanded, her eyes looked confused and... maybe *helpless*? Was that the word? Was Prim ever helpless? Either way, she didn't look like herself. Her vibe was way off.

"Well, I'm not sure, but I think I'm in the process of getting to know your long-lost twin. She's a real delight." He thumbed his finger at the woman with a wicked grin.

Her nostrils flared—from experience, a sure sign he was well on his way to going too far. "Go home."

"Um, nope. I came to see what's going on with you, and you haven't answered my calls or texts in two days. Not gonna happen. So who is this, standing guard like she's patrolling Fort Knox? And why am I hearing strange voices coming from inside your house?"

Prim made a face at him, just like the one she'd

made at the cop after she clocked a guy square in the chops for dumping Freddy Mercury.

He hadn't heard from her in probably eight months, not since her stepfather was released from prison, and he'd texted her to see if she was okay. He'd gotten a short, curt answer and that had been that.

Then, out of the blue, three months ago, she'd called him when she'd found herself in a holding cell for punching some guy who'd dumped a dog on a deserted dirt road.

So Rafferty located the dog, who'd run away and hid in some bushes, sweet-talked the cop, bailed her out, and she'd gone about her merry way with the dog and a court date.

Which was par for the course with Prim. She'd been in and out of his life since they'd both gone off to college. Though to be fair, he wasn't always reachable. As a photojournalist—or as some called him, a conflict photographer—he'd spent a great deal of time abroad in foreign, war-ravaged countries.

But that part of his life was over. Now, he was in the process of figuring out what to do with the *rest* of his life, and he was doing it in the house he grew up in. He needed his roots to ground him, soothe him after his last trip to Yemen.

Imagine his surprise when Prim moved back in to her childhood home a couple weeks ago, totally oblivious to the fact that he was right next door. Or maybe she wasn't so much oblivious as she was completely disinterested.

But he'd come calling anyway—and she'd done what she always did, put up a wall and sent him on his way.

But did that stop him? Nah. He kept smashing his face against that brick wall because he was some kind of weird sadist—a glutton for punishment who just couldn't walk away from the woman he'd always loved.

"Rafferty?" Prim interrupted his thoughts, her tone a mixture of confused and... He still couldn't pinpoint it. "I said, go home. I'm fine. Promise."

"Mistress Nina? Why are you standing out here like some vagrant? Surely there are things to attend inside?" a man crowed as he climbed up Prim's crumbling steps.

A blue man.

Wait. A blue man?

Was his skin really blue or was it the poor lighting from the streetlamp playing with his eyes?

But...another, much younger man stood right behind him and he...he was green. Not Kermit green, maybe more like mint.

Had he really just color swatched a kid?

Sweet Jesus. Rafferty rubbed his eyes to be sure he was seeing clearly.

The green boy with the dark hair and shy smile held up a hand—like, literally held up a detached hand—and waved it at the woman guarding Prim's door. "Help, pl...please, Nina," he stuttered, disjointed and quiet. "It fell o...off."

The beautiful woman took the hand from him as if he were giving her a festively wrapped Christmas package. "Well, fuck, kiddo. Again? Man, why can't we keep this damn thing on you? C'mon, buddy. Let's find some duct-tape and we'll stick it back on."

Duct-tape. They were going to duct-tape this kid's hand back onto his body? Was he hearing properly? Rafferty jammed his fingertip in his ear and wiggled it. Maybe the bomb that went off during his last assignment had left his hearing lacking.

He'd seen some shit in his time as a photojournalist, but...

"Rafferty?" Prim called his name again, only this time she didn't sound quite as annoyed.

He opened his mouth to speak as the little blue man and the green boy and the beautiful pale lady stared at him like *he* was the crazy one—and then the world around him became nothing more than a pinpoint of color and muted sound and he began to fall forward.

He vaguely remembered some sparkles floating around—green and purple, to be precise—when he crashed into Prim.

And that was the last thing he remembered before it was lights out.

CHAPTER

SIX

"Rafferty!" Prim tapped his cheeks to attempt to wake him, but he was out cold—on top of her—in a weird cloud of swirly, colorful sparkles.

Damn, he was heavy. Not that she hated his weight on her...though she *did* hate to admit it. He always smelled like he'd just stepped from the shower, crisp and clean, his dirty-blond hair soft and feathery, tickling her nose as his body sank into hers.

Unable to help herself, Prim took a deep breath and closed her eyes, wanting nothing more than to wrap her arms around him and hold him close.

Raff smelled of a faraway time she'd almost peg as a dream if she didn't know better. A time when they used to sit together on their stoops and talk about everything. Life, school. Their parents, her love of Katy Perry, his vehement dislike of the aforementioned's music. Every night under the stars, winter, spring, summer, fall, they talked. They laughed. They flirted with a teenage romance that never made it past their front stoops.

But those days were long gone, and if she hadn't already fucked everything up the last time she'd seen him in a holding cell, she was going to tonight, for sure.

Nina grunted as she scooped him off her and dragged him, unconscious, into her living room, now full of more people than ever before. "Who the fuck is this dude and did he eat bricks for dinner? Jesus, he weighs a damn ton."

Marty and Wanda instantly hopped up from the couch, their faces full of concern. "Who is this? What happened?" Wanda crowed, grabbing Freddy's favorite worn throw blanket from the armchair and placing it over Rafferty's long body.

Prim licked her lips nervously as she looked at him, immobile on her couch and her heart grew so tight, she thought it might explode in her chest. Goddamn him and his penchant for trying to save her.

She'd avoided him like the plague since moving back here and finding out he was back home, too. The last she knew, he'd gone back to Yemen after bailing her out of jail, when she'd told him she wasn't interested in reconnecting.

Was that a shitty thing to do? Fuck yeah, it was, and Prim knew it. She didn't have anyone she could call to help her after she'd punched the guy who'd dumped Freddy.

No friends or relatives or even acquaintances, and in a spur-of-the-moment act of desperation, she'd dialed his number at the police station as her one call. Mostly because she knew it by heart. Calling him had been a real shot in the dark.

She'd been surprised to find he was even in the country. Prim often wondered if she'd actually hoped he wouldn't answer. She didn't deserve him picking up the phone.

He had, though...and Rafferty did what he always did. He came running to her rescue.

But she'd been in a dark place ever since her step-father's release from prison and what his release meant in her world. She wasn't ready to share that with anyone, especially not Rafferty.

So she'd done what she did with everyone since leaving home at seventeen—she pushed him away.

He'd accused her of using him. And he'd been right.

It disgusted her. Made her skin virtually crawl with self-loathing, but Prim had given up on letting anyone in. In fact, it panicked her to the point of terror. Immobilized her with fear and anxiety, and try as she might to get around it, it was just easier to be a bitch.

She'd gotten off easy after she'd knocked out the guy who'd dumped Freddy. She'd paid for the motherfucker's hospital bill and the court had mandated therapy as a first-time offender.

That was how she'd met Dr. Shay, and while she wasn't even close to ready to talk about what happened years ago and her reasons for keeping people at bay, mostly because she didn't totally understand them herself, she was learning to cope.

And now this. Rafferty, on her couch, passed out cold, likely from shock, because he'd seen something he shouldn't have seen and she was going to have to summon an explanation. So how the hell was she going to explain these people and her fairy-ness?

Looking at him, half hanging off her couch, his enormous body sprawled out, it was all she could do not to brush his dirty-blond hair from his eyes, run her knuckles down his lean cheek.

Stuffing her hands inside her pockets to keep from doing just that, she explained who Rafferty was to the women and Darnell and some green kid with the man named Archibald.

Green. He was green. Jesus Christ. Prim shook her head. She couldn't delve into this aspect of the upside down right now. He'd have to wait.

Instead, she simply said, "He's my neighbor. His name is Rafferty Monroe. We grew up together. I guess he came to check on me because I didn't return his texts."

Usually, to discourage him from texting, she gave him one-word answers. But Rafferty was nothing if he wasn't determined, no matter how many times she ignored his cheerful greetings and funny jokes.

Katy hopped up on the couch, put out that someone was lying on her favorite pillow, and plunked herself down on Rafferty's big chest.

"Look at my sweet girl," Nina cooed, running her hand over Katy's white head. "She likes him. How come Mommy doesn't?"

Marty blinked, reaching down to scratch Katy under the chin. "You don't like him, Primrose? What's not to like about him? He's not hard to look at, that's for sure, and your cat sure likes him. Animals are pretty good judges of character."

She more than liked him. She often thought it felt as though she'd always more than liked him, but...

Prim bristled to hide her emotions. She didn't owe these people explanations about her life or how she felt about Raff. "I didn't say I didn't like him."

"Then why the fuck didn't you want him to come in?" Nina asked plainly.

"Yeah. Why the fuck didn't you want me to come in, Prim?" she heard Rafferty repeat, his voice groggy.

Rolling her eyes to avoid making contact with Raff's gaze, she forced an aggravated sigh. "Because I'm busy. Do you see all these people here? That means I'm busy—with company."

Rafferty grabbed Katy and sat up, looking at all the new faces in her living room, swinging his legs over the side of the couch. "Did I miss some big epiphany in your life? Or maybe you had a near-death experience? Because this looks like a party I wasn't invited to. A party the Primrose Dunham *I* know would rather peel off all her skin than have for a houseful of people."

Her lips thinned as she planted her hands on her hips. "Maybe you just weren't invited, Rafferty? You may have been invited to all the parties in school because you were Mr. Popular, but high school's fucking over."

He patted the place where his heart beat. "I'd be crushed if that were the truth. Now, quit bullshitting me and tell me what's going on."

She squeezed her temples with two fingers. It had been a long couple of days. She was exhausted. Bone weary. She wanted everyone to go away and leave her the hell alone. But it didn't look like that was going to happen. So fuck it. She decided to lay it on him.

Clucking her tongue, Prim sighed. "You wanna know what the fuck's going on?"

Rafferty yanked off his hat and shrugged out of his jacket. "Yeah. I do."

"Okay. I'll tell you. Buckle up, Buttercup. Its story time." Prim cracked her knuckles and blew out a breath. "Friday night, I came home. I heated up a shitty TV dinner because it was defrosting all over my shitty toxic dump of a fridge and my new one's not here yet. I fed Freddy and Katy. I fucked around online, looking for people to hire to fix up this shithole. Then I took a lukewarm trickle of a shower and got into bed. When I woke up, I was in a dungeon—"

"Like a BDSM dungeon?" Rafferty asked, his brow furrowing as he tossed his hat from hand to hand.

What was it with everyone equating a dungeon to sex? "No, Rafferty. A *dungeon*, dungeon. Like *medieval*. Candles on the walls, handcuffs, chains, the whole Renaissance Fair experience."

"Sorry, he offered sheepishly. "I was just asking..."

Prim dismissed him with a wave of her hand. "Know where I was in that dungeon, Raff? *In a fucking jar*. Like the kind of jar my mom used to use when she pickled cucumbers or made jam. That means, I was the size of a damn gnat. I also had on a leotard and a fluffy tutu. But that's for another day. Anyway, plum bananas, right? Know what else I had? Wings! Motherfucking—"

"Cut it out, Prim—"

She jammed a finger into Raff's shoulder to stop him. "I'm not done yet."

Whipping around, she lifted her sweatshirt so he could see her shoulder blade before she yanked it back down after hearing the appropriate gasp.

"Like I was saying, I had *wings*. But I managed to escape and fly the fuck out of the jar when some weird-looking hobbit guy dressed in a brown robe opened it to take me out. I flew as fast as I could, considering I don't know shit-all about having wings or how the fuck to use them."

"Wings," Rafferty mumbled, his face a mask of confusion...

"Wings," Prim reiterated. "Anyway, I flapped those bastards like my life depended on it. Past toadstools the size of houses, past trees with pink and purple leaves, past little woodland creatures, and somehow, I ended up at one of these ladies' houses —"

"That was me," Marty said sheepishly as she raised her hand and looked at Rafferty, who's eyes had gone wide. "I mean, it was *my* house she ended up at."

Prim jabbed a finger in the air. "Right. It was *Marty's* house. The wolf lady's house. Where was I?" she asked as she began to pace. "Oh! Right. I ended up outside the wolf lady's house, where I ran into this monster right here," she said, pointing to Nina, who growled at her in return. "This is Nina. She's a vampire. That's why she's so pale. But I digress."

"Prim, why are you doing this?" Rafferty asked, beginning to rise in protest.

But she pushed him back on the couch with a flat palm to his shoulder. "Still not finished. Anyway, I flew right into Nina's perfect face. She snatched me up in her hand. She's crazy-fast. Like, magician fast. She brought me inside and, long story short, there was a fight about what to do with tiny me. Nina the vampire wanted to throw me back out into the cold, but Marty the werewolf said, 'No! You can't just throw her out into the cold, Mistress of the Dark!'" she mocked, mimicking Marty and pressing her fists to her chest like a damsel in distress.

"Oh, I did not," Marty vehemently denied, making a face.

"Well, maybe not quite like that, but you did stop Nina from hurling her out the door," Wanda agreed, smoothing her skirt over her thighs.

"She sure did," Prim said on a nod. "Then Marty the wolf lady turned into a big, hairy, snarling thing like in the movies because she was mad at Nina the vampire. They got into a fight and while they were fighting, I, being the size of a damn mosquito, was launched like a grenade into a cupboard." Prim paused to be sure she was relaying this fucknuttery in the proper order.

"Get to the fucking point, would you?" Nina complained.

"Shhh." She pressed a finger to Nina's mouth, a finger Nina snapped at. "Just wait," she mumbled, trying to concentrate on the order of things. "Lemme backtrack. I lost my place. It was jar. Escape. Wings. Holy Tinkerbell. Fly. Then Monster with ninja speed. Yelling. A fight. Hair. Teeth. Drool. Ugh. So much damn drool. Thrown into a wall at warp speed. Then... Oh, yes! I remember. Then I was big again, and naked in Marty the wolf lady's kitchen. Then there was more yelling and telling me I was in danger—"

"You *are* in danger, young lady," Wanda muttered in disgust.

Prim nodded and winked. "What she said. Anyway, I told them all to fuck right off, which I'm sure comes as no great surprise to you because I'm an angry potty mouth. Then I left as fast as my bare feet and half-naked ass could move in the snow. But Nina the vampire and Darnell the..." She looked to him in question. What was Darnel again?

She was sure someone had mentioned it in one of their outlandish retellings of how they came to be, but she couldn't remember. "What are you again?"

"Demon. I'm a demon." Then he grinned and tipped his imaginary hat at Rafferty, who blanched as he continued to twist his hat between his fingers—a gesture only she knew meant he was freaked out.

"That's it! A demon. Darnell the demon stopped me and made me let them give me a ride home. Well, stopped is a kind word. Nina grabbed me, threw me under her arm like luggage and shoved me into a big, fancy SUV with lights like the cockpit of a plane. They dropped me here and I thought I'd gotten rid of them, but no such fucking luck—"

"Prim, maybe you should slow down a bit?" Wanda suggested. "Your friend looks positively peaked."

But she shook her head, aghast at the idea. "Why stop now when I'm just getting to the point?" She turned back to Rafferty. "Anyway, then we came here and I couldn't get inside because of course, after being snatched from my bed and locked up in a jar, I didn't have my keys on me. I tried to get in the fucking front door, that damn thing always sticks, but again, no such luck. So then I tried the window and still couldn't get in, but Nina the vampire could because she's freakishly strong—"

Nina boinked her in the arm, her expression annoyed. "Don't call me a freak or I'll eat your face off."

Prim tilted her head and gave Nina a questioning look. "I thought Wanda was in charge of eating faces?"

Nina fisted her fingers with a growl and went for Prim's throat, but Marty stopped her. "Knock it off, Nina! And, Prim? Get to the damn point!"

Prim stuck her tongue out at Nina before returning to her story. "So like I said, Nina pried open the window, which was glued shut by a zillion years of paint and whatever else that scumbag Smitty used to keep the cops out of this dump after I jumped ship. So we got inside, and Freddy and Katy had a little insta-love with Nina the vampire, while Darnell the demon started a fire. I tried to get them to go away, but they just wouldn't split—"

"We're not doing this to inconvenience you, Primrose. We're doing this to—"

"*Help* me." Prim cut off Wanda with a sarcastic tone and air quotes. "Right. They're *helping* me. So then these other two cuckoo birds showed up, luggage in hand like this is some Airbnb because they claim they have new and exciting news about what happened to me. Get this, Rafferty. Apparently, Marty's cousin's brother's sister's BFF who was at a ceramics class—"

"Pottery!" Marty shouted petulantly. "It's pottery, and it was my husband's cousin's BFF, for crap's sake!"

"Details-schmetails," Prim retorted. "Anyway, this BFF said that someone stole me from my bed and turned me into a fairy. That would be the good fairies called see-somethings, as a point of reference. The good fairies gave me powers that some bad fairies, the un-see-somethings, want and they're gonna try to kill me to get them. You good so far, Raff?"

"Seelie and Unseelie. That's what they're called," Darnell pleasantly reminded.

"Yeah, them," Prim drawled sarcastically. "Still with me, Raff?"

He looked up at her, his eyes clouded with a million different emotions she, at one time, would have been able to decipher but now couldn't parse due to the distance between them. "I..."

Prim stabbed her finger in the air. "Exactly! That's what I said. Or didn't say. It left me speechless just like you are right now. Either way, I get your confusion. So then I told them to take their crackerpants asses on out of here *again*, because I think this is some kind of prank orchestrated by Darleen—"

"Who's Darleen?" Raff interrupted.

"She's the bitch in HR at my place of employment who hates my guts. But she's neither here nor there becaaaaause, guess what?" When he didn't answer, Prim pressed him. "Go ahead. Ask me what."

With wide blue eyes, he mumbled, "Uh, *what*?"

"Just before you stuck your nose where it didn't belong to check on me after I've told you to go away a billion times, I found out I can make myself invisible. I don't know how I did it. I don't know why it happened, but while you were out there playing Mr. Nice Guy with Nina the vampire and trying to use your honey/vinegar motto to get past her, I was in here losing my shit because I couldn't see my reflection in the goddamn mirror."

When she didn't say anything else and the room grew deafeningly silent, Prim plopped down on the hearth of the fireplace and waited for Rafferty to process.

He always needed time to make sense of things, which is what made him the far more rational of the pair. Raff always looked at both sides of the story before making a judgement call. He put time and effort into making a logical, fair choice.

She, on the other hand, shot her mouth off and hoped for the best.

Scooping up Katy, who'd abandoned Rafferty, she looked at him with a "Don't you wish you'd gone home now?" gaze.

He ran a hand over his hair, smoothing the chin-length locks away from his face, his mouth open. "I..."

Prim captured his gaze with hers in a challenge. "You what, Raff?"

He moved his mouth again, but very little sound came out and still only one fully formed word. "I..."

Prim set Katy back on the floor and slapped her thighs in satisfaction before rising. "Do you see why I told you to go home? Are you happy you stuck your nose into my business now, Raff?"

"Jesus. Why are you such an asshole?" Nina barked out of the blue. "It's obvious he fucking gives a shit about you. And from the looks of it, you don't have too many people who give a shit—"

"Nina!" Marty hollered with a shake of her finger, her bangle bracelets clanking together. "You stop right there, Miss Ma'am. I find it uncanny that you're calling someone who could be your twin an asshole. Or are you forgetting how many people cared about *you* before we came along?"

"Marty, *stop*. Stop this instant," Wanda demanded, stomping her foot, making Freddy shiver. "I absolutely won't have the two of you fighting about a client. We're a team. We're *always* going to be a team. While the similarities between their personalities are striking—a lack of filter comes to mind—Nina has us and everyone we've helped, *forever*. I'm sure Prim has plenty of people who care about her and—"

"No," Prim said quietly, holding up a hand to keep Wanda from pitying her. "No. Nina the vampire's right."

She could admit the truth. She knew it was just her and her dog and cat. She'd come to terms with it. There was no reason to lie. It didn't hurt as much as it used to—or, she refused to let it hurt like it once had, if you listened to her therapist.

"She really is right. It's just me and Freddy and Katy, and it probably always will be. I'm fine with that. Now, take your tea and sympathy and your rainbow-colored friends and your need to help me and get the fuck out," she said tiredly, even though as she spoke the words, they left her with a strange sadness she couldn't deny.

As she turned to leave the room, Raff did what he always did. He latched onto her arm and pleaded with her. "Prim, don't go. Please. Let's talk about this—"

He stopped short when everyone gasped—just like they'd gasped earlier.

When she turned back around, Raff wasn't there.

Or at least, his body wasn't there.

His clothes stood there, just like someone had plucked his person from them.

But the rest of him?

Invisible.

CHAPTER

SEVEN

"What the hell is going on, Prim?" Rafferty fought not to howl the question. "Who are these people and why am I fading in and out like a TV station that needs tuning? Are we on drugs? Did they drug us? Did they drug *you*? Jesus Christ, what's happening?"

Prim squinted her eyes at him. "You know, I thought drugs, too. Maybe hallucinogens, an acid trip. I don't know. I've never done drugs, but I've seen some shit these last coupla days, Raff. Shit I can't explain."

"We've been trying to explain it to you, Prim. You simply refuse to listen," Wanda—at least, he thought that was her name—pointed out as she came to stand in the doorway of Prim's bedroom.

She leaned against it, stylish and stately, her eyes warm and friendly as she looked at him, or *pieces* of him, in the mirror.

Try as he might, he couldn't summon his reflection in the mirror. Almost nothing but his clothes were fully visible while the rest of him crackled and faded in and out.

"How about you explain it to *me* then. Is this some sort of mass hallucination? Hypnotic state? What the hell is happening?"

The elegant female dressed like Princess Grace shook her head. "No. As you can see over Prim's shoulder, where part of her wing is poking out, I doubt that's something even an expert hypnotist could manage."

Her *wing*. A shimmery, gossamer, multicolored wing. Jesus, Joseph and a camel.

"Then what?" Rafferty murmured as he sat on the edge of Prim's bed, flabbergasted.

She plunked down next to him and clapped him on the shoulder, her eyes full of sympathy—which meant this was serious. Prim rarely allowed herself even an ounce of vulnerability.

"I told you. I'm a fairy with fairy powers. Didn't you listen to what I said out there?"

Raff blew out the breath he'd been holding. "I heard wolf lady and vampire and mosquito and jar and dungeon. I heard a bunch of shit, Prim, and none of it made sense. Zero sense."

She nodded her head and looked down at her sneakers, the scent of her perfume, familiar and soft, wafting to his nose. "Tell me something I don't fucking know, Raff. I don't know what the hell is happening. I keep hoping I'll wake up and I can go back to life as I knew it. But so far, the nightmare continues."

Wanda stepped into the room, folding her hands in a basket in front of her. "Listen, you two, here's what we think. We think when you passed out and fell on Prim, she somehow rubbed off on you, a transfer of power, if you will."

"So does that mean every time I bump into someone, I'm gonna turn them into a damn fairy?" Prim asked. "Because we're gonna have a shit-ton of fairies if that's the case. Or did I give all my so-called power to him and I'm cleared for takeoff?"

Wanda smiled in sympathy, grabbing Prim's hand and squeezing. "No. I don't think that, Prim, and I don't think you're cleared for takeoff either. What I *do* think? I think there's a connection between you two we don't understand, and you have to at least grant us the time to figure it out. We *can* figure it out, if you'll just let us contact the people we know in our world."

Their world? Raff shook his head. What did that mean? What a curious thing to say.

Curiouser still? Prim didn't pull away from Wanda's touch. Further proof she didn't hate all physical contact. Maybe it was just *his* physical contact.

But right now, that was the least of his concerns. He wanted to know what was going on and how he could help Prim, and himself, get through this. "So are you telling me, I'm a fairy, too?"

Wanda nodded with a forlorn sigh. "I think so, Rafferty."

"Am I collecting teeth or granting wishes? You know, bibbidi-bobbidi-boo?" he asked, because those were the only fairies he knew aside from Tinker Bell.

"That's what I fucking asked, too!" Nina barked from the other room. "But sourpuss in there gave me the eyeball of death for asking. See, Wanda? I wasn't being fucking unreasonable. I was being *logical*, not getting all in my stupid chick feelings."

Wanda rolled her eyes before she went all business. "I don't think you're the tooth fairy, but after what I've experienced, I can't say for sure. If Darnell's nose is right, both you and Prim are Seelie."

Darnell's nose? His nose told him they were fairies? He'd ask about that later. But the Seelie bit? It meant nothing. "I don't know what that means."

Wanda sighed. "Listen, why don't you come out into the kitchen where Arch is making some late-night grilled cheese and we can talk. Everything's better on a warm, full tummy. Especially when it's Arch's grilled cheese." She blew a chef's kiss for emphasis. "Then we'll tell you all about what happened to us, how we got where we are, what we think is happening to you, and how we'll try and help you both get through this. Okay?"

He hesitated as his hand began to make an appearance. "Is Arch the blue man?"

She tinkled a laugh lighter than air and winked. "A

troll. Arch is a troll. Also something we'll thoroughly explain."

Rafferty was almost convinced to follow her, but then he stopped. "Wait. The green boy...his hand..."

She smiled reassuringly again. "That's Carl. I can explain him, too. You'll love him. He's the sweetest zombie on the face of the planet."

"*Zombie?*" both he and Prim shouted.

That was when Carl appeared behind Wanda, putting his reattached, duct-taped hand on her shoulder. "Hi..." he said shyly. "I'm...I'm Carl."

"The zombie," Rafferty repeated woodenly.

Wanda reached up and gripped Carl's hand. "*The zombie*," she reiterated.

He nodded his dark head, his sweet face wreathed in a smile. "Yeesss. Zooom...bie."

Sweet Christ.

"So will you two join us?" Wanda asked with a gentle tilt of her head.

"I guess we don't have much choice," Prim muttered. "It's either listen to what they have to say or get the toilet paper and wrap your big ass up so we know where the hell you are."

Rafferty couldn't help it. He sputtered a laugh at the vision of how much toilet paper it would take to wrap his six-foot-four "ass", which had a contagious effect as Prim, Wanda and Carl, all started to laugh, too.

Carl held his hand out to Prim, and lo and behold,

she hesitated only a moment before she accepted it, standing up and following the *zombie* out of the bedroom.

Wanda cocked her head in question, and left with no other alternatives, Rafferty got up and headed to the kitchen, too.

For some grilled cheese and story time.

Now fully visible again, Rafferty sat in a folding chair Archibald had brought with him, at a shaky card table —also provided by Archibald—and finished the last bite of his third grilled cheese sandwich.

He had to admit, Wanda was right. The little blue man with the very proper British accent knew grilled cheese. "Wow. That's the best grilled cheese I've ever had. Even better than my mom's."

Archibald, his blue face full of smiles, nodded his thanks. "The secret to a good grilled cheese, Master Monroe, is to butter both sides of the bread—a sliced brioche. And of course, a good gruyere with a slab of smoked gouda for good measure."

"It was amazing. Thank you." He wiped his mouth, looking at all these new people sitting around a card table in the middle of Primrose Dunham's house, and couldn't help but remember a time—a time before her stepfather, Smitty—when he and Prim sat at her kitchen table, eating Lunchables and apples dipped in caramel her mother had made as an after-school snack.

After Smitty came and laid down the law, those days had stopped, and so had their afternoon hang-outs around the table—*her* table, anyway.

She'd spent time at his house, but not nearly as often as she had before her stepfather came on the scene and filled her days with after-school chores and rigid rules.

Fuck. Now wasn't the time to remember that abso-lute dick of a human being, but he knew Prim was thinking about it, too, by the way she stared off into space, chewing slowly.

Now was the time to focus on what these women had told him as he wolfed down sandwich after sandwich.

Organizing his questions in his head, Raff looked to Nina the vampire, beautiful and angry. "So you claim to be a vampire, right?" Man, she was so much like Prim, he almost thought they might be sisters.

"I don't *claim* shit. I *am* a fucking vampire, and I'd be happy to show you." She flashed her teeth at him. Her pointy, very sharp-looking teeth.

Rafferty wiped his mouth with a linen napkin, something he never thought he'd see in Prim's posses-sion, and shook his head. "I'm good, thanks. I'm just trying to keep everything straight in my head. So now you run something called OOPS? There are others like us who've had this happen to them by accident, correct?"

"That's right," Marty said with an easygoing smile. "We formed the group shortly after Wanda's sister was turned into a demon."

"Dumbest fucking thing we ever did," Nina grumbled, but she patted Carl's hand with a smile as she held Freddy Mercury in her lap. "Except for finding my boy Carl. That was one of the best days of my life."

Carl beamed at Nina, his eyes twinkling when he brought her hand to his cheek and nuzzled it, making her smile at him affectionately. "Me...t...too."

"Dumb?" Raff said. "Why?"

Nina snorted and made a face. "Yeah, dumb. Because of the bullshit we just went through with *you* two fools. No one ever believes us when we fucking tell them what happened to them. There's always a lot of denial, crying. Lots of crying. Bullshit alternate theories about what went down while they try to talk themselves out of what really happened. Then once we get them to accept their fucking fate, there's trouble. Somebody always wants whatever shit they have. The whole damn process is exhausting. That's why it's dumb."

Marty flicked her fingers at Nina. "Because you accepted your fate right away? Because you didn't balk and carry on, all the while swearing like the world was coming to an end?"

Nina grabbed Marty's finger and twisted it. "The fuck I carried on, Ass-Sniffer."

She simply rolled her eyes. "Don't listen to anything Nina says. She has what we like to call a *framily* because of OOPS. The people we help always start the journey hating her guts because she's loud, rude, unfiltered and always threatening to rip something from your body, but those people end up finding out she'd take a hit for them as readily as she'd take one for a blood relative. Nina's a lot of mouth, but she's gushy-soft on the inside, aren't you, Dark Lord?"

Marty pinched her friend's cheek and smiled at her when Nina flipped up both middle fingers from across the table.

"So you were all friends before this happened?" Prim asked as she began to relax a bit in her chair.

She'd been pretty quiet throughout most of the meal, but she'd already heard most of what the women told him, he supposed.

Nina barked a laugh, and Marty and Wanda fell into each other giggling, but they all looked at one another with a fondness you couldn't mistake for anything other than a deep friendship.

As Marty caught her breath, she said, "Friends isn't exactly the word I'd use. Not at first, anyway. At least not until we all were turned. Let's just say we were all trying to make a buck—"

"Selling fucking goop for your GD face and telling people what was in their color wheels, door-to-fucking-door, no less," Nina said sarcastically, but her face had a doting smile at the memory. "It was bullshit. Never sold a stupid thing."

Wanda waved a warning finger at Nina. "But now, Marty *owns* the company, which you might have heard of—Bobbie-Sue and Pack Cosmetics—where we met selling *goop* for women's faces. So there's that. We've been together for fifteen years now, if that says anything about our friendship and how close we've become. We've married, had children, shared our lives just like any other family would, except we're a paranormal family—or *framily*, as Nina calls us."

Despite the circumstances and despite how crazy this all sounded, he'd watched them interact, watched how they moved fluidly as one unit, even just in setting the card table with dishes. He'd watched how they laughed and joked with one another, and he believed them.

He believed they meant well, that they wanted to help. He knew for sure Primrose *didn't* believe them. Not entirely. Or rather, she didn't want to believe them because it meant letting complete strangers into her life, people she'd have to connect with whether she wanted to or not in order to keep herself out of danger.

He just wasn't sure he was ever going to be able to accept that he was a fairy.

"So do you charge money for this OOPS thing? Like a fee to find out what's going on?"

Wanda looked horrified. "Absolutely not! We offer

our services because we've been there, Rafferty. We know what it's like to wander around in a world with not only intense changes to your body, but to your mind. You can't believe we didn't all think we'd gone mad when Marty and Nina were bitten, do you? We were all one hundred percent human once, too."

She paused and placed her chin in her hand, leaning her elbow on the table. "No. We don't charge money. Our interests lie in helping you adjust to something outrageously unthinkable. The only thing we ask is that you trust us. It's probably a bigger ask than money, but it's a necessity in the new world you're going to have no choice but to live in."

He swallowed hard and looked at Prim, who appeared to have zoned back out. "So there's no going back to human?"

"'Fraid not," Darnell said, placing a beefy hand on his shoulder. "But we're gonna help you, Rafferty. I promise ya that."

What else could he do but put his trust in these people? Where else did you turn when you'd gone invisible right before your very own eyes?

He'd been in some damn scary situations, including the one that ultimately made him leave conflict journalism, but this? This was terrifying. Unbelievably terrifying.

"Okay," he whispered almost to himself before he cleared his throat. "Okay. So what do we do now? How do we find out what the fairies want and how do we learn how to live as...fairies?"

Christ. He'd agreed to live as a fairy. All six-foot-four, two-hundred and sixty pounds of him.

"First, we move in and totally fuck up your lives," Nina said with a wicked grin. "We screw with your daily schedules, we frig with your TV time. It sucks—for all of us. You call in sick to work because I'm pretty sure you don't want to be invisible in front of people, do you? Then you derps don't go anywhere without us, *ever*. Got that? Because bad shit is bound to go down. We're with you twenty-four seven, up your asses like a damn itchy hemorrhoid—""

"What Nina means is, until we understand what your powers mean, how to control them, and who's an ally and who isn't, you stay put," Wanda said as she rose from her chair, brushing crumbs from her skirt with a smile. "One of us will go with you to collect your things, but you have to stay here with us so we can keep an eye on you while we find some resources to help."

Hah! Prim was gonna love that.

"Why does he have to stay here?" Prim protested on cue with his thoughts. "Can't you go to his house? It's right next door."

Nina made a face. "No, fucknuts. We stay together at all times. All of us have a role in this shit, strengths that are uniquely our own, and together, we're a bunch of badass bitches. So no. He stays here. Or we can all go to his house—which might be better because your house is a shithole."

Rafferty fought a snort of laughter. Prim's house had once been a thing of beauty. Until Smitty, that is. He hadn't just ruined lives. He'd ruined her family home, her world, and even if it was crumbling around her, she wouldn't want to leave it because he knew she felt her mother in every nook and cranny.

She firmly shook her head, crossing her arms over her chest in an all-too-familiar act of defiance. "Nope. I'm not fucking going anywhere."

"Then *fucking* here it is. Talk amongst yourselves and work this shit, whatever this shit is, out," Nina said with a jeer before she began picking up plates she hadn't even eaten from.

Rafferty sighed. As much as he wanted to connect with the woman he'd loved for what felt like forever, he didn't want to make things worse for her.

He didn't understand why she'd shut him out all those years ago after their high school graduation, and she refused to tell him what happened right before she did, but more than anything, he didn't want her to hurt anymore.

He hated that she hurt.

As the women and Darnell began clearing plates and helping Arch and Carl straighten up the kitchen, he cornered her. "Look, Prim, this is pretty messed up. I get that. I'd go home if I could. But we both know what happened to us. You saw it with your own eyes. Who else can we go to for help, if not these people?"

Her beautiful green gaze, fringed with thick lashes that needed no adornment, searched his, but only for a moment before she put up that wall and closed herself off. "I don't know. I need some time to think. Until then, just let me breathe."

"Prim, we were once friends—"

"In high school, but those days are over Rafferty," she said, her eyes avoiding his, but her tone was pleading. "Why can't you just let them go?"

He wanted to deny they were over. He wanted to find out why they *had* to be over—even as just friends. But from his vast experience with Prim, he knew not to push.

Looking her directly in the eye, he gave her a curt nod. "As you wish."

She stared back at him momentarily, then turned on her heel and stomped off to another part of the house.

And that hurt the same way it always did.

More than he cared to admit.

CHAPTER

EIGHT

Archibald, who Prim had dubbed the organizer of the group, had brought blow-up mattresses and blankets and all sorts of things to make everyone comfortable for their invasion...er, *stay* at her house.

Everyone had gone off to claim a room and get settled while Nina had taken Rafferty to his house to gather clothes and whatever else he needed for an extended fairy-fact-finding mission.

She'd finally been able to grab a shower in her crappy bathroom with even crappier hot water. How everyone was going to be able to groom themselves, especially as much grooming as Marty and Wanda apparently needed, with a trickle of water, let alone cook every day was beyond her.

But they'd made it clear they weren't going

anywhere. So let them suffer the way she did living here.

Her house was a far cry from Marty's cozy, warm Pinterest advertisement of a glam farmhouse. Yet, they'd insisted; this is what they got for pushing themselves on her.

Is that fair, Primrose? How much do you think they love being away from their families and homes, especially during Christmas? Do you think they love leaving behind their creature comforts for a stubborn, mouthy bitch like you? How do you figure in helping you, they're pushing themselves on you? Nina was right. You're being an asshole.

Pulling a clean sweatshirt over her head, past her ridiculous wing, she knew the voice in her mind was as right as Nina. She was an asshole. It's what kept people where they belonged. Away from her.

But how long can you isolate yourself?

Rafferty wants into your life. You know you secretly want him in your life, too. You always have. You can only push him away for so long before he leaves forever. Maybe if you shared with him what happened, you can figure out how to heal it together.

How was she going to stay in such close proximity to him and not launch herself into his arms? How was she going to be in the same space with a man she'd loved for so long, but fought hard to keep at arm's length?

Running a quick brush through her wet hair, she gazed at her reflection in the mirror and grimaced, pushing away all the emotions Rafferty created in her.

He made her feel things she didn't want to feel. He reminded her that once, her life had been pretty fucking great—filled with possibilities.

He reminded her of a time when it had been just her and her mother, Liesl. A time when she'd been mostly normal and they'd done everything together.

Prim wanted nothing less than to remember because it hurt more than any word she could ever craft to explain.

Shaking off her maudlin thoughts, she just wanted to forget for a little while. She was crispy-fried after these past couple of days. What she really wanted to do was curl up under the blanket her mother had knitted for her with Katy and Freddy and sleep for a year.

But as she tried to get comfortable, her wing had other plans. It pressed uncomfortably against the mattress, making it impossible for her to lay on her favorite side to sleep, and she really needed to sleep.

If for nothing else, for perspective that wasn't clouded by overwhelming fear and panic.

"Fuck," she muttered, tossing and turning until she finally decided to get up and sit by the window in her bedroom. That had always soothed her when she was younger. Maybe watching the snow fall would clear her head.

Dropping down into the chair she'd just had delivered the other day and placed by the floor-to-ceiling windows in her mother's old bedroom, she decided to test its comfort.

It was wide enough for her to work from, with plenty of room for Freddy and Katy to sit beside her, and she could put her feet up. She loved the peacock-blue fabric, soft and velvety against her hand.

Tucking Freddy and Katy in next to her, she wrapped up in the blanket her mother had knitted for her one year for Christmas, and stared out the window that faced her small backyard.

The snow fell in rapid white flakes, leaving a curtain of white in its wake. Leaning her head back, she watched as it began to pile up on top of the rusty patio table they used to have dinner at in the summer. It had once been a beautiful place to sit and enjoy a meal.

Lights were strung from the fence, warm and twinkling. There'd been a small garden with herbs her mother grew because she loved to cook. Creeping ivy grew along the side of the house next to the small cobblestone patio, where she'd sat to do her homework in the spring.

Now, the backyard looked like a bomb had exploded in it. Every time she thought she might be able to tackle the idea of renovating, just the idea of how much there was to fix overwhelmed her.

Every corner of her beloved family home was

trashed. But she had a dream of restoring it; it was just going to take time and a whole lotta dough.

With a sigh, as Freddy sank into her thigh and Katy curled up on the back of the chair, resting her chin on Prim's head, the house now dark and quiet, her eyes began to close and for a moment before she drifted off, she felt safe.

She couldn't explain why, but she didn't want to analyze it. She simply wanted to enjoy the moment.

A SMALL SCRATCHING noise niggled at her brain, buzzing and annoying, forcing her to open one eye.

"Get her! Change her now!" a small, squeaky voice ordered.

"I am *trying*, Alfrigg! Can you not see I'm trying?"

Prim's eyes popped open in time to see two very tiny, very weird-looking bugs with human faces and wings.

Wings. Beautiful, gossamer, multicolored wings.

Blinking, she couldn't figure out if, after all that talk of fairies, she was dreaming or they were truly real.

"Change her now! We must bring her back to the Realm of the Hollow before he finds out she's missing, before he finds us and finds out what we've done, Cosmo! We will be severely punished for our mistake! Use all your magic!"

At those words, Prim felt the heat of something she had no definition for begin at the top of her head and fly all the way to her feet, leaving her tingling.

"Bah! Do you not think I'm using my magic, Alfrigg? She resists!"

When her eyes adjusted, she saw a sprinkle of colorful dust floating around her head. Dust that made her cough and gag as Freddy began to growl and nip at the air.

Prim shot upward in the chair, swatting at the dots with wings as she gasped for breath through the haze of dust. "Who the fuck are you? What do you want?"

Her words sent their tiny wings into overdrive, buzzing madly as they launched balls of color at her that served to do nothing more than burn her eyes.

She felt like she was in the middle of a goddamn evil Disney movie gone wrong.

Jumping up, Prim swished her hands in the air in an attempt to catch them, grasping and reaching to no avail.

"Stranger-daaanger!" someone called out as she stumbled around her room, tripping over boxes and the beanbag on the floor, trying to catch the fluttering dots of light.

They flitted about the room, darting at her head, shooting dust balls of color that zigzagged through the air in dazzling swirls of light.

Freddy began to snarl and bark, biting at the air in an attempt to catch them. One of them lobbed a huge ball of color at him, zapping his hind leg and making him yelp in pain.

"You son of a bitch! That's my dog!" Prim cried out, diving for one of the buzzing dots.

Out of nowhere, Carl came rushing into her room, crashing through the door with a poker from the fireplace in his hands. "Baaad!" he bellowed, climbing on the bed and swinging the poker at them like a bat.

They went straight for sweet Carl's eyes, inciting Prim as a rush of rage sizzled up her spine. He was just a kid. A weird green kid, but a kid. One she kind of didn't mind nearly as much as she did the women.

He'd brought her, of all things, a head of broccoli to eat with her grilled cheese. According to Nina it was one of his favorite foods, and that he was sharing it with her was a gift.

A zombie who ate broccoli, not brains. The irony didn't escape her, but she'd be damned if she'd let someone hurt him.

The colored dust had an effect on him that it didn't appear to have on her. Carl began to sputter and shake. He dropped the poker, letting it clatter to the floor as his limbs convulsed.

"Carl!" she screamed, plowing over top of the bed as the two buzzing entities launched their fire at him.

Prim threw herself over his body to protect him when she heard a low growl—a snarl so menacing, so frightening, she was afraid to look up.

But Prim did look up.

Hail Mary full of grace...

That was all she could remember of the prayer in the height of her fear, before her mouth fell open and her eyes went wide at the sight of Nina, her face a mask of absolute rage.

"Get the fuck away from my kid or I'll wipe your ass from the face of this planet!" Nina hollered, her fangs in full view as she lunged for the two tiny dots with a roar of fury.

She lashed a hand out and successfully managed to hit one of them before actually catching it in her hand. She began to squeeze, her eyes bordering on blood red before she yelped, "Motherfucker!" and let go.

Prim clung to Carl, his body quaking and twisting as she stroked his hair and held him close. "Carl, hang on. Just hang on. Help is coming," she whispered, rocking him, trying to soothe him.

Her bedroom window shattered as Nina burst through the glass, chasing after the two dots, the loud crash splitting the air while glass skittered across her littered floor.

Marty and Wanda flew into the room in their bathrobes, running to where she rocked Carl.

Marty took him from her arms. "What happened, Prim?" she cried, cradling Carl.

She licked her dry lips, still unclear herself what

happened. She only knew Carl was hurt, and he was hurt because of *her*.

This had to be because of her, right? Those annoying-AF buzzy things had to be fairies, and they were here because they wanted her. She'd heard them say it.

Carl was hurt because of her and she didn't know what to do to make it right. Tears stung the corners of her eyes as she tried to put together a full sentence.

But all she could manage was, "I'm sorry, Carl. I'm so sorry!"

Without warning, Prim found herself overwhelmed with emotion. She almost never cried, hadn't shed a tear in a long, long time—not since she'd left home after graduation. But seeing Carl looking so helpless, his eyes red, his limbs no longer convulsing but limp and boneless, a rush of tears assaulted her, streaming down her face in fat, salty drops.

"Prim, honey? What's going on?" Rafferty asked, his voice gravelly from sleep as he reached for her arm.

And she didn't resist. Not even a little. Rafferty was so kind. So handsome. Blond, blue-eyed, tall, muscular, but not overly so. Strong thighs, arms meant to hold a girl, a wide chest, ruddy skin.

There'd never been anyone in all these years since they'd parted ways who made her heart flutter the way he did. Who made her want to rethink spending her life with someone. But she couldn't.

Except for in this moment of terror.

She couldn't be sure what came over her. Maybe it was sleep deprivation, maybe it was the insane events of the day mingled with fear for Carl, but she threw herself into Rafferty's arms and began to sob.

"Fairies!" she howled into his chest, her words muffled by his sweatshirt as she clung to him and all his yummy muscles. "I think the fairies came back for me and they were throwing colored balls of dust and they hit Carl and I think he's hurt! Fuck, what if he's hurt because of me?"

Her words came out in a rush of muddled thoughts, partially because she didn't know where to start and partially because Rafferty's arms around her felt so stupid good, she could have stayed in them forever.

"Shh, honey. Slow down. Take a beat."

But Prim shook her head. "They hurt him, Raff! It's my fault."

Rafferty held her close, his hands rubbing soothing circles against her back as he tilted her chin up. "It's okay, Prim. Look. Carl's okay."

She lifted her head to see that Carl was, in fact, all right. He rubbed his eyes, but he smiled that lopsided grin at her. "I...I...am okay, Prim. Promise." He lifted his hand to give her a scout's honor, but if fell off his wrist and rolled to the floor.

Without a thought, Prim ran to the kitchen where she'd last seen the duct-tape and grabbed the roll off her chipped countertop. "I'll fix it, okay?" she sniffled, leaning down and scooping up Carl's hand from the floor without even thinking about the fact that she was about to tape this boy's *hand* back onto his wrist.

She yanked a strip from the roll and ripped it off with her teeth and began to wrap his wrist, trying to control her shaking. "I'm sorry, Carl. I'm so sorry. They were here because of me. This is all my fault."

Carl reached over with his good hand to cup her cheek and shook his head with a smile, his dark hair falling over his pale green forehead. "No. No fault. Okay. I—am—*o*—*kay*."

Tears began to fall from Prim's eyes again, his gentle words a balm to her heart as she taped him up, all the while fighting this unexpected onslaught of emotion.

Marty and Wanda straightened up her room and gathered Freddy and Katy as Darnell's heavy footsteps rang in her ears, signaling his entrance, his eyes wide as he sniffed.

"More fairies?"

"Yes!" Prim shouted, not bothering to question Darnell's uncanny sense of smell. Seriously, who smelled fairies? But it didn't matter. All that mattered was that Carl was okay. "I don't know how they got in or why they want me, but they want me! I heard them say so!"

He put a gentle hand on Prim's shoulder as she frantically tried to reattach Carl's hand. "Prim, slow down. Tell ol' Darnell what happened and lemme see if I can help."

Letting her hands fall to her side when Darnell took over fixing Carl's hand, she blew out a breath before she spoke.

"They woke me up. I was asleep on the chair right by the window and they started throwing colored dust balls at me. I mean, I think they were dust balls, but they didn't do anything to me but make me cough."

Darnell nodded sagely. "Fairy dust. It's magic. Can do all sorts of things, some good, some bad. Strange how it didn't bother ya, though." He paused a moment before he slapped another piece of tape on Carl's wrist. "They say anything to ya?"

Before she could answer, Nina returned via the broken window, her eyes glittering, her mouth a thin line. "Motherfuckers got away!" she spat as she climbed over the shards of glass on the window frame, brushing splinters from her footie pajamas. Then she aimed her wrath at Prim. "Who the fuck were they?"

Wiping the tears from her cheeks, Prim straightened, her eyes narrowed. "I...I don't know. I didn't ask for their profiles and stats. I was too busy trying to keep them from hurting Carl!"

Finally, her backbone had made an appearance.

Rafferty placed himself between them and held up his hands. "Okay, let's talk about this before we get too heated. It's not Prim's fault they showed up out of the blue, Nina."

Wanda, her eyes puffy from sleep, nodded when she put a hand on Nina's shoulder. "Relax, Elvira. She doesn't know who they are any more than we do. Everyone's all right. Carl's fine. Prim stayed with him to protect him. That's all that matters. Please stop being an overprotective beast and help us clean up."

Nina huffed her aggravation, but she began turning over nightstands and scooped up a broken lamp when she grunted and held up something shiny, no bigger than the size of a needle.

"What the fuck is this?" she asked, just before she pointed it at them so they could see what she held between her lean fingers.

"Boss! Nooo!" Darnell roared a warning before he launched himself at the group of women to cover them with his body. "Y'all better duck!"

Rafferty tackled Prim seconds before there was a loud explosion, sending sheetrock and old paneling rocketing through the room in raucous crashes to land on the floor in heaps.

Her heart thrashed against her chest as she squeezed her eyes shut and clung to Rafferty until there was nothing but silence.

When the dust settled, and the old bones of the house stopped creaking, Prim pushed her way out from beneath Rafferty to assess the damage.

She winced.

The entire outside wall of her house, where her

favorite window was housed, now sported a ginormous hole.

A ginormous *glowing* hole.

It was then she wondered if Chip and Joanna Gaines still did consultations.

Because this definitely classified as a *Fixer Upper*.

CHAPTER
NINE

"Holy shitballs," Nina muttered, gingerly placing the needle-like instrument on what was left of her nightstand and backing away with care.

Yeah. Holy shitballs.

Her house had exploded. Not that it didn't need some demolition—it was in pretty rough shape, after all, but if it had been hard to keep the cold air out before? It was going to be an icy hell now.

Yet, as Prim stood up, the glow surrounding the hole mesmerizing her, she noted it didn't feel at all cold. In fact, it was warm as a summer's day.

Walking toward it, her hand out, she felt compelled to touch the singed area where the sheetrock had exploded off the wall, but Nina slapped her hand. "Don't do that, dipshit! We don't know what the fuck it is, for Christ's sake!"

Prim snatched her hand back, but she had to clench her fists to keep from touching it.

Weirder still? The hole didn't lead to the backyard the way logic deemed it should. It led to a long passageway that called to her, tugging at every cell in her body. A vortex of lights swirled and danced before her eyes, and if she listened closely, she heard someone calling her name.

"*Primrose*," the dulcet voice whispered like a siren song, making her lean closer to the hole, a yearning deep within her, pulling at her.

Rafferty was right behind her, his eyes fixed on the enticing glow. "What—is—happening?" he asked, his words stilted, his beautiful blue eyes glazed, but he appeared to have the wherewithal to know something very strange was taking place.

Darnell was the first to answer, standing in front of them and holding up his large hands. "Best I can guess, it's a portal. Y'all gotta stay away from it no matter how tempting. You understand?"

Marty inhaled, pushing her pink eye mask back up on her head. "A portal? To?"

"The Hollow," Prim provided before shaking her head and shivering. How had she known that?

"The what?" Wanda asked, tightening the belt of her robe around her waist. "How do you know that, Prim?"

She flapped her hands, trying to remember what the two buzzing dots had said. "That's what those things said when they were trying to do whatever the hell they were doing to me with those dust balls. They said they had to take me back to The Realm of the Hollow before *he* knew I was missing. Doesn't it make sense that if this is a portal, it leads to wherever they came from?"

"Aw, hell," Darnell said on a heavy sigh. He scrubbed his hand over the top of his head, his eyes worried, his brow furrowed. "This ain't good. We need to board this up now, Boss. That's a whole 'nother world we don't know nothin' about. A world I only heard stories about. Till we know more, we can't let what's in there out *here*."

Prim blinked, breaking the spell the portal had on her, and backed away. "What do you know about this Hollow place?" she asked Darnell.

He lifted his wide shoulders beneath his flannel robe. "Not a lot. I just know fairies dwell there. The Seelies."

She frowned. "But those are the good fairies, right? That's what you said. If they're good fairies, maybe we should go through the portal and find out what they want. What this all means."

"Yeah, they're good, but that don't mean there aren't bad ones along the way, Prim. Good fairies don't kidnap innocent humans. And we don't know for sure this leads to the Hollow. That means, you don't go nowhere near that hole."

Marty nodded her agreement. "And if they were good fairies, why were they shooting their magic at Prim? What are they trying to accomplish? I don't like this. It's suss at best. You both stay put."

"So what is that?" Rafferty asked, pointing to the needle with a frown.

"That," Darnell said, placing a stray shoe box over it, "is a magic wand. Y'all need to stay away from it for obvi reasons, too."

Yeah. Like blow-off-the-side-of-your-house reasons.

Wanda held out her hand to Prim with a smile. "I'll make us some tea and then I want you to tell us everything those fairies said to you. Every single word."

An hour or so and a warm cup of tea later, Prim's story left everyone shaking their heads.

Nina clucked her tongue, crossing her feet at the ankles from her seat on the couch. "So we got a deadly, Barbie-sized fucking wand, a coupla vicious gnats with wings who want to take the newb fairy to their leader, and a big hole the size of a crater in the house that leads to another realm where fairies live. Jesus and shit."

"And they were trying to use their magic on you, but it wasn't working?"

Prim nodded at Wanda. "I think so. They said they had to change me to take me back to him—or something like that. What I don't get is why the fairy magic didn't work on me the way it did on Carl."

"Prolly 'cause you a badass fairy now, Prim. Sorry 'bout my cussin'," Darnell apologized. "I think whatever they did to you was big and they were supposed to keep you there for a reason. But when you got away from 'em, it screwed up their plans."

Prim let a long sigh blow from her lips, trying to make sense of this newest clue to what was happening to them. "But why? Could it be any more random? Who the hell am I to them? I'm a nobody. And what plans? How could they have *plans* for me? None of this makes any sense."

"Maybe they didn't just screw up your abduction?" Raff theorized. "Maybe they did something to you they weren't supposed to and they had to bring you back to this Hollow place to fix it? They did say they were using their magic and it wasn't working, right?"

"They did," Prim murmured, her eyes grainy as sand. "They said they had to bring me back to the Realm of the Hollow before he finds out I'm missing, or they were going to be severely punished. They said they had to bring me back before he found out they'd made a mistake. So who is *he*?"

"Tell me the names you heard again," Marty encouraged, covering a yawn.

Prim rubbed her eyes and hugged Freddy closer. "Alfred? No, Alfrigg...something like that. And Cosmo. I totally remember Cosmo because my stepfather used to drink them all the time."

In fact, he drank them until he was a belligerent, violent, verbally abusive fucking dick of a human being.

Sighing, she shook off the bad memory and waited to see what these gurus of the paranormal had to say.

But as she gazed at them all, hoping to glean some kind of supernatural wisdom, it appeared what they had to say was a big fat nothing.

"How is it, that after all these years, we don't really know any fairies, Marty?" Wanda wondered out loud, rubbing her temples.

She frowned, but then her face brightened. "We did meet a couple when we were trapped in Troll Hill with Sten, didn't we?"

Troll Hill. God, she couldn't take one more single reference to a place that sounded like it came out of the mind of R.L. Stine.

Marty slapped her thigh and smiled wide. "Yes, of course! I've been racking my brain about who to ask for help—who we could reach out to that knows something--*anything* about fairies."

"You mean other than your husband's best friend's sister's uncle at her paint-by-number class?" Prim asked, her tone dripping playful sarcasm

But Marty gave her a pointed look. "I'm going to ignore that little jab at my insider gossip and move right along like the adult I am." She turned to look at her friends. "He took us through a fairy village when we were helping Murphy and Nova. Remember?"

Nina grinned, and the expression was definitely filled with fondness. "Fuck, yeah, I remember that crazy shit. Man, I love Sten. He's a good guy. Remember his buddy Gary? What a fucking trip he was, huh?"

"Gary?" Rafferty asked from where he sat on the floor by the fireplace, his long legs stretched out in front of him and Katy in his lap.

"The giant," Nina answered on a cackle.

Well, naturally there was a giant. Why wouldn't there be a giant in troll land? Didn't that go without saying?

Wanda pulled her phone from her robe. "Anyway, Sten, the King of Trolls, took us through a fairy village to get to his land on one of our cases. It was just like being in a Disney movie. So beautiful. I bet he could at least help us identify what's happening. Maybe put us in touch with Serena?"

Now Darnell nodded his head, too, his smile warm. "Yeah, yeah. Nice lady."

Wanda rose from the couch, tucking her phone back in her robe. "Okay. I've texted Sten and Murphy, let's see what they have to say. For now, we need to board up that hole and keep you two away from it and safe. No hole hopping, got it?" she warned.

"Hole hopping," Nina snarfed, slapping Raff on the back.

Marty rolled her eyes at them before she nodded her agreement with a firm bounce of her head. "We three will sleep in your room, Prim, and you two take the bedrooms we were using. Go get some sleep and we'll see what Sten has to say in the morning."

As everyone rose, stretching and yawning, Prim couldn't help but peek at the hole in her bedroom wall. Even from her debris-filled living room, it beckoned to her.

"Look away, Prim," Rafferty whispered in her ear, making her shiver.

"Go away, Raff," she said on a snort before she scooped up Freddy and hustled up the stairs to yet another one of the bedrooms in complete disarray.

But when she turned the corner of the long hall, she was surprised to find her old room didn't look half bad. The walls were still peeling the old geometric wallpaper she'd begged her mother to let her have, the once shiny wood floors had damp spots from leaks in the ceiling, and there were piles of old newspapers. But someone had stacked them neatly in a corner and put down a pretty floral throw rug in pink and green.

One of the women had put fresh sheets on an air-mattress that sat atop her old one. Sheets that smelled like clean cotton and a spring breeze, with a pale pink quilt to snuggle under and several pale pink and ivory damask pillowcases on plump pillows.

A lavender scarf hung delicately over her torn lampshade, making it look a lot less bedraggled, casting a calming glow over the room.

It was welcoming in a way it hadn't been for a very long time. This used to be her safe haven, her place to dream, her place to find respite from a world that, after her mother's death, had eventually become cruel —ugly.

Until it wasn't. Until there was nowhere safe to hide.

But seeing the small touches the women had made to the room reminded her...there had been a life before Smitty came into it. It was good and kind, and if she could just focus on that time, she could get through this.

Sitting on the edge of the mattress, Prim noted they'd found a picture in a worn frame of her and her mother sitting on the back stoop, her head on her mother's shoulder.

Prim could still smell the perfume she wore, every day, without fail. Beautiful, by Estee Lauder. Just like her.

More tears sprang to her eyes as she looked at that once-happy time in her life, and decided she really must be tired to have this many tears in one night.

Pulling Freddy to her side, she dragged the heavy

quilt over her, clicked the light off and closed her eyes, seeing her mother's face in her mind's eye.

It was only then that she was able to empty her head of all that had passed today and find comfort in blissful sleep, where the scent of clean cotton and her mother's perfume lingered.

CHAPTER
TEN

The boom of a male voice had Prim jumping out of bed and falling to the floor in a pile of her limbs, still limp from sleep.

A glance at her phone told her it was almost ten in the morning, and Freddy needed to go out or he'd use the already damaged hardwood floors as his bathroom.

But looking around, she saw Freddy was nowhere in sight. Her bedroom door was closed and the house smelled of freshly brewed coffee and bacon.

Prim's stomach gurgled. Bacon. She loved bacon. It called to her almost with the same enticing voice as the hole in her bedroom wall.

Pulling herself off the floor, she didn't bother to look at herself in the mirror in the adjoining bathroom. Instead, she flew down the stairs, following the booming voice.

When she hit the bottom of the creaky, worn steps, avoiding the one that had caved in and splintered, she skidded into the living room and stopped short.

A giant of a man with long green hair and orange (*orange?*) eyes stood in the center of her debacle of a living room. He had muscles on top of his muscles and a smile that was warm and friendly.

He bestowed one on her, until everyone—Marty, Wanda, Darnell, Carl, Archibald, and even Nina— gasped.

That was getting old.

"*What?*" she demanded with a small whine she instantly despised herself for. "Now what? Is it my breath?" She felt around the top of her head. "Did I grow a horn? A tail? Why are you all fucking looking at me like I'm the weirdo of this group?"

The big man with the green hair nodded, running his fingers over his mouth as he scanned her from head to toe. "Ahhh, yes. Now I see it. She *is* much like my favorite vampire, Nina, isn't she? It's uncanny."

"Except for those pointy fucking ears you got, Spock," Nina crowed before she tipped her head back and cackled.

Pointy ears?

"Nina!" Wanda chastised, making a face of disapproval. "Don't poke!"

Prim's eyes flew open wide as her hands went to either side of her head. She ran her fingers over her ears—*all the way* up her ears, which stopping at a pointy tip.

Oh my God. No. No, this couldn't be happening.

Prim pushed her way past all the shocked faces and headed for the kitchen, where a shiny silver toaster Arch had brought with him sat on the counter.

That was where she encountered her distorted reflection. But it wasn't so distorted that she couldn't see her wackadoodle ears, enhanced further by her pixie haircut. They sat snugly beside her head, as though she'd put on a pair of fake elf ears. Why had she listened to that damn hair stylist?

"Oh, Gorgeous, trust when I tell you, you have the perfect bone structure for a pixie. Your cheekbones are as high as the Empire State Building and your eyes have that smoldering catty look. You'll be perfection!"

Sure. Except, now she couldn't hide these things on the side of her head that looked a bit like satellite dishes.

A scream of horror she could no longer contain ripped from her throat. "What the fuck is going on?" she bellowed.

The big man with the green hair and orange eyes came up behind her, his eyes filled with sympathy. He held out a large hand to her. "Primrose, I'm Sten Peerson. It's all going to be okay. Will you come sit down and have a cup of coffee so we can talk?"

Marty came up behind her and gripped her arms, tucking her head against Prim's shoulder as she whispered, "It's okay. I promise, honey. He's a friend. A good one, and he has fairy friends and connections who can help us. He has information that can help us help *you*."

Prim looked to her, eyes wide with fear, her limbs trembling. "Are you sure?" she whispered back, her voice shaking, making her loathe her very existence, but she couldn't seem to help herself.

Wanda gripped her hand and squeezed. "We're sure. Come sit down, have some breakfast and coffee. Arch made a frittata and it's divine. You could use a warm meal."

She let Wanda lead her to a new table that had replaced the card table from last night. It was made of a beautiful oak wood, stained in a sandy walnut. Simple, but warm and inviting.

"Where...?" She looked to them all, trying to understand how they made things appear out of nowhere.

"Well, Miss Primrose, the card table will never do," Arch explained, his crisp black suit shining under the lights (which were actually working) of the kitchen as he blustered. "Who can cut even the tenderest of filet of beef on a *card table*? And I certainly can't dress a table properly with all the finest dinnerware on something as crass as a card table. Thus, we remembered this was stored in Mistress Marty's basement and thought surely it would work here. Family dinner isn't family dinner if we're not all seated together, is it?

Now, do sit and I shall bring you breakfast. You must keep up your strength in order to come into your new powers."

Family dinners. Her heart tightened. She couldn't remember the last time she'd had a family dinner—or much else but a TV dinner.

Still, the table was beautiful and she didn't hate it —even if she'd never know enough people to fill it up.

"Mistress Primrose," Arch stared at her pointedly, pulling a wood chair out for her. "Do sit. Make haste, please."

"Thank you for bringing the table and making breakfast." Her words were wooden, but she meant them. They simply didn't come from her mouth with the ease they did for everyone else.

She dropped down into the chair and looked at all the commotion of people milling about her kitchen and almost smiled at the warmth she felt in her chest.

Watched as Arch set about getting her a shiny white and gold plate and placing a healthy portion of the frittata on it while Nina poured her a cup of blazing-hot coffee, setting it down in front of her, the aroma making her mouth water.

"Drink that. You look like shit, and you're gonna need it after you hear what my buddy Gigantor has to say."

Sten laughed, deep and husky, planting a sloppy-sounding kiss on Nina's cheek. "You're my most favorite vampire."

She gave him a shove, but she smiled. "Shut the fuck up, and tell her what's going on so we can get on with it."

"Should we wait for her friend?" Sten asked as he pulled out the chair to her left, at the head of the table, accepting a mug of coffee from Carl before giving him a fist bump.

But Prim shook her head. She needed answers, and if he had them, she didn't want to wait for Raff to get up. Judging from where he'd been in Yemen, it had probably been a long time since he was able to sleep in without being awakened by one atrocity or another. He deserved rest and peace.

Her heart softened when she allowed herself to remember Raff was in the thick of this, too. That he was right here in her house, mere steps away.

"Let him sleep. He's been... Raff is a photojournalist. He just got back from Yemen recently, and I'm pretty sure he's been through it. Probably hasn't had a lot of good sleep in a long time. On top of everything that happened yesterday, he's probably beat to shit."

Wanda nodded. "Yemen, huh? What a harrowing profession. I agree. Let's let the poor guy sleep."

Prim twisted the ring on her pinky finger—her mother's ring— and scrunched her eyes shut, realizing for the first time, she'd never, not once, asked why Raff had come home from abroad. She hadn't even asked how long he'd been back.

Asshole. Asshole. Asshole.

Putting a forkful of the frittata in her mouth to keep from calling herself a bad name out loud, she shoved some food in it.

She hadn't felt particularly hungry when she came downstairs, but then, she hadn't expected a delicacy like this. It beat the living hell out of a soggy, frozen breakfast sandwich with eggs the texture of a sheet of Styrofoam.

"So here's the story, Primrose. May I call you by your first name?" Sten inquired with a tilt of his green head.

She only nodded, shoveling another forkful of nirvana into her mouth and washing it down with the richest, most flavorful coffee she'd ever had in the whole of her almost thirty years.

Sten steepled his hands under his chin. "Here's the story, Prim—or at least what I've been able to gather from my friend Serena, who I hope will be here shortly. You're a fairy."

Prim stopped chewing. "Said the troll from Troll Ville."

Stop being so resentful and rude. This enormous man didn't do this to you, Prim!

Nina slapped her hand on the table, her eyes angry. "Quit being an ungrateful shit and listen to what the man has to say."

Instantly, Prim regretted letting her shitty attitude spill all over this nice man who was only trying to help. She looked down at her plate. "I'm sorry. Nina's right. That was ungrateful."

But Sten held up a forgiving hand. "Now, Nina. Mind your temper. Primrose is in shock, and well she should be. This is jarring at best." Then he eyeballed Prim. "And actually, It's Troll Hill, but let's not quibble about semantics. Yes. I'm a troll and you're a fairy. A Seelie, to be exact. You have all the characteristics—your ears especially."

Her hand went to her ear, covering it, but Sten gently brushed it away, placing it at her side. "Don't be ashamed of them, Primrose. The Seelies are proud people, and their ears and wings are especially envied."

She set her fork down and sat back in the chair, folding her arms across her chest in what some might perceive as defensive. "I guess if I was looking for envy, I'd give a shit. But I'm not. I don't want to be envied. I don't want anything from anyone. I just want it to go the hell away. Can you make it go away?"

"No," he said softly, but with a firm tone. "I can't. No one can. Here's why—and bear with me, because I, with the help of my friend, Serena, have a theory. There are two types of fae. Good and bad. Or as they call themselves, dark—the Unseelie—and light. The Seelie."

Prim nodded, the food, once so delicious, now sitting in her stomach like a heavy weight. "Right. Seelies and Unseelies. They told me all about that."

Sten nodded. "Exactly."

Darnell had come to sit beside her. He reached out and grabbed her hand—which meant what was coming next couldn't be good. She found herself leaning into him for comfort.

"So what about them? How does that fit with what the fuck's going on with me?"

Everyone sat eerily quiet, looking at one another with uneasy glances.

"Say it," Prim demanded, her stomach twisting in knots. "Just tell me!"

Darnell squeezed her hand harder as if to brace her.

Sten looked at her with a sympathetic expression. "We think you were born a Seelie fae and swapped for a human child."

CHAPTER

ELEVEN

When the words wouldn't come out of her mouth, and she stared at them blankly, Nina came ever so helpfully to the rescue. "We think you were switched at birth, dingbat," Nina provided. "Keep up."

Prim clenched her fists together at her side to keep from punching Nina in the kisser. Mostly because while she hated to admit it, she was afraid she'd hit her back.

Marty swatted at Nina, shooting her an angry glance. "Quiet, Mouth. This is a lot to process. Let Prim digest, for the love of Pete. It's a huge event in her life. You know, like when you were turned into a vampire?"

"It's fine. Just tell me all of it," Prim demanded. How did one digest a story like that? He might as well tell her everything and get it over with.

Sten continued, his face hesitant. "Human children

are often kidnapped and, as adults, used for breeding by the dark fae to keep from inbreeding. The child your mother gave birth to... What was your mother's name?"

Prim licked her dry lips, her stomach tight with anxiety. "Liesl. Her name was Liesl."

"We think, and I stress *think*, Liesl gave birth to a human child. However, our theory is, the child your mother birthed either died or was taken and replaced with you, a fairy. Seeing as we suspect your biological mother was a good fairy, because of how you present in appearance, there are two possible scenarios—the child your mother gave birth to died, and your *fairy* mother left you in its place in Liesl's care, and away from harm."

Harm. What harm? She gulped, her mouth gone dry. "Or?"

Sten sighed, his big shoulders rising and falling. "Or, your fairy mother was mixed up in some kind of Unseelie/dark fae trouble, and she swapped you out for a human child. She took the child your mother gave birth to and left you in its place."

Prim tried to stay focused as her thoughts swirled. "But why? And you said trouble? What kind of trouble could she be in that was so bad, she'd take someone else's baby and give up her own?"

Sten's lips thinned. "I don't have an answer for why, or if there was any trouble at all. Only your fairy mother knows the answer to that question. However,

I'm told a legend says a human child is often used as a tithe, an offering for a pact with the devil, and it's possible, though there's no hard evidence, your fairy mother, wanting to keep you, her fairy child safe, left you in the care of a human mother and took the human child she birthed for sacrifice. But remember, this is simply a theory. I have no absolutes."

All the blood drained out of Prim's face. "So you're telling me, my mother, the person I loved more than anyone or anything, wasn't my biological mother...and she never told me?"

Sten reached for her clammy hand and held it tight. "Liesl didn't know, Prim. In fact, if that *is* what happened, she would've had no idea at all."

Wanda came up behind her and wrapped her arms around Prim's shoulders, the scent of her perfume soft and soothing. "I know this is a lot to digest, honey. But we'll help. Your mother was your mother, no matter *who* birthed you. Take that from an adoptive parent. I love my son as much as my biological daughter, and your mother loved you, too."

She didn't doubt her mother had loved her. She'd *never* doubted that. She'd go to her grave not doubting that. But to discover Liesl might not be her biological mother at all? To discover she had a mother who was a fairy? How did she come to terms with that?

Prim let her chin fall to her chest, taking a deep breath. None of this was sitting well with her. None of it. And some of it made her mad as hell.

"So say that again. My *fairy* mother put me here because she didn't want to sacrifice me to the devil? Because that's basically what it boils down to. That's what you're saying, right? But she was okay fucking sacrificing another baby because it was human? What kind of shit is that? What kind of fucking mother does that? How can she be a good fairy if she'd take any old kid, human or otherwise, and offer 'em up to the devil?"

Sten tilted his head, his long green hair falling over his shoulder. "I know this is disturbing and upsetting, Prim. But first, remember, this is all supposition, and second, the paranormal isn't that different from the human world. There's good and evil here, too. Deals with unsavory characters are made in the human world all the time. Drug deals, human trafficking, guns, you name it."

"Okay, that's fair, but sacrificing a baby is..." Prim shivered. She didn't plan on ever having children. Who'd want to have kids with her to begin with? But she couldn't imagine having one and stealing another to offer it to the devil.

That was another thing. The devil? He was real?

Darnell nudged her, clearly reading her thoughts. "Yep. The devil's real. So real."

Prim shrank against him. She figured he'd know. He was a demon. She hadn't given that too much thought, there was so much else to think about, but the girls had assured her that he was a good demon, flying low under Hell's radar.

"It's horrific. *Unthinkable*," Marty agreed, leaning over and giving her arm a gentle squeeze. "But I can't say there isn't much I wouldn't do for my daughter, Hollis. I can't judge this woman until I know the full story, Prim. I hope you won't either."

Sten nodded, sipping his coffee. "If there was trouble, your fairy mother must have been mixed up with something or *someone* from the dark side of the fae, and she had to find a way to protect you."

There was an uncomfortable silence, the only sound the hard swallow of Prim's throat as she listened to this madness.

Putting her head in her hands, Prim fought more tears—which seemed to be her thing these days. "So basically, I've always been a fairy? Why didn't I know this before? I'm almost thirty years old and I've never been able to fucking make myself invisible. That shit would have come in handy a lot sooner than at twenty-nine."

Like in her freshman year of school when her stepfather, Smitty had made one too many comments about how pretty her friend Stephanie was at a sleepover she'd hosted, and Stephanie told her mother, and her mother confronted Smitty.

After that, Stephanie was never allowed to hang out with Prim again because her stepfather was labeled a perv.

In fact, no one was ever allowed to sleep over again. Not that she wanted to subject anyone to her stepfather...but she hadn't been invited to anyone *else's* parties ever again, either.

Or maybe some invisibility would have come in handy when Lowell Patterson had snapped her bra so hard, it broke and she had to throw it away. But then fuckwit Lowell dug it out of the trash in the girls' bathroom like the weirdo he was and showed her entire tenth-grade chemistry class she was still wearing a training bra.

Where was her invisibility then?

Where was her invisibility when her mother died when she was still in high school, and Smitty—

Prim gulped and straightened. Nope. Not today.

Marty cupped her chin in her hand and leaned her elbow on the table. "We're assuming that's why you were abducted, honey—because someone found out about you and they want you back."

"Because? For what?" Why did she matter now?

"Because your power does something important," Sten stressed. "We don't know what or why, and if Serena would just get here, maybe we could find out more. Regardless, you mean something to them."

Rubbing her temples, now aching from information overload, she still didn't totally understand. "So they took me to this Realm place and did what? Pressed the stupid 'on' button and suddenly I'm a fairy?"

Sten's eyes went sympathetic. "I know it sounds crazy, but essentially that's what happened, Prim. They activated your powers, which were strong enough to turn your friend Rafferty into a fairy, too, simply by bumping into you. You have to learn how to temper those powers with other fairies who can teach you, and an oracle who can guide you."

Prim was so confused, her head spun and panic had begun to set back in. "An oracle... What kind of dungeons-and-dragons shit is this? This is ridiculous! How am I supposed to believe any of this?"

Nina popped her lips. "You see that fucking hole the size of a tractor trailer in your bedroom we boarded up this morning? See how it glows? You see that half-assed wing poking out of your back? You see your pointy fucking ears? *That's how.*"

Under normal circumstances, she'd appreciate Nina's no-nonsense, unfiltered reminders, but today? Today she wanted to clock her in the face.

The only thing keeping her from doing that was again, the fact that she'd carried Rafferty like he weighed as much as a pillowcase. And those teeth. Jesus, those teeth.

Thus, she opted to ignore her. "So the weird buzzy things the other night? Alfrigg and Cosmo. They wanted to take me back to their creepy leader? Because they did say they were going to be severely punished by *him* because of their mistake."

"We think so. But we don't know for sure, and we

don't know if Alfrigg and Cosmo are Seelie or Unseel-ie," Sten answered.

"But we also don't know if my fairy-mama is good or bad either. I mean, if she swapped me and took a human baby to give as a sacrifice, how good can she be? I don't want anything to do with that kind of homicidal batshittery."

"Which is why we're not leaving your side until we know who can be trusted," Wanda assured her with a smile. "We just need to wait for Serena and hopefully, she'll be able to provide more information."

Sten looked at his phone and shook his head, concern in his eyes. "I don't know where she is. She said she'd meet me here. I'm starting to get worried."

"Maybe she's off sacrificing an innocent baby in a volcano," Prim said sarcastically, unable to keep her dark thoughts from seeping out of her mouth. "That must take some serious fucking planning."

"Who's sacrificing babies?" Raff asked as he saun-tered into the kitchen, his eyes widening when he saw the new table and chairs.

Arch scurried over and pointed to the empty chair across from Prim. "Sit, Master Rafferty. I shall bring you sustenance. You must be famished after such a long sleep."

Prim couldn't even look at him, no matter how sexy he was still rumpled from sleep. Wearing low-slung gray sweatpants and a navy T-shirt, his skin tanned, his eyes bluer than blue. He ran a hand through his dirty-blond hair and avoided eye contact with her, as well.

When he moved his hair, he couldn't hide his ears, but he took the slight gasps from Wanda and Marty in stride.

"I know," he confessed, smiling at them. "My ears, right?" Raff grabbed the tip of one and good naturedly winked. "I woke up with them."

"And you're not shitting chickens," Nina asked, sounding surprised.

"Not yet," he joked.

Nina pointed at him with an approving grin. "You are bad ass, motherfucker."

Arch pointed to a chair. "I said, sit, Master Rafferty."

He smiled his thanks at Arch and took a seat, looking at everyone gathered around the table. To his credit, he didn't even flinch when his gaze fell on Sten in all his orange-eyed, green-haired glory. "How come I didn't get an invite to the paranormal pow-wow?"

How were they going to explain this whacked turn of events?

Prim answered with her usual glib retort. "We voted you the fuck off the island."

Sten laughed and passed a napkin to him. "I'm Sten Peerson, by the way."

"Your friendly neighborhood troll," Prim provided, knowing she was being obstinate and rude.

Raff nodded, but if he was surprised, he didn't let

on. Raff accepted everyone at face value and always had, no matter what they looked like or where they came from, which just might make what had happened to them a little easier for him to deal with.

He held out a hand to Sten. "Rafferty Monroe. So why didn't you guys wake me? What'd I miss?"

Sten shook hands with a welcoming smile. "Prim said you probably needed a good night's sleep. I hear you just returned from overseas?"

He nodded, looking down at the mug Arch placed in front of him, his eyes avoiding everyone as he wrapped his hands around it. "Yemen. Got back about a month ago. Took some time to decompress on a beach in Cabo, then came back to figure out what I'm going to do next."

Next? Did that mean he was here to stay—or simply recharging for his next death-defying assignment?

Sten nodded his understanding. "I hear your job can be pretty stressful."

Raff did what he always did—he nodded with a smile and deflected conversation away from him and his work—work that would likely bring most people to their knees.

Prim had seen the pictures he took. They were beautifully horrifying to the point that when she looked at them, she felt like she was right beside him. He made his subjects that real.

But Raff's smile brought lines around his eyes and

a darkness probably only Prim could identify. She knew him, and when he hurt, he shrugged it off but the signs were there.

The same signs that had been there when his mother was killed. That had been one of the worst times of his life, when they were in eleventh grade. She'd never forget him calling to tell her his mother had been found in their local grocery store parking lot, murdered, but he'd pushed through because that was who Raff was—always worried about someone else.

In that moment, seeing his vulnerability, Prim felt like dogshit for not at least checking on him—for keeping him behind the wall where she hid from everyone on the other side. But she always worried if she gave an inch, Raff would take that as an in—and she wasn't ready to let anyone in.

And that's not selfish at all, is it, Prim? You self-absorbed jerk.

Prim reached across the table and touched his hand briefly. "You looked beat last night, Raff. Plus, it's probably a good damn thing you got some sleep, because wait till you hear the batshit-crazy stuff the troll has to tell you." Sitting back, she nodded to Sten. "Go ahead. Tell him what you told me."

As Sten explained the entire story again, and Raff listened, Prim watched him absorb the information that she was born a fairy, how she'd transferred her fairy-ness to him, and what the future looked like as of now.

He sat for a moment, sipping his coffee, taking small bites of his frittata before speaking. "Am I hearing this right? I'm a fairy because Prim's powers accidentally rubbed off on me, but she's the big deal here? She's the one they want to bring back to the mothership?"

"That's what we think," Sten agreed.

Nina nudged his shoulder with a flat palm and a playful grin. "How does it feel to have a girlfriend who's the big fucking cheese?"

Before Prim could vehemently protest, Raff barked a laugh.

He winked at Nina, his eyelashes sweeping his cheek. "I'll let you know when I have a girlfriend's who's the big fucking cheese. Until then, what do we do to protect Prim, until we know for sure what the fairies want from her?"

Sten held up a hand as his phone buzzed a text. Watching his face fall, Prim knew something was desperately wrong.

"Dude? What's up?" Nina asked, concern in her voice.

He cleared his throat. "It's Serena. She's missing."

TWELVE

"Prim?"

She turned to find Raff, his eyes full of concern as he approached her. She sat outside on her back stoop while Nina babysat her from the window to the back door, marveling at how hard it was to stay away from the hole in the side of her house.

The ragged glowing edges literally called her name, evoking a yearning so deep inside her, she almost couldn't breathe from the longing.

But she'd managed to stay seated by stuffing her hands inside the pockets of her puffy jacket, her ankles crossed, staring at the beautiful white snow piling higher and higher against the fence.

She didn't understand the lure. She wasn't sure she *wanted* to understand it.

How would she ever understand any of this?

When Sten got the text from his wife, Murphy, that no one had seen or heard from Serena since their last phone conversation when she'd agreed to meet him at Prim's, she felt that old panic rise up in her stomach and she'd needed air. Serena was possibly the only person with a lead to what was going to happen to them next.

Tucking her chin inside her jacket, she forced herself not to react when he touched her shoulder, even though she wanted to throw herself into his arms.

Prim was worried about Sten and his friend. He'd looked crushed when his wife said they couldn't find her, and she couldn't help but feel partially to blame.

After all, they were trying to help her, and that icy exterior she'd so proudly boasted when Sten had explained their theory made her feel like a bag of dicks. She'd never even said thank you. Which made her the ungrateful bitch Nina had so succinctly labeled her.

"Is Sten okay?"

Raff brushed the snow from the place beside her and sat down. A sideways glance told her he'd done his best to cover his new ears with a hat, but it wasn't thick enough and the tips were somehow poking through the fabric. "He's really worried, Prim. He said the fairies aren't exactly the kind who are generous with information-sharing. So Serena was important to us figuring out where to go from here."

Prim shivered. "I hope she's okay. I wish I could do something—anything. But fuck if I know how to help myself, let alone anyone else."

"Sten's friend Gary is trying to figure out what's happening."

She snorted, cold air blowing from her mouth. "The giant."

"Come again?"

"Gary. He's a giant. At least that's what Nina the vampire said."

His laugh was ironic. "Why doesn't that surprise me?"

"What's left to surprise you with after last night?"

Raff nodded with a smile. "Not an untrue statement."

Now there was this other thing between them. The thing she'd done. Having had time to catch her breath, she'd come to the realization of how selfish she'd been about Raff's situation—*again*.

She'd never be terribly sensitive. Primrose Dunham was well aware of how often she trampled on people's feelings with her big size tens, and mostly she didn't realize it unless someone pointed it out to her. But believe, they happily pointed it out.

Dr. Shay said she'd dulled her empathy to stay in survival mode—a defense mechanism, of sorts—or some such shit that made sense when she'd diagnosed it over a Zoom call.

Thankfully, she'd also said Prim wasn't totally devoid of empathy. The numbness she felt about the world around her hadn't completely consumed her, so she wasn't inhumane.

Dr. Shay had even used Freddy as an example. Saving Freddy from that swine who'd dumped him and left him with a leg that would be twisted and crooked for life meant Prim wasn't a joyless husk of a woman. So yay for her.

But animals in need weren't her problem. She'd loved animals all her life.

People—any kind of people—were the problem.

However, she at least had enough empathy left in her to know she'd done this to Raff, and the guilt for telling him to go away was eating her alive, now that the haze of fear had muted a bit.

This fairy thing wasn't only about her and her feelings.

She'd been so determined to keep him at arm's length, trying to keep him from entering her isolated little bubble of pathetic, she'd shirked ownership in all this. And he deserved an apology.

But rather than show her embarrassment and guilt, because words and sharing her emotions weren't her strong suit unless they involved cussing, Prim poked her head out of her shell just enough to test the water. It made her a coward, but baby steps.

"You mad?"

"About?" he asked, his voice gravelly and low.

She closed her eyes and inhaled. "About what I did to you, Raff. *I* did this. Me. It's my fault you look like an episode of *Star Trek*."

He cupped her chin, leaving her fighting not to tear his fingers from her flesh to quell the tingles he created. "Don't talk stupid. Of course, I'm not mad. How were you supposed to know you were the ultimate in fairies?"

Shaking her head, Prim looked away at the fence that needed repairing and the tree limbs that needed trimming, sagging with the heavy snow. "I'm really sorry I did this to you, Raff. I know this probably fucks a lot of shit up for you."

"How so?" he asked about as casually as he was asking her the time.

Prim made a face of disbelief. "*How so?* Raff, I work from home. I can get away with ears and wings. At least until my annual review with that hag Darleen. You go to war-torn countries and take pictures for magazines. How will the people of Yemen or wherever feel about you having wings if you get them?"

He sighed, folding his arms over his knees and clasping his hands together, the same way he'd always done when they sat together so many years ago.

"First, I'm not going back to Yemen. Second, I don't have wings, but the invisibility thing sure would have helped over there."

Prim sat quietly for a moment before she said, "Yet. You don't have them *yet*. And you're not going back to Yemen? Why not?"

Raff looked down at his feet. "I'm not going back to *anywhere*, Prim. I've been doing this for seven years. It's time for a change."

Her heart felt his words, felt them to the core of her being. Something had happened over there—the reason he'd taken some time off to decompress before he'd come home.

It had been a long, self-centered time since she'd thought about anyone else's pain but her own, but she knew Raff, and she knew he was in pain.

Putting a hand on his thigh, Prim whispered the words she'd always whispered to him when he was troubled. "I'll be your paper towel, Monroe."

It had once been an old joke between them. When either of them had a problem, they'd say, "Spill it." One day, right after her mother told her she was marrying Smitty, and Prim had been beyond distraught, Raff had come over after school, found her crying, and told her to spill it.

Prim had joked through the tears that the "spill" was too big to clean up. Raff, in his typically creative way, told her he'd help her clean it up—he'd be her paper towel and absorb all of her sorrow.

From that day forward, it had always been their private joke. One among many, but an important one in later years.

Raff looked at her for a moment, as if he were really seeing her again, obviously remembering their ritual from so long ago...but he suddenly shook his head. "Nah. No spills here, Dunham. No mess to clean up."

She knew that was a lie, and it hurt that he wouldn't confide in her. But how could she pressure him to tell her what was going on when she could barely allow herself to think about why she'd cut off all ties with him?

It's a real slap in the face, huh? Does it sting, Primrose? Because you deserve it.

She refused to share anything with anyone because it was harder to share than hide. But mostly, she didn't share because she was ashamed, and the secret she held tight to her chest was bigger than she'd ever be.

Grabbing Raff's hand, strong and cold, Prim held it tight for a moment before letting go. "I'm still sorry I did you like that."

"You know, I've been thinking about this. A fairy? I mean, it could've been something cooler, like a vampire or a werewolf. But a fairy? How am I gonna explain that to the guys on the bowling league?"

"Sexist much?" If anyone could wear a pair of wings and still look manly, it was Raff.

"Fucking patriarchy. It's hard to shake. My apologies."

Prim giggled, tucking her jacket around her as

more snow began to fall. "The next time I turn you into something, promise I'll try and make sure it includes big pointy teeth and a lot of drool."

Raff laughed the way they used to, but then he sobered. "So...this thing about your mother..."

She nodded, staring off into the curtain of snow. "I've been thinking about it. You know, I don't get it. We look almost identical. If you look at some of the pictures I have of my mom when she was my age, we look exactly alike. She always used to say that. Is that some kind of fairy voodoo? Did they sprinkle some of that dust ball madness over me to make me look like her?"

Rafferty's shoulders bunched upward. "Could that notion be any crazier than some of the other stuff that's happened? But that's not why I asked. I'm asking if you're okay. You just found out your mother likely isn't your biological mother. I realize we don't know for sure, but if it's true, that's huge, Prim."

Yeah. It sure was huge. But... "I don't care whose bits I came from. Liesl will *always* be my mother. She was the best mother ever, and if what Sten says is true, and she swapped me out for a human baby, my fairy mama was a homicidal maniac. She belongs on Investigation ID, not making friends with the kid she dumped. I'll pass on that bullshit, thanks."

He looked surprised. "I really expected you to be far more upset. I thought you'd be angry, feel betrayed, call your whole life a lie, that type of stuff."

146

Now she looked down at her feet. To deny how much she'd loved her mother was to deny her very soul. "I won't lie and say this isn't freaking me out. It is. But my whole life wasn't a lie. My life until... My life was great. My mom was the greatest. Maybe she didn't know I wasn't biologically hers, maybe she did...and if she did, she loved me just as hard. So does that part matter?"

Raff sat silently for a moment, the snowflakes sticking to his thick lashes. "No. I guess it doesn't."

Then she remembered *his* mother, and what happened, and the guilt clawed at her stomach again. "I'm sorry... How's your dad?"

Mr. Monroe was a kind, gentle, quiet soul, and when his wife was murdered, he'd silently fallen apart for a while.

Raff's smile was wan as he sighed. "He's really good now. Moved to Oregon. He loves it there, and I have to admit, the pictures he sends are beautiful. He met a really nice lady named Tara, pronounced *Tar-ahhh with a long a*, thank you very much, and she's done wonders bringing him out of his shell."

Prim smiled, too. No one deserved a happy ending more than Mr. Monroe. He'd been an important figure in her life for as far back as she could remember—always warm, always welcoming, and nuts about Raff's mother, Sandy.

But what he'd been through when she was murdered had been ugly and brutal.

She wanted to ask if there was any new information after all these years, because Sandy Monroe's murder had been unsolved, but that wound was so raw, still so wide open, she couldn't.

"I'm glad to hear your dad is happy. I was surprised when I came back and saw he kept the house."

Raff's nod was slow. "He kept it for me, thinking I might want to have some place familiar to hang my hat when I came back to the States."

"You still have that poster of Angelina Jolie hanging in your bedroom?"

Grinning, he nodded. "Not much has changed over there, that's for sure."

"Well, you can update it as you go. It's still in really great shape."

But once more, Raff shook his head, his voice quiet. "I think I'm gonna sell."

Prim froze, her fingers turning to ice inside her jacket pockets. If Raff sold, she wouldn't have to see him in their side-by-side driveways and either avoid making eye contact, or duck into her car with a quick wave.

But as much as she avoided him, as much as she told herself she wished he'd leave her the hell alone? The thought of him selling rattled her; made her feel lonelier than she'd ever felt before.

Rather than reveal that. Rather than asking him to

stay so she could blatantly ignore him some more, she kept her response casual. "Bet you'll get a good price for it."

"We'll see." Then he changed the subject. "So you don't want to meet her? Your fairy-mama?"

"She allegedly sacrifices babies, Raff. To the *devil*. Do you want to meet someone who gives bribes to the fucking devil?"

He shivered. "Yeaaah. The *devil*..."

The way he said it, with such wonder, Prim knew he was in as much disbelief as she was over the fact that the devil really existed. "Is it me, or is that shit bonkers? Did you ever really believe Sister Juanita when she said the devil was real and we were going to Hell for lying about who stole Father Moynihan's wine?"

Raff mocked an offended look. "We did not lie. It wasn't us."

"No. It was fucking stupid Patrick O'Hare, but we knew who did it."

He held up a finger and shook his head with a playful smile. "But Sister Juanita didn't ask us *who* took it. She asked if *we* took it, and we didn't. So I think we're safe from the bowels of Hell for today."

"Hey, lovebirds, nice trip down Memory Lane, but we're goin' on a road trip and if I gotta go, you two fucking Tinker Bells do, too," Nina said from the kitchen doorway.

"A road trip? The hell. I can't go anywhere like this, Vampire Lady. I have a damn wing poking out of my back and pointy ears," Prim protested. "I'm not going out in public."

"Prim," Wanda called, holding up a jacket that looked like it would fit around a mountain, wearing an expression that said she'd brook no back talk. "You *will* put this on and you *will* go out in public. Now come along. It's time we get you two out of the house and out of your heads. We're all just sitting around here waiting and it's doing no one any good to brood. It's the most wonderful time of the year, it's snowing, and we're going to celebrate the beauty of the season whether you like it or not."

They were away from their families at a time when they should be cuddled up near a fire, watching Christmas movies and decorating their trees. Instead, they'd sacrificed all of that, those memories they couldn't get back, to help her, and now Raff.

Don't be an ungrateful asshole, Prim. Just this once, do something for someone else.

Marty stuck her head over Wanda's shoulder and grinned. She wore a marshmallowy, fuzzy hat and cute elf-shoe earrings in glittering red and green. "Get your butts in here, front and center."

As she rose and brushed off the snow from her jeans, Prim felt good, a warmth pervading her insides despite the cold.

That feeling came from finally talking to Raff after all these years. Almost the way they once had.

That's what happy feels like, Primrose. It's like sunshine on your face and fucking soft, fluffy kittens. Freshly baked Christmas cookies, a hug. This means you're happy.

Yeah. She was happy.

CHAPTER

THIRTEEN

"C'mon, Rafferty, you chickenshit! Afraid I'll kick your ass again?" Prim called in a teasing tone from the top of a snowy hill at the park near their houses.

Raff was busy situating Carl on a tube, making sure he was secure. "Just keep your dang drawers on, Dunham! I got your chickenshit!"

It had been Nina's suggestion to go tubing, despite her grousing about not wanting to leave the house.

They'd grabbed hot chocolate from a local food truck, piled high with whipped cream and dredged in cinnamon, along with some warm, crispy, soft-on-the-inside glazed donuts, pulled some tubes from the back of Marty's SUV (how they managed to produce every single thing needed, in the exact moment for every situation it was needed, was a mystery) and off they went.

Of course, there was no beating Nina the vampire. She'd plopped her ass down on one of those inner tubes and nearly created sparks as she'd zoomed down the hill, slicker than snot, cackling the whole way.

But Prim had come close, and along the way, she'd creamed Raff, who'd fallen off his tube after hitting a bump that left him flailing in the air before landing in a drift, laughing hysterically.

Christmas music played from the speakers on the stage where, in the summer, their town often hosted local bands and music festivals. The town had decorated the gazebo with twinkling colored lights and an enormous wreath, and strung lights in the trees on either side of the tubing lane.

Everyone was laughing and joking, and while Marty and Wanda had opted out of the fun in favor of tailgating in the back of the SUV, they cheered and catcalled them from the warmth of the car.

Prim closed her eyes and inhaled, finding it easier and easier to live in the moment and actually enjoy the memories the park brought. Much like her mother, Christmas had been her favorite time of year, too, and looking down at their town from this view, Prim could see why. Main Street was idyllic, all lit up and decorated with boughs of evergreens and red ribbons.

She and her mother used to come here every winter to tube, until she got sick. It was their way of kicking off the holiday season. They'd pack sandwiches and a thermos of her mom's special butterscotch hot chocolate with tons of gooey marshmallows. She'd also make Rice Krispie treats with M&Ms in them, Prim's favorite, and they'd listen to the music and simply be together.

When Smitty came along, as controlling as he became, her mom still found a way to sneak them off to spend a couple of hours at the park until she was too sick to do so.

At that age, she didn't know how to talk to her mother about how Smitty made her feel. Sometimes, she wasn't even sure her mother realized Smitty had taken over every aspect of their lives. But when Liesl met him, she'd been unaware she was in the beginning stages of her fight with cancer.

He'd come in all charming and affable, wining and dining her mother, bringing gifts to Prim. As their relationship progressed to marriage, Prim had still been wary, but she could never put her finger on what bothered her so.

Once Liesl married Smitty, it began as a subtle change. She had chores that went with his spare-the-rod, spoil-the-child mentality.

Little by little, she wasn't allowed to do much of anything but go to school and study. After the incident with Stephanie, something he'd successfully kept from her mother thanks to her illness, Smitty tightened the rope around Prim's neck until she almost couldn't breathe.

But in her mind, telling her mother about it or

complaining was absolutely out of the question. Liesl was in and out of the hospital during rounds of chemotherapy, and sometimes so sick, all she could do was sleep. No way would she trouble her mother with her worries.

"Mommy! Look! It's one of Santa's elves!" a little girl yelled at the top of her lungs in excitement, pulling her from her dark thoughts about treacherous Smitty.

She wore a pink and red snowsuit she could barely walk in, her chubby cheeks red from the cold. She waddled right up to Prim and tugged her jacket.

"Can I see your ears? Pleeease!"

Her hand instantly went to where her hat had risen up over her right ear. Shit.

"Alaina! That's rude!" her mother chastised, huffing and puffing as she trudged her way up the hill, a sled in her fist. She looked at Prim with an apology in her eyes. "I'm so sorry. She's beyond excited about Christmas."

But Alaina was a curious, determined little lady. She tugged at Prim's jacket again. "Can I touch 'em? Please?" She fisted her hands together in prayer.

Her mother rolled her eyes and grabbed her daughter's hand. "Alaina! You cannot touch the nice lady's elf ears!"

Prim knelt down in the cold snow. "I don't mind at all." She leaned closer to Alaina and let her run a gloved hand over the tip.

Alaina giggled. "They look so real," she whispered with clear awe.

"Oh, my stars," her mother agreed, her eyes wide. "They do..."

Prim stood up with a chuckle, brushing off her pants. "The mall doesn't play."

Alaina's mother laughed nervously, almost as though she were relieved. "Of course! You work at the mall."

Prim saluted her and winked. "Elf number three, at your service."

"Hey, nugget," Nina called, waving to Alaina with a smile so sweet, Prim almost fainted. She put a fist out to the little girl and waited for her to bump it.

Alaina's eyes widened as she got a clear view of Nina. "Ohhh, you're like a fairy princess, but with mermaid hair. You're so beautiful!"

Nina grinned softly. "But not as beautiful as you. So, are you excited for Santa?"

She jumped up and down as best she could in her snowsuit and pumped her fist in the air. "Yes!"

"C'mon, honey," her mother urged, holding out her hand. "Let's go get some hot chocolate and let these pretty ladies enjoy their night."

Alaina grabbed her mother's hand, but she didn't leave without a parting shot. "Okay, bye, but... Hey, lady, can you please tell Santa I want a unicorn soooo bad! Oh, and an iPad and a motorcycle..."

As her tiny voice faded, both Prim and Nina laughed. "She's gonna be a fucking handful someday."

Prim agreed...and then she remembered Nina's daughter Charlie, and the guilt she felt for keeping her from her family stung once more. "You have a little girl, right? Charlie?"

That made Nina beam, and if she wasn't already beautiful enough, she was even more so when her little girl was mentioned. "Yep. Still a baby by vampire standards, if not in damn years."

"Vampire standards?"

"We age slow. *Really* fucking slow. Charlie's eleven in human years, but she looks like she's about three."

Prim blinked, digesting yet more whacky paranormal information. Then something occurred to her. "Holy shit! You're not in your twenties?"

"Uh, no. I'm pushing GD fifty."

"Damn," Prim muttered, tucking her chin to her chest. "You're old...*er*... Older! I thought you were my age."

Nina leered at her. "But not too old to kick your fucking skinny ass."

Prim gulped, but she knew when she was outmatched, so she clamped her lips shut and looked down the hill at the glisten of the snow beneath the moon.

"That's some fucking primo snow, huh? Like damn glass," Nina commented.

Prim made circles in the fluffy covering with her

booted foot, tucking tighter into her enormous jacket, which had actually managed to hide her wing. "Yeah. It always is this time of year. I love to tube. It used to be one of my favorite things to do."

Nina examined her, her eyes beautiful with the twinkle of Christmas lighting them. "Until?"

Prim blew out a breath, her lips tightening as if doing so would keep the information inside her mouth. "Until it wasn't."

Nina shrugged like it didn't make a bit of difference as she looked at Prim with eyes that scrutinized. "You don't hafta tell me shit, kiddo. It ain't no skin off my nose. Though, it might lighten your gloomy ass up to un-fucking-load. But whatever."

Without a hint of a warning, the words spilled out of her mouth. "My mother died of breast cancer when I was in the beginning of my senior year in high school. She was really sick for a long time, most of my high school years, and then she was just gone. *Dead*. That's what happened."

Nina put a hand on her shoulder and squeezed. "Damn sorry about that, kiddo."

Prim nodded, looking down at the snow-covered hill, fighting hot tears. Why was she always crying lately? "Yeah. Me, too."

"So you two came here a lot?"

"Yeah," she whispered, her heart tight, pounding hard in her chest. What the fuck was happening to her? Prim cleared her throat and gave a clearer answer.

"Every year at the beginning of the season like clockwork, for as long as I can remember."

Nina let her hand drop as she watched while Carl and Raff flew down the hill, laughing like loons, Carl tucked safely in Raff's lap. "Where's your pops?"

"His name was Brett, and he died before I was born —like two months before. Hit and run. So I never met him. I've only seen pictures of him and only know what my mother told me."

According to her mother, he was a terrific guy who swept her off her feet when they were both working at a law firm as interns during college.

The pictures Liesl had of her father always depicted them smiling and happy, looking at each other with so much love.

Her mother regaled her with stories of him, of his generosity, how excited he'd been about Prim's arrival —so excited, he'd bought the house she now lived in to surprise her mother.

"Grandparents? Aunts? Uncles? Any other living relatives?" Nina asked.

"None living. It's just me. You want my fucking blood type, too?" she asked defensively.

Nina replanted her hand on Prim's shoulder and stared her directly in the eye, one eyebrow raised. "I'm probably not the bitch to ask."

Prim couldn't help it, she sputtered a laugh. "Right. But can I ask something else?"

"You can always fucking ask," she joked.

"I did a little reading on vampires earlier this afternoon. I googled them, actually, and I learned some shit."

Nina made a face, tucking her hands into her dark hoodie. "Like?"

"Like, why didn't you have to ask to be invited into my house? The internet says you can't come in unless I invite you, and I didn't invite you."

"Because I'm the baddest vampire bitch in the land."

While Prim didn't doubt that, she didn't think it was the answer. "Funny vampire is funny. Now the truth?"

Nina flapped her hands in dismissal. "That's all just bullshit nowadays. Maybe it existed way back, but vampires and actually most of the paranormal have come a long damn way since then. I go where the fuck I wanna go."

Prim was aghast. "Even into churches?"

Nina snorted, and Prim found it ever fascinating that no condensation puffed from her mouth. "I was raised Catholic just like you. I had some issues at first, but nothin' a little tolerance-training and time didn't fucking handle. Same thing with sunlight. Now I could preach a GD sermon midday in July in Texas and not flinch. Not even a little."

Her Catholic upbringing trembled in fear. "You really are a badass. So okay, you can deal with sunlight and the Father, Son and Holy Ghost, but what about the...the blood drinking? I mean, that's real, isn't it?"

Nina planted her hands on her hips. "Yep, but before you go all fucking stupid, I drink *synthetic* blood. But the instinct to drain dumb people dry remains. Being a badass, I manage to curb that shit, too. Basically, I eat hamburger instead of a filet every day so you fucking morons can live."

Prim licked her lips and stuffed her hands inside the enormous jacket pickets as she gave Nina a sheepish glance. "One more question? Swear it's the last."

"Remember what I said about stupid people," she warned.

"Can you explode into a colony of bats?"

Nina growled, making Prim squeak with a giggle before grabbing her tube and jumping onto it, using her palms to push off and get away from the vampire as fast as possible.

Nina's laughter followed her the entire way down the hill until she slowed to a stop, conveniently in front of the hot chocolate truck.

Grabbing her tube, she set it against an icy tree and trudged through the snow to grab more hot chocolate, the sounds of Nina, Carl, and Raff's laughter, ringing in her ears.

Just as she was about to step up to the truck's window, someone grabbed her arm and pulled her into a shadowy space between a knoll the back of the truck.

Panic seized her. Was it a fairy? Were fairies this strong?

"What the fuck?" she yelped, trying to yank her arm from the solid grip as her eyes adjusted to the dimness with only the hum of the truck's generator in her ears.

"Look who it is after all this time," a greasy voice whispered in her ear. "Didja miss me, Prim?"

Her heart began to race, and without rhyme or reason, Prim froze. Her fight-or-flight immobilized.

She knew the time would come. Though, she was surprised at how long it had taken. But she knew he'd eventually come back to make her life miserable. Like mold, he was hard to kill.

Yet, she couldn't make her feet move. Instead, they felt like blocks of ice.

But she did manage to issue a weak threat. "Get off me, Smitty. Get the *fuck* off me."

He laughed his dark, ugly gurgle of a snigger. No matter how lighthearted the subject, Smitty always managed to turn it into something insidious with that disgusting laugh.

"Still talking like the foul-mouthed tramp you always were?"

He was the very reason she swore. In some mental act of passive-aggression, she used crude language as a way to inertly lash out at him, to make him angry, fully realizing no good would come of it but doing it anyway.

She'd first noticed his distaste for a good cuss when her mother had lobbed a swear word after burning her hand on a hot dish.

Smitty had lost his mind, something he did often after becoming entrenched into their lives. He'd told Liesl he'd better never hear her use that kind of language around him again. *Ladies*, according to the law as deemed by Smitty, didn't swear.

That incident had stuck with her, and the year after her mother died, while she was still living with Smitty, waiting every day to turn eighteen so she could get away from him, she'd started swearing as often as possible, taking secret pleasure in seeing his face turn beet red with anger.

Nothing tickled her more than watching that red rage start at the base of his neck and work its way up across his cheeks.

Smitty gazed into her eyes. He was only taller than her by a couple of inches, but those inches were intimidating when she was a kid and obviously remained so today.

He hadn't changed much. He was older, but he was still good-looking with lean cheeks and piercing blue eyes, a reminder why her mother had fallen for him.

Dressed as though he were headed to a winter-themed event at a fancy club, he wore a dark green turtleneck under a long trench coat.

He eyeballed her entire length with lewd eyes. "Looking good, I see."

"Still an ex-fucking-con, I see," she spat back, straightening a little.

He'd intimidated her—or maybe the word was terrorized her—almost from the moment he'd enter their lives, but that last year? That last year after her mother died, and she was waiting to graduate in order to claim the money her mother had set aside for her, had been a literal Hell on earth.

He grinned, his handsome smile betraying the oily blackness that lived inside him. "Aren't you happy to see me, Primmy? It's been a long time."

"Ten lifetimes wouldn't be fucking long enough. Now let go of my arm," she demanded, remembering all those nights when she'd gone over and over the heated confrontation she'd have with this man if she ever saw him again.

She was going to show him she was no weak pussy. She'd spit in his disgusting face after she told him what a monster he was.

She'd dreamed of paying him back for letting her mother die alone, for not telling Prim she was in her final moments, for not allowing her go to Liesl.

Yet, here she was, acting like said weak pussy.

He let go of her arm and replaced it by gripping her chin. "Someone needs to wash that nasty mouth of yours out with soap," he snarled, squeezing her jaw until her teeth chattered.

Where's all that rage now, Prim? Now, when you could use it, you've gone all shrinking violet? Who the fuck are you?

Prim summoned the guts to slap his hand from her jaw. "Get the fuck off me and go the fuck away."

He moved in closer, his presence looming, overwhelming her with his vileness. "But we have so much to talk about, Primmy. You have something I want…"

And another thing. She hated that damn nickname he'd given her. Primmy. "I *said* fuck off, Smitty, and stop calling me Primmy. It's Primrose. Now, I don't have shit to say to you. Back the fuck off," she hissed in his face through clenched teeth.

Instead of backing off, he moved in closer, so close she could smell the vodka on his breath. "Or you'll do what?" was his sinister reply.

Yeah. What would she do?

You're gonna get your ass together and live out your dream of pulverizing this motherfucker, Primmy. *That's what you're gonna do.*

Summoning every last ounce of courage she possessed, using all the rage she'd swallowed time and again when he'd swept in and invaded their lives with his rules and demands and controlling ways…when he'd verbally abused her mother…

She owed him.

"Yeah," he sneered, his rank breath assaulting her nose. "Nothing to say? That's what I thought."

Closing her eyes, and clenching her fists, instead of

fighting off the absolute raw hatred she felt for him, she leaned into it.

Deep. Hard.

Prim lapped it up. Savored it as if it were a sumptuous, velvety piece of chocolate on her tongue.

"*Fuck. Youuuu!*" she howled, so loud, with such force—a bolt of light actually shot from her mouth.

A weird ball of color literally rushed from between her lips and smacked Smitty in the chops with so much power, it knocked him clear across the park—where he crashed into a big maple tree and slumped over at the waist.

Oh.

Oh, shit.

FOURTEEN

"Hey, fucknob, guess what? You get to choose your own adventure. How do you want to die, you goddamn crusty, dickless piece of shit?" Nina screamed in Smitty's face. "Should I make it fast, or super fucking slow? Because I love slow. I like it *real* slow."

As Prim stood frozen, staring at what she'd done to Smitty, Nina had flown down the hill in a blur of white snow and dark hair streaming in ribbons of black behind her, hauling Smitty up by his throat and slamming him against the trunk of the tree with such force, the tree shook from the ground up.

Snow fell in clumps from the branches, landing on them and splattering to the ground.

Smitty's feet dangled helplessly as he tried to speak, his face red and distorted.

Marty rolled up behind Nina and grabbed her by

the shoulders, her fingers tightly gripping the vampire's flesh. "Let go, Nina," she warned with a hiss. "Let go *now*."

But that didn't affect Nina in the slightest. She gripped his neck harder and jammed her face into Smitty's, her eyes narrowed and full of fire. "You ever fucking touch her again, if you ever *think* of touching her again, go anywhere the fuck near her, I'll eat your dick clear off your body and wrap it the fuck around your pencil neck, you motherfucking pissant. You feel me, Sport?"

"Nina!" Marty whispered close to the vampire's ear. "Let him go before you draw attention and cause trouble for Prim. Do it, Vampire!"

Smitty could barely move as he watched the two women, let alone acknowledge Nina's threat, but he didn't have to. She opened her hand and stepped back, letting him fall to the ground with a hard thump and a glare.

"Prim!" Raff yelled as he raced down the hill toward her, stopping short to grip her by the arms and pull her close. "What the hell just happened? Are you okay?"

"I..." She opened her mouth to speak, but her surprise prevented any words.

How could she explain what had just happened? She'd screamed with such force, she'd sent a man reeling. Who did that?

Wanda flew up beside her, pushing Prim's hair

from her eyes and cupping her cheek. "Honey, are you okay? Who is that?"

Prim couldn't help it—she burst into tears, falling deeper into Raff's arms as Wanda rubbed her back with her palm in soothing circles.

Her entire body trembled violently as she cried into Raff's shoulder, and he whispered, "It's okay, Prim. It's okay. I'm here. I won't let him hurt you."

She gasped into his chest, relishing the smell of his jacket mixed with his cologne and the cold air.

"That's right, you pussy! Move the fuck along or I swear on your tiny dick, you'll wish I'd killed you!" Nina screamed so loud, it made Prim shake harder.

There was a scuffle of feet and loud, almost strangled grumbling before there was silence and nothing but her raw sobs.

Afraid to look up from the safety of Raff's arms, she burrowed farther into his warmth, forcing herself to inhale deep breaths.

Nina leaned in from Raff's side and put a finger under Prim's chin to gaze into her eyes with concern, wiping her tears. "You okay, kiddo? Did that fuck hurt you?"

She shook her head, unsure how to accept all this fawning over her. It had been a long time since she'd felt this raw, this overwhelmed with emotion. It had been a long time since she'd let anyone get close enough to fawn over her.

"No...no. He didn't hurt me. I'm okay," she

murmured, pressing her cheek to Raff's chest, absorbing his heartbeat.

Carl stuck his head around Nina's, nudging her out of the way. He pressed his cold nose to hers. "Bad...bad man. Ni...Nina make him go, o...kay?"

Prim smiled at Carl in all his boyish handsomeness, cupping his cheek. "Okay," she whispered.

Carl thumped her on the back and smiled, giving her a thumb's up.

"Come on, sweet girl. Let's get you home, yes? Enough wintering for today," Wanda said gently, taking her by the hand and leading her back to the SUV, making her shed more hot, silent tears.

Prim went docilely, all the while feeling enormous guilt for how they continued to be kind to her, to make her feel as though they'd known her forever instead of just a couple of days, and she'd shit on them endlessly while they did it.

In that moment, she vowed to try to think before she spoke, to at least allow for some caution in her words—to stop fighting the warmth these people thrust upon her in their effort to help her.

Because she was exhausted from keeping people out—from isolating herself.

She was really going to try.

Really, really try.

"Ooooh," Prim breathed, rubbing her swollen eyes when they stepped inside her house with the new front door that no longer felt quite as dilapidated as it had only this morning.

"Sur...sur...prise!" Carl called with a huge grin, giving her a hug before pushing her into the doorway, where the scent of pine and sugar cookies wafted to her nose.

Arch greeted them in the living room, standing by an enormous bare Christmas tree in the middle of her floor-to-ceiling windows, an earnest smile wreathing his blue face. He approached her and gave her a light hug before setting her from him.

"Mistress Primrose, your beautiful home awaits. I hope you'll enjoy many, many happy Christmases here," he said softly.

The tree, a beautiful Douglas Fir, sat proudly in front of her windows, at least eight feet tall, its green branches regal, even bare.

But it wasn't only the tree that surprised her—it was the entire room. No longer were the walls peeling, the windows sagging, the floor uneven and warped.

No—the walls were smooth as a baby's butt, painted in an oyster white, with thick taupe trim around the windows and floors.

In fact, it looked very similar to the pictures of several rooms she'd pinned on Pinterest. The floors were a light oak, gleaming under the new canned lights in the ceiling that beamed soft, incandescent rays over the room.

To compliment her kiwi-green couch, there was a velvet loveseat in light gray with a throw blanket in orange and green casually tossed over the back. Tons of throw pillows in her favorite colors and geometric shapes, plump and soft, lined the surfaces of her furniture.

A roaring fire blazed in her fireplace, no longer crumbling but completely overhauled in pale red and light brown brick, with a dark willow basket filled with firewood on the hearth.

The new mantle, a chunky piece of wood stained a few shades darker than the floor, held fuzzy green and white Christmas stockings with Freddy and Katy's names on them.

Prim almost couldn't take it all in, her breath became so caught in her throat.

But that wasn't all of it—her kitchen had been a love letter to disasters everywhere. Where once hung those orangey oak cabinets that were falling apart and crooked, now were hunter green cupboards with brushed gold handles. And there were so many of them she lost count.

The backsplash in brick matched the new brick on the fireplace, and an enormous copper sink sat neatly under the window where her mother used to watch her play out back, while she did the dinner dishes. Shiny steel appliances replaced her old, battered ones, gleaming under more beautiful lighting.

The countertops weren't the old yellowed laminate she hated so much, but a light blond butcher block, also stained to match her floors.

Above the dining room table Arch had somehow magically produced the other night, hung a huge sphere light in brushed gold to match the pulls.

It was exquisite. All of it. This was everything she'd hoped her house could be, but she'd been overwhelmed by the enormity of the task of renovating it.

"How the hell...?" she breathed.

Marty smiled and gave her a hard hug. "We know people," was all she offered, but Prim shook her head.

"No," she said, fighting more tears. God, her eyeballs were going to fall out of her head from all this damn crying. "This is more than that. The furniture, the cabinets, the floors...how? We were only gone for four hours!"

Wanda's laughter tinkled as she pulled off her scarf and hung it on a shelf with peg hooks by Prim's new front door. A peacock-blue door, no less, with a square, stained-glass insert.

She pinched Prim's cheeks and winked. "See? Being paranormal isn't all bad. Look what we can accomplish with our super-speed."

"But you guys were with me..." she protested, still in shock.

"But I wasn't, Miss Prim, and neither were the

bosses' husbands," Darnell said, holding out his arms to her with a grin. "Sten helped, too. He'll be back in a little bit. He went to see Gary."

Prim put a hand to her mouth as she walked into Darnell's arms and let him envelope her in his big embrace. "I don't know what to say…"

"You don't gotta say nothin'," Darnell said, affectionately patting her on the back with a thump. "Just don't go touchin' anything. Lot of it's still dryin'. Even being paranormal won't speed *that* up."

She snorted a laugh before she looked at them all, her lower lip fighting a tremble. "Thank you. All of you. I don't know how you got it so right, so *me*, but… thank you. I'll pay you back for all of the materials—"

"The fuck you will. Some of this shit's been in Marty's basement forever, the damn hoarder. It was just gonna sit there and end up donated anyway."

Marty rolled her eyes, throwing her hat at Nina's head. "I'm not a hoarder. Some of the furniture is from shoots we did for Pack Cosmetics. We really were just going to donate it, but now it's going to good use, and you have to admit, it looks amazing. It worked perfectly for the sort of mid-century modern-boho vibe you favor, don't you think?"

Prim nodded, equally dumbfounded and thrilled. "How did you know I'd love this? I mean, I love *everything*, all of it. Right down to the geometric area rug."

"Pinterest," Marty answered with a wink. "Your

vision boards gave us all the answers we needed. Now, there's still plenty of work to be done. Tons of finishing touches, like that hole the size of a crater in your room, but we'll have to wait on that until we know what we're dealing with. Those stairs are a fright, and of course the bathrooms, but this is a beginning, a *new one* for your *new* life," she emphasized. "And as a huge plus after that sputtering fountain trickle of a shower I took this morning, the heat and water are working."

On impulse, Prim launched herself at Marty and hugged her tight, inhaling the scent of peaches and sage. "Thank you. I don't deserve this after the way I treated you. You hardly know me, but thank you. I can't explain how much this means..."

Raff came up behind them, his eyes dancing. "If you guys are in the market for renovating, I have a house, too, you know. I mean, my life is going to be new as much as Prim's, right?" he teased.

Nina flicked his hair, knocking the knit hat off his head and exposing his pointy ears. "Don't hold your fucking breath," she teased.

Arch clapped his hands then, drawing everyone's attention to a pile of totes he stood beside. "Now, my angels, no more tears. We have a *home* to decorate for Christmas. Shall we?" he encouraged with a wink and a get-your-butt-in-gear expression.

In a flurry of laughing chatter and movement, everyone grabbed a tote, popping them open and pulling out ornaments and greenery and all manner of things Christmas.

Some were hers, some—like everything else—had magically appeared out of nowhere, but they were filled to the top with decorative festivity.

Prim swallowed hard and blinked to prevent more tears as someone turned on Nat King Cole's "White Christmas", her mother's absolute favorite. She marveled at this beautiful space, filled with people laughing and joking.

In her isolation, she'd never have considered how full her heart would feel, letting so many people into her home.

But it did. Her heart felt full, thrumming in her chest, overwhelmed by more long-lost emotions.

Raff nudged her with a grin. A grin so handsome, it felt like she was seeing it for the first time—without the haze of her anger clouding everything around her. "C'mon, slacker. Grab a tote and get to decorating while we wait for Sten."

She scooped a smaller tote into her arms and set it on a new end table, popping it open and smiling. "They found some of my mother's stuff..." she murmured, holding up the clay snowflake she'd so painstakingly made in the second grade.

Raff nodded, his gaze warm. "Seems they did."

"You told them about the attic, didn't you? Where did they find all of this?" she said softly, holding up the snowflake with hardly any glitter left on it.

She hadn't been up there since she'd moved back, knowing there'd be memories she wasn't ready to face. It was hard enough seeing the house in the condition Smitty had left it, but to see her mother's things might have been the straw that broke the camel's back.

Raff smiled at her, tucking a lock of hair behind her ears with tender fingertips, probably realizing she was thinking about her mother.

"Remember when we used to hang out up there, in that corner by the trunk with your grandma's stuff?"

Her attic was enormous, spanning the entire house. She and Raff played up there all the time when they were in elementary school, imagining they were pirates or kings and queens of a made-up kingdom.

She nodded, looking down at her feet, her heart aching for that simpler time. "I remember."

He had a faraway gaze for a second, before he smiled again and held his hands up. "Anyway, I remembered that's where your mom used to put a lot of holiday decorations. I just pointed the way in a text to Darnell."

Her chest went tight right along with her throat. She didn't deserve his kindness. She didn't deserve any of what was happening.

"So you knew what they were doing this whole time?"

He shrugged with a crafty grin. "Maybe."

This was all too much. She didn't know how to

accept all these good things being thrown at her, but she was going to try.

Standing on tiptoe, while Christmas music played and lights began to twinkle on the tree, Prim pressed her lips to his cheek, closing her eyes and savoring his skin against hers, the rough patch of hair forming on his jaw.

Raff turned then, his mouth grazing hers.

They'd never kissed. Never once. Even as many times as she'd wanted him to kiss her, it never happened—and she'd accepted that long ago.

Because despite her romantic yearning, they'd been friends. Good friends, once.

But her life had been such a shitty mess for so long, she'd avoided interacting with him as much as possible before they'd graduated from high school— even though he never went a day without checking in on her.

As much as she'd pushed him away, he'd left the lines of communication open with cheerful texts, and eventually emails, from wherever he was in the world.

She'd been so wrapped up in her humiliation and embarrassment about the controlling conditions they'd lived in, conditions her mother had been too sick and helpless to do anything about, and she'd been too terrified to tell anyone about, afraid they'd take her from her mother. Never once had Prim considered telling Raff.

He'd been busy trying to move on with his life in

high school after his mother was killed and dating an assortment of girls, one right after the other—he didn't need her problems fucking up his teenage experience—especially because of what happened with his mother. She didn't want that.

But mostly, she didn't want Raff's pity.

She couldn't bear his pity.

And when he went away after college to his first assignment in Africa, she'd let more and more time pass between answering his texts to purposely distance herself further.

Prim's teenage dreams of them dating had fallen to the wayside.

But tonight, when his lips touched hers, and her head exploded, she remembered how many times she'd wanted him to kiss her.

Tonight's kiss confirmed she'd not been wrong when she'd fantasized about this very moment.

Raff's lips were soft but firm, pressing against hers with gentle insistence until his arms went around her back and he hauled her against him.

She went willingly, forgetting everything around them, the only sound the crash of her heartbeat in her ears and their ragged breathing. The Christmas music became a distant, muted thump. The laughter from the people in her house muffled.

There was nothing but them.

His body was hard against hers, strong and taut, yet melting into her frame until she couldn't decipher between the two of them. His tongue slipped into her mouth, eliciting a soft groan from Prim, making her wrap her arms around his neck, cup the back of his silky-soft head and fall deeper into his arms.

This kiss—this delicious, explosive, long-awaited kiss—was so much more than she could have ever imagined, more than she'd ever, in all her teenage years, dreamed.

It was even better than the one she'd once imagined sharing with Zac Efron.

I mean, seriously, who could be a better kisser than Zac Efron?

FIFTEEN

The spell was broken when she heard Nina yell, "*Die Hard* is *so* a fucking Christmas movie, Ass-Sniffer! Don't talk stupid."

Marty let out a ragged sigh. "Just because Christmas is the setting, doesn't mean it's *about* Christmas, you beast. It's about a crazy guy, trying to steal money from a rich guy at a Christmas party. That there's a Christmas tree in the background does not a Christmas movie make, Elvira."

"Well, you two, what do you say? Is *Die Hard* a Christmas movie?" Wanda cooed with a giggle when they snapped apart as though they'd been caught slamming each other in the backseat of a car. "Yay or nay?"

Prim was too frazzled to answer, but Raff saved them. He cleared his throat and took a step back from

Prim, leaving her suddenly feeling very alone. "I gotta go with Nina on this one, Marty. Sorry."

Marty blew a raspberry at him and pointed to the Christmas tree, her bangle bracelets jingling. "Whatever. Get over here, Stretch. We need someone to decorate the front of the tree while Darnell does the back."

Raff nodded, but before he went to help, he whispered to Prim, "Will you meet me on the back stoop after dinner?"

He didn't appear nearly as discombobulated as she was, but she managed a smile—because yes. She'd meet him on the stoop. She'd meet him on the face of the moon.

"I'll be there," she replied, inhaling deeply.

Freddy pawed at her leg, with that look in his eyes that said poop was imminent. She hadn't walked him since this all began. He loved to walk in the snow, and she definitely needed some fresh air.

Prim scooped him up and kissed his snout. "I've been a bad mommy lately, haven't I? Let me get your leash and we'll go, okay?"

His long ears perked up as she went off to her new kitchen to find his leash.

"In the pantry right in the middle of the far bank of cabinets, Mistress Prim. Do take care not to muss the paint inside. It's still drying. And make haste. Tonight, we shall feast on an Italian pepper beef dish with homemade French bread so divine, you might shed a tear," Arch said as he worked at the big six-burner stove, cooking up something that smelled like Heaven.

On impulse, and certainly without any thought that she was actually expressing an emotion, she came up behind Arch and gave him a quick hug, gripping his shoulders. "Thanks, Arch. For...for everything. You're the best."

He patted her hand without ever turning from the pot he was stirring. "Ah, Mistress Primrose, you do flatter me. Off with you now. Be swift!"

Kneeling down, she latched a very excited Freddy into his harness and leash as he wiggled his long body in excitement.

Nina was glaring at her when she stood back up. "How many fucking times do we have to say you go nowhere alone?"

She rolled her eyes at Nina and snickered. "I'm not fucking going anywhere alone. I was actually going to ask you to join me, so I could have some sparkling conversation and be blessed with your razor-sharp wit."

Nin stooped at the waist and picked up Freddy to drop a kiss on the top of his head. "Mommy's got jokes, huh?" Freddy licked Nina's face, his eyes adoring.

Darnell rolled up the sleeves of his ugly Christmas sweater—and it was *ugly*—and held out a hand to Prim. "I'll go, too, Boss. Nuthin' better than a nice walk in some cold snow to git you right with the world."

Prim took his hand and asked with an impish grin, "Is that a relief after living in the fiery depths of Hell?"

Darnell barked a laugh as he led her out the front door. "Look who's funny today. Get some wings and you're ready to go out on the road with your standup, huh?"

She chuckled as they pushed their way down the snow-covered steps. Someone had shoveled them off earlier, but the snow was coming down so hard you wouldn't tell.

Taking a deep breath when Nina set an exuberant Freddy on his feet, as they began walking, Prim really looked at the houses on her street for the first time since she'd been back, instead of hiding from the moment she left her car until she could get inside.

A smile lifted the corner of her lips. There'd been a time when she'd loved this street and her neighbors.

Everyone had decorated for the holiday, the way they'd always done. There were snowmen and reindeer, inflatable Santas and elves, trees adorned with twinkling lights.

Her Jewish neighbor, three houses down, had a menorah in his big bay window and even a light-up dreidel.

All of the houses here were a mixture of newer Victorian and Craftsmen. An odd combination to some, but home to her. Each yard had a tree of some kind...maple, oak...and in the fall, it was quite a sight for the foliage lovers.

"Nice neighborhood ya got here, Prim," Darnell commented, hooking her arm through his while Nina flanked her on the other side. "You grew up here, right?"

"I did," she confirmed, watching Freddy saunter happily in the snow. "I never lived anywhere else until I went to college."

They stopped when Freddy found the base of Mr. Robertson's tree at the end of the road especially interesting.

Nina planted a hand to her shoulder and lifted her chin with a fingertip. "So that skeezy fuck you blew a new O-ring...you wanna tell me who the hell he is?"

Damn. She'd almost successfully forgotten about what she'd done, fully realizing she needed some kind of explanation for the light that shot out of her mouth, but afraid of what it might be.

The question ruined the warm bubble of Raff's kiss she was floating upon.

And nope. She didn't want to tell anyone anything about Smitty. "No," she answered quite plainly.

"Tough titties. Who was that asshole and why was he hangin' onto you like you were the last bitch on Earth?" Nina pressed, her eyes fixed on Prim's face.

Darnell rubbed her arm, his dark eyes glowing with understanding and sympathy. "Boss is just tryin' to help, Prim. We gotta know everything to help you the right way."

"He has nothing to do with this. With me being a

fairy," she said stiffly, looking down at the ground while Freddy fiddled. At least, she didn't think he did... how could he?

Could he?

Nina popped her lips in obvious impatience, the dark night making her pale face almost glow, her angry expression clearly visible. "Then why did he say you have something he wants? What the fuck does he want?"

"You heard that?"

Nina stared at her hard. "I heard everything, Prim. I'm a fucking vampire. I hear the guy in the house three streets away taking a dump. So yeah, I heard what he said. What does he want?"

Shit. Shit. Shit. How could she explain Smitty, and why wouldn't he and his ugly memory go the fuck away?

She shrugged, trying to play him off as nothing more than a nuisance. "That was Smitty. My stepfather, and I don't know what he wants. I swear, I don't. I haven't seen him since the night I graduated high school, because he just got out of jail a few months ago."

"For?"

Jesus. Prim felt like she was being interrogated by a member of NCIS. But as Nina waited for an answer, her eyes burning a hole in Prim's cold face, she knew she didn't have a choice because what if it could help figure out what was happening to her?

Looking away from them, Prim repeated what she knew. "He did almost a dime for drug possession. Third-degree felony. He got out on early release for good behavior a few months ago, but this is the first time he's contacted me."

Darnell whistled, tucking her to his side. "Was he dealin' while he lived with you and your mama? When she was sick?"

Apparently, he'd been doing it the whole time he'd lived with them. "That's what the police said when they brought me in for questioning. That he'd been involved in dealing coke and fentanyl for years. They'd just never been able to catch him until..."

Until someone he sold that crap with ratted his ass out.

She thought when she ran away from his drunken grip the night she graduated, she was done with him forever.

But she'd never forget that night when they'd hauled her out of her dorm room and took her to the police station for questioning.

The cold, damp green room with two detectives staring her down with angry faces and throwing scary words around like life in prison and conspiracy. It felt as though she was guilty by association for the way they treated her.

She'd answered as best she could, everything she knew about Smitty. He'd told them he sold pharmaceuticals, and that was why he was away so often.

He was selling something all right, but it wasn't diet pills and vitamins. And after her mother died, he didn't bother to hide his rough friends or his drinking.

That last year at home for her had been a living nightmare. Smitty'd stopped making her do chores in favor of hanging out with his druggie friends. Sometimes, it was as if he didn't even know she was still there.

Sometimes.

Day after day, not knowing who she'd wake up to find sleeping on the floor or the couch was the penalty she paid for suddenly being excused from his rigid rules.

One time, there'd been a filthy scum of a man passed out on her bedroom floor when she woke up. The house became a shit-pile of dirty clothes and cigarettes filling up ashtrays, beer bottles left with the fermented stench of alcohol permeating the air.

Her only solace was knowledge of the money her mother had left her, money Smitty knew nothing about. With her scholarship and that money, she was able to escape him until the police contacted her and he was convicted.

She'd used some of the money her mother left to pay the taxes on the house for all these years, until, through therapy with Dr. Shay, she decided she was ready to come back and face at least some of her demons.

Darnell hugged her, pulling her next to his stout

body, warming her as she shivered. She hated Smitty. She didn't want to talk about him anymore. It hurt too much to remember that time in her life. It hurt to remember all the things he'd taken from her—kept from her.

Nina clenched her fists together, but her eyes softened. "I don't need you to tell me the deets to know what the fuck happened after your mother died, kiddo. I think I already know, and I oughta beat that fuck with his own arm for it. But if you want to, I got ears. I'll listen. I'll *always* listen."

Prim gulped. Except for Raff, who she was too embarrassed to confide in, had ever willingly offered to listen to her before this until Dr. Shay, and she'd been court-ordered to do so. But to be fair, she'd never wanted to tell anyone either.

"We don't wanna make you talk about somethin' that hurts so bad, but we also wanna help. To help you, we gotta look at everyone in your life who might wanna hurt you, Prim, and he sho' sounds like he wants to hurt ya, from what the boss here told me."

Nodding, Prim reassured him, "I know you guys are just trying to help. But I don't think Smitty has anything to do with what happened to me...I mean, the fairy thing anyway. Though, I don't doubt for a fucking second he'd barter a baby to the devil."

She knew firsthand what he'd barter to stay out of trouble and pay off a debt.

Nina squinted as a curtain of snow fell on them. "I think he'll watch his ass after what you did to him."

Prim scoffed. "After what *I* did? Me, Nina the vampire? You almost took his damn head off."

She cracked her knuckles before stuffing her hands into her hoodie pockets. "I'da taken his limbs off, too, if Marty wasn't such a damn party pooper."

Licking her lips, Prim decided to tackle this new power head on. "What did I do, anyway?" She still wasn't sure she understood it.

Darnell chuckled. "I think you can use sound as a weapon. So when ya yelled at that creeper, you blew his ass outta the water."

"Wow..." she murmured. "Anything else I should know that might come up? I mean, besides invisibility and the power to eviscerate a man with my voice? Am I going to be able to beat people to death with my wings?"

Darnell winced. "Well, yeah. You can do that, too. Leastways I think you can. I hear they're pretty strong. But we gotta get 'em in working order first."

Nina tugged her arm and directed her back down the street. "Don't forget you can turn into a damn gnat with sparkly wings and fly."

Right. She could fly. Though, she could hardly remember leaving that dungeon and how she'd made her way to Marty's. But tonight, she was glad she did.

"About that. How did I go from being almost six feet to the size of a Lego? Does that just happen? Why hasn't it happened again? Will I just morph the fuck out like you guys do with your teeth and fur? Or am I just going to be the biggest fairy in all of fairyland, stomping around on all their little houses made out of toadstools? The one they point and laugh at behind her back?"

"Just open your big fucking mouth and yell at 'em. That'll shut that shit right down," Nina advised with a cackle, leaning down to scoop up Freddy, who'd indicated he was too tired to go on by stopping dead in the middle of the street and laying in the snow like a wet noodle.

Prim couldn't help but laugh out loud into the cold, dark night. "Damn. Where was all this when Darleen from HR was riding my ass about wearing work boots to the office? I could have sent her into outer space."

Nina's look was astonished. "Darleen bitched about you wearing boots? What the fuck kind of rank bullshit is that? Work boots are fucking life. Fuck Darleen."

Prim held up a hand toward the cloudless sky. "Testify."

As they strolled leisurely back to the house, softly commenting on the decorations and the beauty of the snow, despite the fear of what came next, Prim felt safe, protected in a way she never had before, or at least not in a very long while...and it scared her.

Petrified her. These people weren't going to be here

forever. They'd help her figure out her fairy problem and they'd go back to their lives and then it would just be her again.

A day or so ago, she'd wanted nothing more. But tonight? Right now, she didn't feel as strongly about it as she had even just a few hours ago.

As they rounded the corner, shuffling through the snow, the cold air making her teeth chatter, Prim allowed herself to relish being in the safety of these people who hardly knew her, but felt like they'd always been in her life.

Dr. Shay had encouraged her to make a friend. Just one. Open the door to the possibility of a friendship just an inch or so.

She'd scoffed at the idea. Spit in the face of the suggestion. Friends wanted to know things...personal things...things she didn't want to divulge to anyone, ever.

Bet ol' Dr. Shay'd be really proud to see the gaggle of women and men surrounding her now. In fact, her life had suddenly become a regular Grand Central Station.

How's that for opening the door?

Lost in her thoughts, Prim didn't realize they were at her house until two things happened.

First, a light so bright—almost blinding—blazed through her new front windows in a multicolored, crystalline glow, pulsing as if it were breathing.

Prim blinked. "Raff?" she whispered.

"Holy shit, Mothra got his fucking wings!" Nina mused with a cackle.

Second?

Darnell began to yell to Nina. "Boss, we need to get help, *now!*" he cried.

As Prim spun around, she saw Darnell scooping something out of the snow. A tiny creature with pink and gold wings weighed down by the heavy snow, leaving them hanging behind her back, her beautiful face peaceful despite her slack body.

"Who is that?" Prim asked Darnell in a frightened whisper.

"It's Serena. This is Serena!"

CHAPTER
SIXTEEN

He stood at the window, watching Prim, Nina and Darnell as they walked off into the night, Freddy Mercury skipping ahead of them, crooked leg and all...and Raff smiled at how nuts he was about Primrose Dunham.

She was rude, cussed like a trucker, opinionated, unfiltered and angry as hell. She hadn't always been so angry at something he couldn't understand, something she wouldn't talk about, but she was all those things and more.

His friends would call him crazy for still loving her after all this time, but he knew the Prim who once laughed easily. Who saved strays, who'd had a gerbil named Zac Efron, who'd loved Sour Patch Kids (especially the watermelon ones) and who always stuck up for the underdog.

Even when no one stuck up for her.

She'd been his best buddy—the only girl he invited to his house after school for peanut butter and Fluff sandwiches. The only girl who could eat more of those sandwiches than he could. Prim was the girl he'd played old school Zelda with, the girl he'd gone ice skating and tubing with. Then she'd become the young woman he'd spent countless nights dreaming about.

The young woman who one day had stopped coming over after school for sandwiches and Zelda because Smitty wouldn't allow her to do anything until her chores were finished, and even if she completed them, there was her homework and her mother to take care of.

Prim had become withdrawn, sullen, and eerily quiet several months after Smitty moved in. His mother said she was just adjusting to a man in her mother's life, that maybe she was a little jealous of the attention her mother paid Smitty.

Raff wanted to believe that, but selfishly, and like most teenagers, he only thought about how much he missed his friend.

He'd tried to talk to her—plenty of times. Like all the times they sat out on her back stoop when Smitty was gone on his trips to wherever the hell he went. But she brushed him off, and she'd been doing that almost ever since.

Every time he thought she'd let him in, she clammed up and put him back in his friend box where she'd decided he belonged. Though, when his mother was killed, and all during the investigation, she'd been by his side.

He hadn't been able to articulate how he felt, how devastated he was by his mother's untimely death, but Prim didn't appear to need words, and she definitely didn't push him to do anything other than sit with his feelings—with his pain—while she held his hand.

Prim was simply there. Quietly. Solidly.

And then she wasn't, *again*. And this time, she was even more withdrawn than ever before. He'd tried in every way possible to talk to her, reach her, but she'd always pushed him away. His dad, broken and bereft over his mother's murder, was in no shape to deal with his teenage angst, so Raff had kept it to himself.

But he'd never stopped loving her...

They'd graduated and gone off to college. He'd done his best to stay connected with her, but she'd done as little as possible in return, and while it hurt like hell, his life had changed on a dime when he'd been offered his first job as a photojournalist by a magazine to take photos of the decades-long war in Afghanistan.

He decided to take the job in part because it excited him, but also because it was time he made a change in his life, something away from their small town and the painful memories.

That one job led him all over the world, and his life became hectic. Still, he found ways to keep in touch, and Prim blocked his efforts at every turn with one-word responses and stilted phone calls and emails.

Finally, he'd left things alone for longer periods of time—mostly because he realized he'd likely never know what made Prim decide to turn the light switch off on their friendship with such abruptness...and his life overseas took a turn that had changed him forever.

But tonight? A shift between them had happened, and he knew she felt it, too.

For him, he'd just kissed the love of his life. The woman he'd loved since he'd first officially met her in science class in the first grade. They were even born only minutes apart, but because Prim was born first, she always joked that she was the eldest of their dynamic duo.

Of course, he didn't know it was love back then. Back then he'd just thought she was more awesome than his favorite cartoon, *X-Men: Evolution*. That was saying something for how cool Prim had been.

"It's beautiful, isn't it? The snow. So peaceful."

Raff nodded. "Yeah..."

"Hey, you okay?" Wanda asked, coming to stand beside him.

He couldn't stop smiling. "I am. I'm really okay."

Wanda tilted her head and looked up at him, her eyes gleaming beneath the Christmas lights on the tree. "Have you always loved her?"

He nodded, his chest tightening at the question. "Always."

"How long have you known each other?"

"We officially met in the first grade, but we've always lived next door. We share the same birthday—almost right down to the minute."

Wanda cocked her head, her chestnut hair gleaming in the light of the tree. "Almost?"

He grinned at the memory. "We're just a couple of minutes apart. Prim came first, of course."

Wanda smiled. "Of course, as all strong women do. How old are you two?"

"Twenty-nine," he answered easily.

Then Wanda's face changed to thoughtful. "Has she always been this..."

"Cranky? Mean? Foul-mouthed? Angry?" He shook his head. "No. Not always. There was a time when... she was different. Before her mother married that jackass Smitty. It changed her. It changed everything. Not at first, but slowly, and then her mother got sick and..."

Wanda placed a hand on his arm, warm and gentle. "I'm going to try and ask this as delicately as I can, and you don't have to answer if you don't want to, but did he...did he hurt her?"

Raff had wondered that from the start, and he'd hinted at it many times, but Prim vehemently denied any sort of sexual abuse. "If you mean physically, I don't think so. He was a controlling bastard, but he didn't hit her or her mother. Still, I always kinda wondered..."

Wanda bit her lower lip. "We've been wondering, too. She's terrified of him, Raff. We could smell it."

"*Smell* it?"

Wanda tapped her nose. "Half vampire, half were-wolf, remember? Our senses are heightened, and Prim was terrified of that disgusting man. Not to mention, he smelled putrid, and I'm not talking about the alcohol on his breath. I'm talking about his filthy soul."

Raff clenched his fists together to avoid punching a wall. His anger mingled with his sense of awe at these women and their capabilities. "I knew she hated him, from almost the moment he came into their lives, but if I find out he... I'll hunt him down myself. I'll kill him."

"I think you'll have to get in line," Marty muttered, coming to stand on the other side of him. "Wanda's right. That swine smells like toxic waste. So what do you think he wants with Prim now? We googled him and found out he did time for felony drug possession, among other things, but we all heard him say she had something he wanted. Any idea what that could be?"

Raff's heart began to pump harder in his chest. What did Smitty want, and would he have to beat the answer out of the asshole to find out?

"I have no clue. After her mother died and Prim went off to college, my dad said things got pretty wild over here. Loud parties, upset neighbors, police calls. Dad was in the process of moving to Oregon when

Smitty was arrested. I guess I could ask him if he knows anything, but I doubt It. He was pretty wrapped up in his grief after my mother..."

"Was killed," Wanda finished for him, her tone hushed. "We did some digging on you, too, and we read the article in the local paper about her. I'm so sorry, Rafferty. She was a beautiful woman, and I bet she was a great mother."

He let his chin hit his chest to hide the deep pain his mother's unsolved murder still ignited in him. "She was the best. And in a close second place, Prim's mother, Mrs. Dunham, was pretty amazing, too. They were friendly for a long time, until she married Smitty. I mean, they didn't go out for drinks or anything, but they chatted from time to time. If one or the other needed sugar or an egg, they had each other's backs."

Marty tucked her hair behind her ears. "So your mother didn't like him either?"

"No," he murmured. "In fact, I remember a few times when my mother tried to bring food over for them when Liesl was sick, and Smitty wouldn't even let her in the door." Raff paused with a frown. He was beginning to see a theme here. How had he missed it? "So...he was isolating them. Isn't that one of the terms they use these days to describe a narcissist?"

Wanda blew out a long breath. "One of many, yes. Listen, Raff, we're no doctors. We can't say for sure Smitty is anything other than a prime piece of garbage. The way you describe him keeping Prim and her mother from everyone screams a bunch of different things. It could've simply been to hide his drug deals. I'm fairly certain he wouldn't want anyone snooping around, and if Prim's mother fell ill, she surely couldn't do much about it."

"She was really sick for almost three years before she died." He'd never forget the difference only two months in her life made. Mrs. Dunham (he'd never stopped calling her that, even after she married Smitty) had gone from pale and thin, to frail and almost breakable.

Out of the blue, he remembered something—and it burned his gut. "There was an incident with a friend of Prim's. Her name was Stephanie. I don't know what happened exactly. I just know it had to do with Smitty. Prim would never talk about it. Maybe that's what she's been dealing with all these years. Maybe he..."

Oh, God. Oh, Jesus Christ. Had Smitty sexually assaulted Stephanie? Or *Prim*? His blood boiled, and it was all he could do not to smash his hand through the window.

Marty clucked her tongue and crossed her arms over her chest. "Listen, Smitty is the least of our problems at this point in terms of what's happening to you guys, fairy-wise. If we had to, we could take care of him before you even blinked. But he's still a big personal problem for Prim. He's the reason she's shut herself off from everyone and everything, of that I can assure you and I don't need a degree to know that. It's why she's so damn angry. Hurt people, hurt people, Raff."

Raking a hand through his hair, Raff didn't know how to respond. "We were friends for a long time. I don't understand why she didn't tell me. Maybe that sounds totally out of touch, but I swear, I never saw anything but a strict stepfather who kept her on lockdown."

Marty rubbed his arm. "We're not blaming you, honey. You were children. What we're saying is, we think she's traumatized. We suspect she shuts everyone out as a coping mechanism."

Wanda sighed, her eyes thoughtful. "We know a little about this because of Nina."

He lifted an eyebrow. "Nina? I'll admit they're a lot alike in many ways, but I think Nina's the one doing the traumatizing. Was I the only one who saw her almost rip that guy's head off his shoulders?"

Marty jabbed a finger in the air. "She does that because she's a protector. Animals, the elderly, the bullied. She's cranky and rude as hell, but there was once a little girl who didn't have anyone to protect her from her drug-addicted mother and an absent father.

"That's how our girl copes. She cusses up a blue streak, she tells it like it is, no holds barred, and she defends the weak—the helpless. The difference is, our fiercely protective, loyal vampire knows *why* she does what she does now. She's been through some intensive therapy to find out. But Prim doesn't know how to deal with why she hates the world or why she's so damn afraid of it, Rafferty."

Unbidden tears sprang to his eyes, tears he swallowed until his throat burned. He ached for her, right down to his soul. Why hadn't he pushed harder? If he had, would it have pushed her over the edge?

"So I've only made things worse by invading her space all this time, by trying to get her to open up. I'm an asshole."

"No. *No*, Rafferty," Wanda whispered, leaning her head on his shoulder. "You're not anything of the sort. You're someone who's always been there for her. You can't help fix the problem when you don't know what's broken. So you did the best you could. None of us know what's broken in Prim, and we have no right to diagnose her, but we think that's why you see so many similarities between Nina and Prim. Because outwardly, they truly are a lot alike. Angry, combative, unfiltered. It's the inside that's different...and only Prim can fix that."

Raff didn't want to hear platitudes and reassurances. This wasn't about him. It was about Prim. She needed help, more intensive counseling than what her court-ordered therapist could offer, and he was going to do everything in his power to encourage her to pursue her mental health.

Marty gripped his hand as if reading his mind. "We know someone who counsels the paranormal. Her name is January Malone, and if she can help the beast that lives in Nina, she can help Prim. She's an amazing lady. The fairy business aside, I promise we'll help her through this, Raff, and you, too."

He looked at them in wonder and had to ask, "Why are you doing this? You don't even know us. You're not doing it for money, fame. I don't get it. Can there really be this many good people all in one place?"

Wanda looked out the window, off into the night lit up by Christmas lights, her gaze far away. "Isn't this the way it should always should? People helping people?"

He smiled, tears rushing to sit behind his eyelids again. The sentiment bringing back the ugly memory of why he'd left photojournalism for good this time. "If only..."

Marty broke the moment of silence by giving his arm a nudge. "So, you're a photographer."

"I am," he said quietly. He *was*. He didn't know if he could be again.

"Oh, Raff," Wanda said softly. "You take the most beautiful pictures. What a gift you have. Honestly, that one of the mother breastfeeding her baby outside of a crumbling building left both Wanda and I in tears. You must have seen so much."

He nodded as they all stood, looking out the window. He had.

"I sense it troubles you a great deal..." Marty led the beginning of a conversation he wasn't ready to have.

"Your nose, right?"

Her smile was gentle. "Yep. I don't just sniff asses."

He barked a laugh. "Noted."

"Maybe, just *maybe*, it's okay to let Prim's troubles take a back burner for a second and focus on you and what's happening inside your heart, deal with what troubles your soul. You'd probably be more helpful if one of you is healthy not just in body, but in mind," Marty suggested softly.

Wanda gave him a light pat on the back. "If you're ever so inclined, Dr. January's doors are open to you, too."

Raff swallowed hard. "Appreciate that."

Marty and Wanda drove their hands though each of his arms as they watched the endless snowfall. "Now, on to other fairy news. You ready?"

He winced. "For?"

"For some news from Sten and his friend Gary."

"The giant?" he asked tentatively.

He wasn't sure he was ready to meet a giant. His anxiety suddenly ratcheted up a notch. With the suspicions the women had about Prim's past and the possibility they were going to find some answers, he felt downright panicked.

"Yeaaah," Marty answered. "He's pretty big—and green. But he's a great guy. "You'll like him. He's an Earth Troll, for clarification."

"You know, I've been looking up fairies and trolls and all the folklore that goes with. I can't believe it's not too far from accurate. Wings, manipulation of sound, invisibility, a magic wand."

"Believe," Marty said on a light chuckle. "Neither can we. But Gary's real, and he's on his way with Sten. I don't think he'll fit in the house, but we'll figure that out when he gets here."

As Raff paused to consider the idea that Gary wouldn't fit in the house, a rush of heat assaulted him.

Without any warning, he suddenly felt something pushing against him—from the inside out.

Raff almost fell over at the force leveled against his back. He wasn't a small man, but it felt like someone had yanked something out of his spine, making him reach out to catch himself against the window frame.

Jerking forward, the pull of his skin turned into a stretch—and then nothing but blinding light scissoring its way through the room, making everyone cry out.

"What the...?" he yelped.

And then there was the buzzing. Like a fluorescent light that needed replacing or a bee gathering pollen from a flower.

If not for Marty and Nina, he would have fallen on his face, taking the Christmas tree and half the house with him.

"Marty!" Wanda called out. "Don't let him fall!"

Marty grabbed his arm and pulled him forward, keeping him upright until he steadied himself and found his footing.

The glow instantly muted, allowing him to see Marty and Wanda, both rubbing their eyes. "What the hell...?"

That was when Raff saw his reflection in the windows. In fact, outer space probably saw his reflection, too.

Raff's mouth fell open, his eyes going wide and the only thought in his head happened to be quite comical.

WWTBD.

What would Tinker Bell do?

CHAPTER
SEVENTEEN

"Serena?" Sten shouted from the direction of the kitchen, as Darnell carried her inside and gently draped her across the gray loveseat.

Prim ran and grabbed a blanket to cover her with, her heart throbbing in her chest. This was the elusive Serena? The fairy who'd helped the women in Troll Place—or whatever they called it?

As Prim eyed her, trying to stay out of the way, she marveled at her size. It was a crazy thing to wonder at a time like this, when Serena was injured, but how did she go from big to small and vice versa? She presented very average in height, slender, curvy, and beautiful in repose.

"What the frack happened?" Marty asked Darnell as Sten sat on the edge of the loveseat, moving Serena's soaking-wet, wavy red hair away from her gamine face and tucking it behind her ears—ears that looked much like Prim's.

"We found her outside in the snow, Boss. She was unconscious, just layin' there like she passed out." Then Darnell sniffed the area around Serena, his lips thinning. "Fairy magic. Some fairy's been up to no good. I can smell it."

Wanda pressed her hand to her cheek, her eyes worried. "Are you sure it's not *her* magic?"

Darnell shook his head as he pulled off his knit hat, his face worried. "Naw, I know what her magic smells like. It ain't hers."

"I have her phone!" Nina called from the doorway, holding the cell up. "It was on the ground, covered in snow, and it's fucking cracked."

"Rice!" Raff hollered from near the windows, his big wings buzzing with an electric hum as they swatted the air. "Put it in some rice," he repeated. "I'd help, but..."

Prim had forgotten what she saw outside the window, leaving her to wonder which issue to tackle first. As everyone else surrounded Serena, she decided Raff looked like he was who she could help most.

Biting her knuckle to keep from screaming with laughter, because it was neither appropriate or decent, she asked, "What the fuck happened, Raff?"

There he stood, by the Christmas tree, illuminated, handsome, *winged*.

And they were beautiful wings. Gold and silver

with splashes of pale blue and green, spanning almost from one end of the room to the other. It was awe-inspiring and terrifying.

Raff shook his blond head, the tips of his pointy ears peeking through his hair. He made a face at her. "I have no clue, Prim. I was just standing here, looking out the window, watching the snow as I chatted with Marty and Wanda and *kablam*! Wings. Big, flappy wings."

Prim held up a tentative hand as she moved closer. "Can I touch them? Will it hurt?"

His jaw tightened and his stance widened. "I don't know. I mean, they didn't hurt much when I sprouted them, but they're heavy as hell."

She traced a finger over the outline of them, surprised at how delicate they felt, considering Raff had classified them as heavy. The gossamer wisps glowed brighter when she touched them, beautiful colors pulsing to life.

If she was an envious girl, she'd be positively green right now. Compared to the sad lump she had on her back, which didn't show signs of changing, Raff's wings were a far cry from what she'd been given.

"If you weren't the size of a fucking moose, we could put you on the top of the tree, buddy," Nina teased, ducking when Raff's wings gently flapped, knocking a few Styrofoam Christmas ornaments to the ground. "So what the fuck happened?"

Raff shook his head, running a hand over his stubbled chin. "Gee, Nina the vampire, I have no idea. I was hoping you, Paranormal Guru, could tell me."

Nina shrugged and made a face, but her eyes glowed. "I have no fucking clue, except the boy has become a fucking man. You're all growed up, buddy."

Raff rolled his eyes. "Funny. Not helpful, but funny."

"Sten said he might have something from Serena's phone, and Gary's here. He's got some shit to tell us, too."

"The *giant*?" Prim squeaked.

Nina thumbed over her shoulder toward the back kitchen door. "Yeah. In the backyard, because we can't figure out how to fit him in the house without fucking taking half of it out. You think you can walk with those things?"

Raff winced, eyeing his wingspan. "I'm not sure I can without knocking everything over. Thoughts?"

Nina got behind him. "You go, I'll be your wingman." Then she laughed. "Hah! Get it? Wingman?"

Prim let them go ahead of her, stopping to see how Serena was doing, but she was still sprawled under the blanket. Someone had brought a towel to dry her hair, and Carl leaned over the back of the couch and held her hand.

"Sten? Is she going to be all right? Is there anything I can do to help?" she asked, placing a light hand on his broad shoulder.

Sten's lips went grim, his expression worried.

"There's nothing you can do, Prim. She's under some type of spell, as best I can see. Someone didn't want her to get here, that much is clear. We need to get her back to her people so they can tend to her. Go hear what Gary has to say and then we'll figure out what to do next."

Prim moved from foot to foot nervously. Seeing this woman, a genuine fairy, made her uneasy. She was likely a perfectly lovely person.

She had on a cute little sparkly white leotard and a pink and gold tutu that matched her wings. She was beautiful, her face serene as she slept, her chest rising and falling in gentle breaths.

She looked harmless, but then she thought about Alfrigg and Cosmo and how they'd tried to fry her face off, and she wasn't so sure.

Had she come to tell her something about her mother? About what to do next? Had she gotten hurt trying to help her?

If Prim didn't feel guilty before, she felt like positive dog shit now. All these people were trying to make things better, but everything felt like it was getting worse.

Giving a squeeze to Sten's shoulder, Prim decided to help where she could and made her way to the kitchen, where Nina guided Raff by yelling, "Left, Mothra! You're gonna knock all the new fucking cabinets down, you derp!"

A crash ensued, wherein all the gorgeous copper

pots, hanging in a row above her new peninsula, fell to the ground in a clattering heap.

"Sorry!" Raff yelped. "I've never had wings before, okay?"

Prim fought a laugh by covering her mouth—until she looked out the window over the sink, where a man so big, so handsome, so *green,* sat in her backyard.

Wow. He sure didn't look like the guy on the can of green beans. He wasn't hard on the eyes either.

She leaned into Nina and whispered in hushed reverence, "Is that..."

"Gary? You bet your fairy ass it is!" After positioning Raff at the window overlooking the backyard, which she yanked open so he could hear what the giant had to say, she grabbed Prim's hand and pulled her outside into the snow.

Gary sat with his legs crossed, a green haze of man in the middle of a snowy white background. Naked from the waist up, his torso as tall as her house.

Every time she thought she'd seen it all, there was this. A green man who was a stone-cold fox and taller than her house.

Would there ever be a time this wasn't absolutely fucking crazy?

Launching herself at the man the size of a Redwood tree, Nina stretched her arms wide to cup his face in her hands, hands that looked like they belonged to a Barbie doll, compared to the giant's face. "How the fuck are you, buddy?"

He chuckled, low and deep, making the earth actually quake while knocking snow from the tree limbs. "My favorite vampire in all the realms!" he exclaimed, scooping her up in his palm and pressing Nina lightly to his cheek. "I'm real good, little lady. How's you? The family? My little Charlie?"

Nina grinned as Prim stood below in complete awe. "Good. Everybody's good."

He set her down on the ground and lowered his head to peer at Prim, who felt like she was Cindy Lou Who, staring up at the face of the Grinch. "And this lovely morsel? This must be Primrose," he said with a wink, his deep voice resonating in her ears."

Prim twisted her fingers together, anxiety making her shiver. "I'm Prim. Nice to meet you." She didn't know whether to hold out her hand or not, but she didn't need to worry. Gary swept her up in his palm, despite her sputtering.

"Nice to meet you, too. And don't be afraid of me, please. I won't hurt you. I'm a peace-loving guy. Now this," he pointed to a wide-eyed Rafferty, "this is the other fairy. Rafferty, right?" He leveled one of his eyes to peer into the window at Raff, who stumbled backward until Gary reached through the window and plucked at his T-shirt with two fingers, standing him upright.

Poor Rafferty looked like he might collapse on the spot, but he squared his shoulders, or tried to anyway, and straightened. "Yes. That's me, Rafferty Monroe. The *other* fairy."

Gary smiled wide, his teeth sparkling white against his green skin. "Pleased to meet ya, Rafferty."

"So whaddaya got for us, my guy?" Nina asked.

"Get comfortable, Prim, and have a seat," he said, nodding to his palm, where she stood in absolute frozen terror. "It's okay. Sit. I'll keep you warm. Promise," he said with a naughty wink.

Prim used his thumb as leverage until she slid to her backside and sat cross-legged. He was right. His palm was warm and toasty.

In all the books she'd read, in all the fairy tales her mother had told her, this went beyond anything she could have ever imagined.

Nina tucked her hands into her hoodie. "Sten says you heard some rumors from the Realm of the Hollow. What the fuck's going on?"

Gary nodded "And it might be just that—a rumor. Anyway, rumor has it, there's some scrit. You know, like an ancient scroll of some kind? A prophecy of sorts."

Both Raff and Prim nodded. "And it says?" Raff asked, his expression hopeful.

Gary scoffed, nearly blowing Prim over. He tipped her back upright with an apologetic grin. "Sorry, sometimes I don't know my own strength. Anyway, the problem is, no one knows exactly *what* it says. Not totally. The only thing they've been able to decipher is some gobbledygook about a fairy given up at birth. That could def be Prim, but how can we be sure? If you listen to the lore, fairy babies were swapped all the time."

Prim swallowed, her nerves atwitter. "Okay, but seeing as I escaped a Mason jar like some goddamn firefly, the chance it could be me is pretty likely? Have you heard of any other people being snatched from their beds and stuffed in a jar recently. It's definitely as good an explanation as any."

Gary bounced his head. "All true. Anyway, the scrit says, and I say this with mucho hesitation because how do I know if the scrit reader is right? It's in an ancient language—"

"Get to the point, Gary," Nina interrupted. "What the fuck does it say?"

"It says, if the fairy given up at birth isn't killed, it will destroy both the dark and the light. Meaning, the Seelie and the Unseelie will be no more. As in, it'll wipe out their entire race. Total annihilation."

Wasn't this the cue for a dun-dun-duuun?

Prim licked her lips and pressed her fingers to her temple. "And *if* I'm the fairy given up at birth, I'm the one they want to kill." Sweet baby Jesus in the manger.

Gary winced, his green face pained. "That's what I'm hearing."

"So could that be why those two fairies came to try and take Prim?" Raff asked. "Because they want to kill her? Is that why they took her in the first place?"

"Alfrigg and Cosmo, Sten said, right? Those two fairies?" Gary asked, his eyes narrowing.

Prim nodded. "Uh-huh. That's what I heard them call each other. They said they had to take me back before *he* realized they'd made a mistake. Now that I think about it, I guess they meant mistake as in, I got away. I escaped the Mason jar they had me trapped in."

Gary grumbled. "Those two are wee little henchmen. Butt kissers who do any dirty scoundrel's bidding. Sort of like bounty hunters in the human world."

Fear ripped through her, sending her pulse racing. She was no chickenshit, but no one had ever wanted to kill her before, either.

Anger from all the fear of this entire fiasco left her feeling so out of control, she wanted to throat punch someone. "Okay, so do we find Alfrigg and Cosmo and beat the fuck out of them until they tell us who this oracle is who had them kidnap me?"

"Fuck, kiddo," Nina said, shaking her head. "I hate to admit it, but I like you more and more."

Gary tsked that notion. "No. No, Miss Prim, we do no such thing. You're mighty powerful if you're who the rumors say you are, but you're not ready to take on those beasts. First, you need to be taught how to use your powers by an oracle."

Prim made a face of disgust. "Why the hell would I want one of those if all they want to do is kill me?"

"Because just like Sten told ya. There are good and bad people everywhere. Not all fucking oracles are bad," Nina assured her.

"You want one of those because he can help you learn how to shrink and fly and use your magic wand. You've already seen what your voice can do to someone. You don't want to create a tsunami in the fountain at the mall, do you?"

"Wait. Hold right on there. She gets a magic wand?" Raff muttered. "Do I get one, too?"

"Only if you wear the tutu," Gary teased before he sobered. "Listen, this is serious. You saw what that wand Nina found did to your house. A wand I'm very carefully taking back to the Hollow. We have to figure out if the baby the prophecy speaks of is Prim and if so, who gave her up, and is that fairy a part of this."

Prim only grew angrier at that answer. "She can't fucking have it both ways. She can't save me by sacrificing some poor human baby, only to turn around and want to kill me. That makes zero sense."

"That is a very good point. Regardless, we also have to request a meeting with the Queen of the Seelies. Her name is Queen Pria, FYI—a nice lady by all accounts. We have to find out what to do from here, how to keep you safe from harm, and she'll know."

The hole in the side of her house started calling her name again, and she almost knew what came next without even asking, but she asked anyway on the off chance there was a way she could sit this one out and couch potato on her new love seat while devouring a PB and J with an ice-cold glass of chocolate milk.

But that would make her a complete coward, leaving her salvation up to everyone else, wouldn't it?

"So what's next?" she squeaked, feeling very small and outnumbered, and it wasn't only because Gary's hand was so big.

Gary clucked his tongue. "I think you know what comes next, don't you?"

"I have a feeling it's going to involve that hole in my house and glitter. Lots and lots of glitter," Prim answered, trying her hardest to be brave.

Gary roared with laughter, making some of the lights in the neighboring houses blink on. "So much glitter. So much."

EIGHTEEN

Four days later, Prim kissed Freddy and Katy, showering them with all the love she had just in case...

She couldn't think it as she looked at those sweet faces.

Looking to Arch, she smiled at the little blue man who'd become so dear to her in the last few days. The man who'd baked cookies with her. The man who taught her what mise en place meant, and who educated her on the different cuts of meat.

The man who'd held her hand on the couch while they watched *The Great British Bakeoff*.

"I left a note with their feeding schedule and the number of their vet, if you have any problems," she whispered, suddenly overwhelmed with their parting.

Arch took Freddy in his arms and snuggled him under his chin. "I'll handle everything, of course, Miss

Prim. Please don't fret. I'll take the best care of them and you'll be back before you know it. Isn't that right, Master Fredrick?" He plopped a kiss on Freddy's head.

Then he held out an arm to her and without hesitation, she went into his embrace. "Thank you, Arch. I don't know what else to say but thank you. These last few days have meant..." Tears stung her eyelids—again. It was the most ridiculous thing. She'd hardly ever cried until this happened. Now, she was a sloppy, snotty, sobbing glob of a human.

Arch held her close and whispered, "Never forget what I told you, Mistress Prim. You are worthy. I shall say this until you finally heed. *Primrose Dunham is worthy*. She's a gift, yet unopened for all to enjoy."

He *had* said that, several times, and the more he said it, the less she found herself resisting fighting the notion that she wasn't the dregs of humanity because she couldn't stop Smitty.

Of course, Arch didn't know what troubled her so deeply, but he said he knew it was something—something he hoped someday she'd trust them enough to talk about. But until then, he'd remind her every day she was important. That she mattered.

"Thank you, Arch. I'll see you when I see you, okay?"

He chucked her under the chin. "You most certainly will. I shall await with coconut drop cookies and a peanut butter and jelly sandwich the likes of which you've never seen."

Dropping one last kiss on Freddy's head, she set Katy down and turned to give Carl a hug. "Thanks for reading to me every night before bed, Carl. I hope, when this is over, you'll come by every once in a while and read to me again. We still have to finish *To Kill a Mockingbird*."

He chuckled, thumping her on the back before giving her a hard hug. "Atti...cus isss good. You...you are good. Very good, too. See you...sssoon."

Prim pressed her cheek against his cooler one and whispered, "Soon, buddy." And then she turned and headed to her bedroom where the women, Darnell, Raff and Sten waited for her to begin this madness.

This morning, they'd pulled the boards down from the hole in her bedroom. The whole time, she'd fought to look away and not run off into the vortex in an impulsive act of bravado.

Gary had confirmed that indeed, Sten was correct —the glowing juggernaut of a hole was a portal to the Realm of the Hollow.

And after three days of prep, during which OOPS and the others grilled Prim and Raff—whose wings had finally left the building—about the hazards of fairies and what to expect in the Realm, complete with pictures and lessons on bowing before royalty and a bunch of other bullshit Prim couldn't remember, they were off to speak to Queen Pria.

To see if she could not only save the dark and the light from ending, but Prim's ass in the process.

They'd only been able to glean a couple words from Serena's phone, and they weren't terribly helpful. *Nun* and *lie*. In the overall scheme of things, they essentially had nothing.

Gary had taken Serena and that deadly wand back to where she lived to get her some help, and they hadn't heard anything much other than she was still stable.

As Prim hauled her backpack over her shoulders with a wince when it grazed her still unformed wing, or the hump, as she'd begun to jokingly call it, Raff held his hand out to her.

He'd kept his distance for the last few days, leaving Prim to think maybe that kiss that had blown her mind hadn't done the same for him.

Did you ask him what was wrong, dumbass?

No. She hadn't. She wouldn't. She couldn't. She was too afraid to hear the answer. But something else was up with him, also, and she couldn't pinpoint what. She wanted to, but he'd felt unapproachable.

"Ready?" he asked, deep and rumbly, his eyes lined with weariness.

Ready? Was she ready to find out who'd dumped her and stolen a baby to sacrifice to the devil? This and other news at five.

No. No, she wasn't ready.

Instead of saying anything sarcastic, Prim simply nodded and took his hand before they stepped into the whirring vortex of sound and color. "Ready."

He stopped for a minute and looked at her, just before they walked into the long passageway that led to the Hollow, and said, "Know what this feels like?"

"Dead fairy walking?"

Raff snickered. "No. Like the Legend of Zelda. Like we're going on a quest."

Yeah. It kind of did.

Prim looked into his bluer-than-blue eyes. "Except, I only have one life. Link had a bunch."

"But remember that one level where you were half dead? You had like a quarter of a heart left. You walloped Ganon and you were barely breathing. You *can* do this, Prim. *We* can do this."

Her heart swelled in her chest at his earnestness. She didn't deserve Raff. He never stopped being supportive, and why she never *recognized* it as supportive instead of invasive was something she needed to explore with Dr. Shay.

These last few days, it felt like she was thawing. As though she'd been in a deep freeze for all these years since leaving home, and now she was feeling all the feelings. Sometimes they hurt enough to double her over. Sometimes they felt so good, she smiled to herself.

And she'd decided, once they had this crazy fairy thing squared away, she was going to figure out how to live—really live, let people in—without feeling so afraid.

"Lovebirds? Let's get the fuck on this. Christmas is

coming. Like fucking literally, and I got shit to get done." Nina rolled her hand in a move-it-along gesture.

Prim straightened her spine and tightened her hand in Raff's, forcing her feet to move.

She followed behind the women, with Darnell and Sten in the lead as they moved deeper into the swirl of colors and that odd humming that sounded like a siren song to her ears.

Three hours later, her legs felt like they were going to collapse and they were *still* walking. "You guys think there's an airport around here?" she joked as the endless tunnel of light and sound yawned before them.

"It won't be long now," Sten said, pointing to what appeared to be nothing.

"Yeaaah. Not long now." Raff nodded as though he knew something they didn't.

Prim grabbed his arm, realizing his eyes had taken on an almost glazed look. "Raff? What's happening?"

Her words made him blink. "Huh? Nothing's happening."

"There!" Wanda shouted, the clack of her low-heeled shoes echoing in the tunnel. "There it is! Oh, it's just like I remembered!"

Prim squinted. If she narrowed her eyes, and tilted her head to the right, she could almost see lights at the end of the tunnel. But of course, she didn't have vampire vision.

Raff stopped then, his body stiff, his eyes glazing over as he stared straight ahead.

"Dude." Nina gave his arm a light shove. "What the actual fuck? C'mon. Get your ass in gear. We're almost there."

He blinked and looked at them as if seeing them for the first time. Then he shook off whatever was troubling him. "Sorry. Let's go," he said with a determination that was evident in the way he strode forward, strong and tall.

Sten stopped them all just before they entered the golden hue, holding up his hand. "This is it. The Hollow. Listen to me very carefully. Gary's meeting us here. You talk to no one until he does. Fairies are infamous for their trickery. They'll try and sell you things that don't exist They'll make things appear that aren't real. They love to tease and taunt and they aren't always appreciative of outsiders. We need to make an appointment to see the queen immediately, and that means getting to her kingdom safely and finding her advisors. That's it. Understood?"

Sten had drilled that into their heads since they started this intensive fairy boot camp, so she nodded her confirmation. She also tried hard not to acknowledge the pull she felt toward that damn light and instead focus on what he was saying, but the need was beginning to overwhelm her.

Breathe. Inhale. Exhale. Breathe.

That's what Sten had told them to do, but it wasn't

offering a whole lot of help until Marty and Wanda moved up beside her and grabbed her hands.

When everyone else nodded, Sten forged ahead, walking into the golden light.

Her first step onto the ground crunched as the gold light bathed them all in its glow, making them almost look like they were in some kind of animated cartoon.

Nina's hair was glossier (if that was at all possible), Marty's bracelets shined blindingly, Wanda's pretty eyes looked as though they were dancing.

When Prim looked down, she realized, they were standing in snow.

But not the kind of snow you get in upstate New York, as much as she loved it. This particular blanket of white shimmered, glistened in rolling slopes.

"Holy..." Prim couldn't finish the sentence for the beauty before her. The landscape was picturesque, almost like a Christmas postcard.

As her eyes adjusted and the glow dimmed, a vast village sprawled before them. Tiny huts the size of Barbie's beach house scattered among the snow-covered trees, sitting on the ground and hanging from branches.

Fruits, or what she suspected was fruit, gently swayed in lilac and peach colors, with splashes of pink and blue for good measure.

Lights twinkled and buzzed in muted array, flitting from place to place. It was quiet, so peaceful without any of the typical noises one heard living in a village, that it soothed her.

And yep. There were toadstools in all the colors of the rainbow, sprouting from the hills, their dotted tops covered in snow. Ferns—not green, but in colors matching the fruit—whispered with the gentle breeze, poking out of snow-covered hills.

Without thinking, she stepped forward and grabbed Raff's hand and squeezed. "Can you believe this place?" she asked in a hushed whisper.

Raff shook his head in clear disbelief, pulling her closer to his side. "No...it's like...every fairy tale we ever watched as kids. It's amazing."

"Is that little Prim?" a voice boomed.

Had anyone, in her life, ever called her *little*?

Her eyes flew upward when something blocked the sky, now turning purple and pink. Prim cupped her hand over her eyes. "Gary?"

"Glad you made it!" he said with a cheerful smile, planting his hands on his lean hips. "It's beautiful, your birthplace, isn't it?"

"Is it wrong of me to hope this is all some big mistake and I'm not the one whose head they wanna lop the hell off?"

He bent his torso so they were eye to eye. "No. But until we know for sure, my pretty, we have to get moving before night falls. Is everyone ready?"

"Any news on whether the queen will receive us?" Sten asked.

Gary pulled a phone from his pocket the size of a billboard sign and scrolled it. "Nothing yet, but the closer we are to the kingdom, the safer we'll be. And in light of that safety, shall we?" He motioned for them to keep moving. "I have the perfect place for all of you to rest up."

Prim tapped his shin, her head easily still a foot away from his knee. "How's Serena?" She'd thought as many good thoughts in these last few days as she possibly could for the woman who'd tried to help her.

Gary's face went somber. "Still under that infernal spell and we don't know how to break it. No one can wake her up. But that leads me to another cautionary concern. No one can find Alfrigg and Cosmo. I was careful about asking around about them, but they're nowhere to be found.

"If anyone gets wind of you being here, Prim, and you are the baby in that prophecy, it won't just be those two henchmen looking for you. It will be every hunter in the land. I can only assume it's you they want. It's the only rational explanation for why they came for you. Until I know otherwise, we act as if you're their prey."

Their prey. Prim shivered. "Understood," she said from trembling lips.

"Your head has a bounty on it, my dear, and I can't figure out who wants you killed. There's been no more chatter of it when I'm within earshot since I last saw you. Whoever leads this campaign for your life is to be feared, and they've done a grand job of making sure all the fairies know it. Their lips are sealed tighter than a ten-gallon drum."

Prim sighed, her heart beating harder in her chest. "Got it." Mostly.

Marty rubbed her arm in sympathy. "Okay. So, this means...?"

"This means, getting information will be difficult at best. This also means we must take the least-traveled roads to the queen's castle and they aren't always pleasant. Many of the very hunters I've mentioned litter the roads and bridges along the way, so we must keep Prim and Raff hidden from everyone, including the good fairies. We need to keep all of you hidden to avoid discovery."

"Then let's get this fucking show on the road," Nina urged. "Point me in the direction, big guy."

Prim didn't think she could take another step. The soles of her feet burned and her eyes were grainy, but it was either that or end up dead.

Dead hadn't been on her bingo card just a few days ago.

She'd like to keep it that way.

CHAPTER
NINETEEN

"It's not exactly a plush chalet in the woods," Gary said with a wince when he saw their expressions upon first glance at their accommodations. "But it's warm, and we won't die of exposure."

"About that," Prim said, wondering out loud something she'd been randomly thinking about since she'd met the giant. "Why aren't *you* dying of exposure, Gary? You're half-dressed."

He chuckled as he plucked the rickety cabin door open with two fingers. "I don't feel the cold the way you do, lovely lady."

"This is yours?" Raff asked as he took in the very rustic nature of the cabin, with its lumpy tin roof and crooked logs.

A thin stream of smoke blew from the chimney, and while it looked as though it might fall over with a good stiff wind, there was, of all things, a turret on the roof.

Gary's answer was amused and secretive. "No. It's a *friend's*.

Now scoot. Inside, all of you, Night will fall soon and we must keep you hidden."

The journey here had been long and especially cold, making her hump of a wing ache, but she was determined to shut her big fucking mouth and be grateful for what these people were doing for her.

As snowdrift after snowdrift passed, as they took cover under silver-leafed trees and concrete bridges to hide from other travelers, she continued to be grateful.

"Let's do it, people!" Gary called with impatience.

Everyone scurried inside, where a warm fire awaited them and seven tin dinner plates were neatly laid out on a roughhewn wood table.

"Hellloo!" a tiny voice called out, the flap of wings lightly clapping together greeting Prim's ears.

As she looked around at the interior of the cabin, with its warped planked floors and enormous stone fireplace, Prim decided this wasn't so bad. At least she wasn't dead, right?

A small ball of light zipped into the sitting area, where plaid blankets sat on the back of a worn sofa and on top of a coffee table made of something she couldn't identify.

"I'm Farrah, and I'll be your host tonight! Please come in and sit down. Make yourselves comfortable."

Sten's eyebrow rose as he looked to the open door where Gary stood and whispered teasingly, "Farrah, eh? How come I didn't know about *Farrah*?"

Gary gave him a randy wink. "What? We have a lot in common. Plus, she's really good at keeping a secret."

Sten barked a laugh. "You old dog. Congratulations!"

Farrah buzzed over to Gary and gave him a peck on the lips then the tiny fairy clapped her hands, her sparkling wings flapping madly, and directed them to the table. "C'mon, you lot, before the food gets cold!"

Everyone scrambled for a chair, seating themselves as Farrah brought bowl after bowl of food, filled to the top and steaming hot.

Prim wasn't sure what much of it was, but one granola bar and an energy drink at lunch hadn't exactly been the meal of kings. So as she filled her plate with assorted meats and unusual-looking cheeses in pink and green, her mouth watered.

Farrah filled their tin cups with some sort of shimmering liquid that tasted of cinnamon and pears.

Everything was unexpectedly delicious, and she stuffed herself until she thought she'd burst.

As they all enjoyed the meal, as the group chatted and laughed, making the best of the situation, Prim decided to ask her first friendly live fairy about her wing, and that crazy thing she'd done with her voice to Smitty.

She picked up her plate and made her way to the sink, where Farrah canoodled with Gary through the window.

Gary cleared his throat, his green cheeks burning bright red. "We have company, my love."

Farrah squeaked, buzzing to hover in front of Prim's face. "Apologies. Is everything all right?"

Prim smiled at this tiny sprite of a woman with aqua-colored hair that sat in a high, wavy pony on her head. "Dinner was wonderful. Thank you. I don't mean to intrude, but..."

She flapped her tiny hands. "No intrusion at all," she reassured, flying to land on a basket set on top of the crude wood cabinets. "Bet you have some questions, don't you?"

Prim gave her a sheepish glance. "Do you mind?"

"Hit me!" she chirped, crossing her tiny legs as she perched on the edge of the basket.

"First, I'm probably the biggest fairy to ever hit the Hollow, and Raff's no slouch either. I know at one point I was smaller, because I was in a jar, but how do I do that...again?"

She jabbed a finger in the air with a wide grin. "You, m'dear, are a fairy raised in the human world— which means you can switch back and forth. It just takes practice, and once you meet your oracle and some of your guides, they'll teach you how."

Well, that was a bit of a relief. At least she wouldn't be Gigantor in a land of little people. "And my hump...

I mean, my deformed wing? Why won't it either go away or fully form? Raff got his wings with no problem."

She chuckled a melodious laugh. "Everyone's different, Prim. It's like boobs," she said with a shake of her torso. "Some girls get them early; some get them later."

It was all she could do not to cover her own boobs —or lack thereof. "But some never get them at all."

"You hush!" she chastised with a shake of her finger. "You have boobs. Are they the size of melons? No. Are they just right for Prim and her long limbs and enviable tiny waist? Yes! You're beautiful, and your wings, when they pop, will be too."

Beautiful was a ridiculous assessment of her, but she'd take it.

Shoving her hands inside the pockets of her jeans, she felt a little better, but there was still more troubling her. "What about the invisibility and that awful thing I did with my mouth?"

Farrah's eyes lit up and she clapped her hands together in glee. "You can manipulate sound! That's a rare gift, my friend. It positively screams royalty."

"Royalty...?"

"It means whoever your parents are, either one or both are royalty. Only royals can manipulate sound. Or it's possible someone gifted you that specific power. The people responsible for your capture bestowed the gift of sound manipulation."

That didn't make any sense, and she said as much. "Why would they give me something so powerful if they want me dead?"

Farrah's brow furrowed. "I don't know. I'm as confused as everyone else. I guess for now, we have to go with the theory that you were swapped at birth and the powers come from a biological parent. I can't explain why they give them to you only to turn around and try and kill you. None of us understand it. That's why you must see the queen."

Prim looked down at her fingers, twisting her mother's ring around her pinkie. "It didn't feel like much of a gift. It felt like assault with a deadly mouth."

Farrah flew toward her then, hovering in front of her face, her eyes soft with sympathy. "But I'm told he was a very bad man. He deserved what you did to him, Prim. Regardless, you'll learn to control it. This I promise you."

"And the invisibility thing?

She grinned. "We can all do that. Watch!" She snapped her fingers and disappeared, before reappearing right before Prim's eyes.

God. This was bizarre.

More than anything else, her next question had been burning a hole in her brain since she found out there was a whole other world or realm or whatever-thefuck they called this, aside from Earth. "Do I have to live here? I mean, do I have to leave New York and come live in a tiny Barbie house?"

Farrah snorted. "No, silly! Your life has been lived in the human realm. Just like Sten's wife Murphy and her sister Nova. They travel from realm to realm with the greatest of ease. Once we know your position here, the rest will fall in line. Of course, you'll want a place to stay in the Hollow. Sort of like a vacation hideaway, but that can all be sorted when we get you fixed up. Raff, too, if he'd like."

Okay then. She was up for a vacation hideaway. "Is there anything else I should know?"

"Have you been hearing any voices?"

"Um, voices...? Maybe just the ones that were calling me whenever I was near the hole in my house."

Farrah nodded, her aqua pony bouncing. "Yes. That's the call of your new people. At least I think it is. But I mean, specific voices. As if someone's talking to you, but they're really in conversation with someone else."

Prim shook her head. "Nope. Not yet anyway." And thank fuck. Jesus, she had her own voice in her head, she didn't need another one.

"In time, I'm sure. When you meet your oracle, he'll teach you."

"Here's a thought," she muttered. "What if they don't want me here? What if we've done all this, and these oracles and guides and whatever else don't want anything to do with me? I mean, I'm allegedly the one who's going to end the dark and the light, right? If those two henchmen who kidnapped me and then came back for seconds wanted me dead, *someone* sent them to do the job. Couldn't it have been this Queen Pria, trying to protect the Realm of the Hollow, who sent them?"

Farrah sighed, her expression thoughtful. "Therein lies the crux. I don't for a moment believe Queen Pria would approve that, no matter what this supposed scrit says. Our queen is good and kind. She loves her subjects. She'd find a way to make this right. She'd never order your death. Which means someone else is spearheading this."

Prim looked down at the braided rug on the floor by the rusty sink and took a breath.

Farrah flew to her, pushing her chin upward with her tiny body. "Look at me, Prim, these women, Sten, Gary, they'll find out who's behind this, and when they do, I'm certain the queen will punish them severely. We'll keep you safe until our last breath."

God, this was all so heavy, she didn't know how to keep her head held high, but she was going to try. "Okay, so on a lighter note, I heard something about a wand. Do I get one of those?"

Farrah giggled, brushing Prim's face with her soft wings. "When you graduate fairy school, young lady. All in due time. However, I will admit, it's one of the coolest gadgets I own. Wanna see?"

Prim laughed, too, feeling a little lighter as Farrah produced her wand and they chatted about all the amazing things she'd do with it once she was given hers own.

For the first time since all this began, she felt a little bit of hope.

Even if a bunch of mean fairies wanted her dead.

SHE CLIMBED the winding stairs to the turret at the top of Farrah's rickety cabin, praying her big feet didn't take out the rotting steps.

Prim needed a moment to herself to gather her thoughts before they began this next part of their journey, and seeing as she couldn't go outside—in order to keep her safe—she opted for the next best thing.

Entering the tiny room, she caught her breath at the shadow sitting on the bench that spanned the width of the windy turret.

"It's just me," Raff said quietly.

Her heart instantly fluttered the way it once had where Raff was concerned...before she became so numb inside, she felt nothing but rage.

"Do you want to be alone?"

He shrugged his wide shoulders. "Nah. Come and sit with me and look at this incredible sky."

She hooked her leg over the splitting wood of the bench and took a seat, unsure what to say, because Raff hadn't said much to *her* in the last few days since fairy bootcamp had begun...or since that kiss.

The kiss she couldn't stop thinking about when she wasn't worried someone was going to whack her.

"Would you look at that sky, Prim?" he whispered. "It's incredible.

She looked up and gasped as the wind in the turret whooshed, echoing.

Indeed. Indeed it was. Fluffy blue and pink clouds drifted by, their backdrop an indigo blue. Stars you could almost reach out and touch, fat and lemon-colored, winked back at them, forming shapes.

The vast landscape below was mostly barren. Miles and miles of snow-covered land, glistening under the pale pink moon.

"It's like nothing I've ever seen before," she whispered in awe.

"It reminds me a little of the night sky in Yemen," Raff said, sounding very far away.

"They had pink and purple clouds in Yemen?" she teased, hoping to lighten his clearly ominous mood.

Raff shook his head, pulling off his knit hat and tucking his hair behind his ears. "No. I meant the sky. It's a sort of deep blue. It's beautiful."

"Will you miss it?"

He lifted his chin and swallowed hard. "Not Yemen itself."

"But someone specific?" Prim experienced a stab of jealousy, which was ridiculously unfair. How dare she have the nerve to be jealous when she'd never once even asked how he was doing while on the job.

Even odder still, she'd never asked if he'd been involved with someone *anywhere*.

Know why that is, Prim? Because you're afraid, chickenshit.

That was very fair. She'd purposely avoided asking questions because she didn't want him to ask *her* questions.

Raff let his head hang between his shoulders. "Yes. Someone specific."

When he didn't say any more, she gulped. Dare she ask? The silence between them engulfed her, swallowed her up until she knew the right thing to do was at least ask.

How could she have never once inquired about his mental health? Surely, he'd seen some horrible things. His pictures alone told her that.

God, she was a massive jerk. In the interest of self-preservation, she'd sacrificed everyone's feelings.

All this thawing out was beginning to wear her down. It was everything all at once and it scared the hell out of her.

Instead of pressing or pushing, Prim wrapped her arm around Raff's broad back. "You don't have to tell me. You don't have to say anything. I'll always be your paper towel. No matter what."

Raff leaned into her then, letting his head rest on her shoulder, heaving a long sigh. "Her name was Amal. She was like everyone's grandmother in her village. Her sons had both been killed in the war and she was alone, except for her cat and her neighbors who all looked out for her."

Prim sat, listening to Raff breathe, waiting until he was ready to continue.

"Even when she had so little and virtually lived in poverty, she brought me homemade cakes and water. We developed a friendship—a deep one. Whenever I was there, I always went to visit her in her village, and she always welcomed me with open arms. Some of the best conversations I ever had were with Amal—broken English and all."

"How did you meet?"

She felt Raff smile against her shoulder. "Very unconventionally. I saved her beloved cat, Jabal, from a bombed site. He was stuck under some heavy rocks, and I got him out. She made me Bint al-sahn, a honey cake, as a gift of gratitude. That sealed the deal for me. I brought her supplies, food when I could. I even tried to find a way to get her out. To bring her here. But I never got the chance."

Prim sat quietly, saying nothing. Instead, she ran her fingers through his thick hair and listened.

He sat up and ran a hand over his face, as though he could wipe the memory from his mind. "I saw it happen. I'd just returned from another assignment, and I was headed out to see her. I knew the danger had ramped up recently, but that's my job, right? To take pictures of dangerous things. I was just entering the village, and as always, when Amal had word I'd been spotted, she'd wait by her crumbling front door for me."

Prim's stomach turned, her heart chugging so hard she heard it in her ears.

Raff let his head hang low, his chin touching his chest. "So there she was, smiling and welcoming me... waving...and then *boom*. It was over in half a second. Some insurgents bombed her village, wiped out almost everyone. If I'd just been a little earlier, we would have gone for a walk, and I could have prevented..."

Prim fought a gasp, even though she'd been almost certain of the outcome before he told her. "Oh... Oh, Raff. Raff, I'm so sorry," she whispered, pulling him to her and pressing her lips to his stubbled cheek before letting her nose rest on it.

"If I'd just gotten there a minute sooner..."

Survivor's guilt. Dr. Shay had talked about this in reference to her guilt over her mother's passing. How horrible. How devastating.

"I... Were you hurt?"

"Not really. I got scraped up and a stitch or two in my arm from some shrapnel when I managed to dig out Jabal, who went to a loving home via an adoption program here in the US, but I didn't care about me." He paused, his words tight and slow. "I dug... I swear, I tried to find her body...I couldn't... I tried..."

A tear slid from Raff's eye then, one that landed on

her lips, salty and warm. "Of course you did. *Of course*, Raff," she murmured.

He sat up and straightened then, shaking off his sorrow in the same way he had when his mother was killed. "After that, I took a break. It was time. Seven years is a long time to see what I've seen. I don't know how people do it for a lifetime, but I don't think this is for me anymore. So that's why I'm back. I'm in the process of rethinking my life and where to go from here."

Yeah. Same. Then, her selfishness reared its ugly head. How could she have been so blind to all he must have suffered—even if Amal hadn't been killed, Prim knew he'd been exposed to the horrors of war.

Why hadn't she *ever* bothered to ask how he was, for fuck's sake?

Remorse stung her gut like salt on an open wound, almost doubling her over. "I'm sorry, Raff. I never asked. I..." How could she explain what an awful person she was?

"It's okay. I get it," he said, quite suddenly much lighter. "You have a lot on your plate, too."

He'd only asked what was on her plate a million times over the years, and she'd only shut him down a million more.

Without warning, without thinking it through, Prim said, "About that kiss the other night..."

He stiffened against her. "Maybe we shouldn't—"

But she thwarted him by pressing her finger to his

soft lips as tears welled in her eyes. "Let me finish. We have...stuff, Raff. We have so much stuff going on inside us, and we need to fix it. We have to. *I* have to. All these years, I let you chase after me, look after me, care about me, and I threw it back in your face because I have...stuff. I never asked about your life, about how you were doing, about *anything* because of my damn stuff."

He grabbed her finger and kissed the tip. "It's okay, Prim..."

She put her finger back on his lips and shook her head. "No, Raf. *No*, it isn't. It'll never be okay that I was so fucking selfish. Never. Right now, that doesn't matter. Here's what matters—we both need to fix ourselves before we do anything else. But I need you to know...it meant something to me, and no matter where we go from here, that kiss will always be one of the most important things in my life because I love you. I've *always* loved you—"

"Hey! Secret lovers!" Nina called, poking her head inside the turret. "Got some news from the palace."

They both turned, Prim feeling Nina's vibe, and it wasn't good. "What's going on?"

"Someone's kidnapped the queen."

TWENTY

While the women and Sten, Darnell, and Raff sat around the big table and tried to devise a plan to save the queen, Farrah had gone off to investigate and bring back any information she could get her tiny hands on about what was happening in the kingdom.

All they knew for sure was a coup had occurred.

"I say we go fucking balls to the wall, storm the castle and make those fucking little traitors tells us what the hell's going on," Nina said from clenched teeth, her fangs poking out of her mouth.

"Listen," Sten said, holding up a hand. "We can't just rush in there and beat the life out of everyone, Nina. That's not how we get answers. If the queen is in jeopardy, Prim and Raff's chances of surviving are slim to none. She was likely our only hope of finding the root of this problem and begging for mercy for Prim's life."

"Why the fuck not? It's my experience that a little torture always makes 'em talk."

Marty patted Nina's hand to calm her. "Take a beat, Elvira. We need to figure this out rationally and make a plan. We never go in without a plan."

Wanda nodded, smoothing her hair back from her poreless face. "Marty's right. So, I vote we wait and see what Farrah and Gary have to say when they get back. Until then, no one beats the life out of anyone and we all stay put."

"Agreed," Sten said with a sharp nod.

Darnell scratched his head before folding his hands in front of him. "Any idea how this happened? When?"

"According to Gary's source, she was taken earlier this evening. She's pretty heavily guarded, so that says to me it was an inside job."

An inside job. This felt way too *Mission Impossible.*

"So someone under her employ helped to have her kidnapped? But why?" Prim wondered out loud. "What did she do? I don't get where she figures into all this." Then she paused and it hit her. "Farrah said the queen was kind, that she'd never order a hit on me. Maybe this queen is a casualty of the war on me? Maybe she found out those little goons tried to kill me and tried to put a stop to it? It's pretty coincidental that this is all happening now, isn't it? Right after they made an attempt on my life?"

Sten pushed his long green hair behind his shoulders. "That makes a great deal of sense, Prim. Or it might not be at all related. Maybe someone wants to overthrow her? I don't know the inner workings of fairy bureaucracy. They're mostly a peaceful lot. Sure, they love to create chaos from time to time, but I can't remember the last time a mutiny occurred. I don't know what anyone would gain. But I do know what it's like to have someone want all the power."

Nina cracked her knuckles. "It feels pretty damn suspicious to me that this is fucking happening now, with all the shit going on with Prim and Raff. Do we know if those little freaks Alfrigg and Cosmo served the queen? That would at least tie this shit together. I don't know how, but it's something."

"I haven't a clue," Sten replied, scrolling his phone. "And I still don't know what the hell these two words from Serena's phone mean. *Nun* and *lie*. That's been bugging me since we found her in the snow."

So many unanswered questions...so many variables...

Panic had begun to set in as Prim twisted her mother's ring on her pinkie finger. If the queen had been abducted, who was going to save her from whoever wanted to knock her off? Who was going to help Raff adjust to being a fairy if she ended up dead?

Her stomach gurgled, the delicious meal she'd eaten earlier revolting in her stomach.

At a loss as to what to say or how to help, she decided she still needed that moment to herself. Her talk with Raff, the news of the queen being kidnapped, all of it was piling on top of her until she felt like she weighed a thousand pounds.

She silently left the small room and slipped back up the stairs to the turret, letting the wind whooshing about cool her hot cheeks.

Closing her eyes, she took deep breaths, trying to gather everything that had happened tonight.

So for starters, she'd finally been able to connect with Raff about something other than her, and he'd shared something deeply painful. His pain, so raw, so palpable, had rocked her, had cleared the haze of her own bullshit long enough to see she wasn't the only one hurting, and she wanted to fix it.

She wanted to be mentally healthy for Raff, but more than anything, for herself. She desperately wanted to find peace within her soul.

Secondly, she'd told Raff she loved him. It had slipped from her mouth like melted butter. A secret she'd kept for so long, for almost as long as she'd known him, had just popped out.

She wouldn't take it back because she'd meant it, but her timing couldn't have been worse.

"Prim? Oh, Prim, honey, is that you?" asked a voice

so familiar, so comforting and gently sweet, shook her to her core.

She lifted her head, her jaw unhinging. No. It couldn't be...

"*Mom?*" she whispered. How was this even possible?

"Uh-huh," her mother said with her beautiful smile. "It's really me."

Tall and willowy, Liesl held out her slender arms to Prim. Her dark hair, long and wavy, billowed around her face, her red lips in a beaming smile.

The longing to go into her mother's arms, to apologize over and over for not taking better care of her when she was so sick, for not being with her when she died, tore at her rapidly beating heart.

Pressing her fingers to her lips, Prim blinked. "How? *How are you doing this?*"

"Come sit with me and I'll tell you all about it," she said with a loving smile. "Come."

Her mother held out her hand, and just as she was about to take it, as she was about to finally have the chance to make things right, to tell her mother how sorry she was that she hadn't fought Smitty harder, Prim heard a gruff voice yell out.

"Prim, *no!*" Nina bellowed in a blur of motion as she reached for Liesl, scooping her up by the front of her silky shirt.

The act of Nina grabbing her mother incited Prim, sending her pulse into orbit. She didn't even think twice. She didn't think about how strong Nina was or how she'd likely rip her limb from limb, all she saw was her mother being snatched away from her—and she reacted.

Prim leapt from the bench and hurled herself at Nina, grabbing her by the hair, twisting the shiny locks around her fist. "Leave her the fuck alone!"

"Prim!" she heard Marty holler. "What's going on?"

"Get the fuck off me or I'm going to pop your goddamn eyeballs out!" Nina roared, still holding Liesl by her shirt.

"Prim! Help me!" her mother cried, helplessly hanging in the air as Marty successfully pried Prim's hands from the vampire's hair.

"I'll kill you if you hurt her!" she screamed at Nina, going for her again, but Wanda entered the tiny room and wrapped an arm around Prim's waist like a steel band.

"Stop this now, Primrose!" she yelled, giving Prim a hard shake in an attempt to make her stop struggling.

"Primmy, make her let me go! Help me!"

Primmy...

Nina, her eyes on fire, held up her mother and shoved her in Prim's face. "This isn't your fucking mother!"

It was then her mother's face changed right before her eyes. No longer the beautiful, clear-skinned, dark-haired beauty, but in her place, a handsome man...one who'd aged well, despite his prison sentence.

Smitty.

Motherfucking Smitty.

She didn't bother to think about how he'd gotten here or why, she just wanted him to hurt, the way *she* hurt, for somehow using her mother's image to trick her.

She wanted him *dead*. Bloody. Broken. Battered to bits, shredded the way her insides were torn and tattered.

Rage assaulted her, so swift and so fierce she saw all the colors of the rainbow, making every nerve ending she owned burn bright with hate.

With a growl, she curled her fist into a ball and hit him with all her strength—and she kept taking whacks at him, over and over, for everything he'd ever done to make her life a living hell. Striking him until her knuckles bled and her arm felt like it might fall off.

"I hate you, you sick fucking pig!" she spat with a howl, spittle flying everywhere. "I'll kill you for what you did to me! I hate you! *I hate you!*"

But even covered in blood, Smitty grinned wide, full of his particular brand of sickness. "Still a filthy little tramp, huh, Primmy?"

She didn't remember much after that, though she did remember clawing at his face, trying with all she had to rip him from Nina's grip, but Marty stopped her, grabbing her arms and holding them so tight, it felt like they might break.

"Goddamn it!" she heard Nina yell, as she jumped over the side of the turret's balcony. Then she was gone in blur of limbs and hair.

Marty turned her around and pulled her close, holding her tight, whispering soothing words into her ear, calming her as she sat Prim down on the bench and rocked her. "It's okay, Prim. It's okay... Shhh."

In seconds, Nina was back, hoisting her slender legs over the side of the balcony. "The slippery fuck got away."

Prim's ragged sobs heaved from her chest, ripped from her lungs as Marty rocked back and forth, the scent of her peachy perfume soothing.

Wanda knelt in front of Prim, her eyes worried. She brushed Prim's hair from her face, wiping her tears with tender fingers. "Oh, Prim. What's happening? Please tell us. *Please,* honey."

Nina sat down on the other side of her, taking her hand and tucking it into her lap while Prim caught her breath. "Listen, kiddo, you have some shit you need to work out. Some *serious* shit. What the fuck did that piece of slimy hot shit do to you, and how do you want me to kill him? Because I'll catch the skeezy mother-fucker, and when I do, he dies."

She shook her head as hot tears flew down her face, landing in her lap. Words. How would she ever speak the words? "I... I can't. I just..."

Marty smoothed circles over her back. "You don't have to talk to us, but, Prim... Oh, honey, you're *so very angry*. Something awful happened to you to make you shut down like this. You have to talk to someone about it. A professional, someone who can help you."

She sobbed harder, all of the anguish, all of the hatred she'd felt for so long welling up and spilling over to leave her feeling nothing but shame and guilt for her poor treatment of these woman.

"I'm sorry," she sobbed. "I've been so selfish and rude to you. You guys have done nothing but protect me and feed me and try to figure out who wants me unalived and... I've been a real asshole the whole way."

Nina chuckled. "You're not selfish so much as you're a chickenshit. You're so busy keeping your shit together, keeping all that rage inside so it doesn't spew all over everyone around you, you don't have time to think about fuck all else. Is that selfish? Maybe...but you're also protecting people from your-self—from your crap. Mostly you're protecting your-self, but you gotta either let someone in and get it off your chest or let it the fuck go, kiddo. You can't live like this. I damn well couldn't."

Her eyes found Nina's, searching them. "I don't understand..."

"Surely you don't think Nina was always this nice, do you?" Wanda teased, chucking her under the chin.

Nina rolled her eyes, but she nodded. "There isn't anyone who's gonna understand you better'n me, kiddo, because like it or not, we're the same, Prim. We're the same fucking person."

Prim took a deep breath and shook her head, fighting to find a smile. "No way. I'm nothing like you, Nina. Not a fucking single similarity," she joked.

"Joke all you want, but you know it's true. We're rude and isolating and we say shit other people won't because they don't want to hurt anyone's baby feelings. We don't put it as fucking nicely as everybody else, but we tell the truth. The difference is, I know *why* I say it. I talked to someone who helped me to fucking understand, and she said something that I never forgot. Hurt people, hurt people."

Hurt people, hurt people.

Marty dropped a kiss on Nina's cheek. I'm so proud of your loud, rude ass, Elvira. You worked hard to get here."

Nina swatted at her, but it was with a smile. "Fuck off, Blondie."

"Nina's had some intensive counseling, and it's mostly paid off," Wanda explained with a crooked smile, patting Prim's thigh.

Nina tipped her chin up and forced her to look into her almond-shaped black eyes. "Okay, so where the fuck was I? I remember. You're not like me at all," she tipped her head back and laughed. "Except, you're just like me. You shut yourself off from everyone because it fucking hurts too much to let anyone in. They'll just disappoint you, amiright? You had a shitty stepfather, who did something shitty to you that you don't want to talk about. Because to talk about it would be to say the shitty thing out loud. Put it out in the universe. Make it real—and you can't believe you let it happen. You feel like it's *your* fault."

Prim swallowed hard, her eyes filling with more stupid, unwanted tears, overwhelming her. Why was she crying all the time?

She held up a hand and shook her head. She couldn't. She wouldn't. "Stop. *Please stop*," she whispered hoarsely.

"Just listen, Prim. Listen to what Nina has to say," Marty whispered.

"Guess what? You don't have the market cornered on a shitty parent. I had a shitty childhood, too. I had a father who was gone all the time, driving a truck to avoid being home with my fucking drug-addicted mother. He was off gallivanting across the damn country, bringing me back pencils from rest stops as some kind of fucked-up way to make up for leaving me with her. And then *she* pawned me off on my gramma Lou. It was just me and Lou for most of my life—until I met these nutty bitches and my husband Greg."

Prim licked her lips, relaxing her hand a bit in Nina's. Her vampire skin was cold, but it was comforting just the same and it almost felt like if she let go, she'd fall into an abyss and there would be no climbing out. And still she stayed silent—because she couldn't form words.

"It's true," Marty confirmed as the wind blew her hair around and her eyes grew wet. "We told you how we met, but when Nina had her *accident,* she had to come to terms with a lot more than just becoming a vampire."

Nina nodded. "Truth. When I met these nutty bitches, it wasn't just me anymore, kiddo. It was me and them, but I had to fucking work to let 'em in—to find a way past the disappointment in my life, my disappointment in people. I didn't trust anyone except for Gramma Lou, who was the best, BTW. I isolated myself. I lashed out just like you fucking do. Some people withdraw, some people come out guns blazin' because we're GD determined to be heard."

"And I think it's fair to say, you come out guns blazing, Prim," Marty confirmed, and that was more than a fair assessment of exactly who Primrose Dunham was.

Nina gripped her hand tighter. "And it was hard to let these nutty bitches in, to let them help me, because I didn't know how to ask for help and until them, no one had ever really helped me aside from Lou. Christ, it was so fucking hard. I was embarrassed that I came from a place with dirty needles, a cracked-out mother, and a lying, cheating father who couldn't stand to be with me because I reminded him of my mom. Doing the work is hard, but you gotta do it. I need you to tell me you'll at least fucking try."

"We'll help," Wanda said, her eyes brimming with

tears. "We'll help, if you'll just let us.

All these warm words of support and comfort, all this sympathizing with her despite the fact that she felt like an awful person, became almost too much.

Something in her shifted then, something big, something that had been lodged deep in her for so long, she didn't know what it felt like *not* to carry it.

"He was going to sell me for a night as a way to...to pay a debt to some guy he was doing drug deals for."

After all this time, after keeping that secret so close to her chest, she couldn't believe how plainly she'd said it. How it spilled out of her mouth with such ease.

In response to her confession, Marty tried quite unsuccessfully to hide a gasp. "Dear God..."

Prim clenched her fists together and closed her eyes. "When my mom was dying, Smitty didn't tell me the nurses at the hospital told him it wouldn't be long. He never said a word. Not a fucking single word...and he knew. *He knew.* So when I showed up to visit her while he was off partying with his freak friends, she... she was gone. She was just gone..."

"Oh, Prim," Wanda said, her voice shaky as she cupped her cheek. "Oh my God, I'm so sorry."

She would never forget walking into that hospital room and seeing her fragile, beautiful mother with a sheet over her face. She would never forget the smell of antiseptic and urine, the dead silence of a room once filled with beeping heart monitors and tubes from her mother's IVs.

She would never forgive Smitty for robbing her of her last opportunity to say goodbye to the one person in the world she loved more than anyone or anything.

And she would never forgive *herself* for not telling someone how awful he was not just to her, but to her mother. For not at least trying to find them a better situation because she was so afraid of him and his endless threats.

"And you blame yourself for that shit, don't you?" Nina pushed.

A sob escaped her throat, ragged and painful, but she gritted her teeth and told them the truth. "I blame myself for not getting her away from him," she hissed, her anger rife. "For not telling someone what he was like, but I was so scared, and right after she met him, she was always so sick. He knew I had nowhere to go, and he reminded me of it all the time. He told me if I tried to get away, he'd find me. I was always so afraid of him and what he'd do to us if I ratted him out. So I shut my mouth until that night...until..."

"Until that fucking prick decided to offer you up like some kind of fucking sacrifice to pay off a debt?" Nina spat. "I swear on all that's holy, when I get my hands on that fuck, I'm going to kill him."

"It was the night of my graduation. I was so happy because even though Smitty was controlling my entire life, he had no idea my mother had put money away for me for college. She'd been doing it since I was a baby, starting with the money my father left when he died. With that and a scholarship, I was going to be free as a fucking bird from that pig. Free of night after night with his disgusting friends drinking and doing lines, while I tried to study and just get through high school. I was finally going to be free..."

Wanda's chest heaved, clearly fighting her repulsion, but she didn't say anything and Prim couldn't seem to stop saying all the things.

"If I hadn't overheard them in the kitchen, the kitchen where my mother baked me cookies, where we planted seeds in a Dixie cup for a vegetable garden... If I hadn't overheard him make the deal with this guy, if I hadn't watched him spike my soda, he would have..."

Marty swallowed so hard, Prim actually heard it over the rushing wind in the turret, but then her face hardened. "Nina's going to have to get in line."

"Ditto," Wanda spat, wiping tears from her face.

"So you got the fuck away, right? Got away and never looked back. But while you did that, you decided for all the time no one heard you, or maybe more accurately, for all the time you were too fucking afraid to say anything because you were terrified of that puke, no one was ever going to *not* hear you again."

When Nina spoke those words, the pieces of this puzzle she'd been pondering for so long slammed together.

Her nod was slow. "Yeah... I think I decided for all the times Smitty shut me down, I was finally going to speak up. I was going to make my voice heard, no matter how harsh, how ugly. In fact, he's why I swear so much—because he said ladies didn't use foul language. And the ones who did were tramps, lowlifes."

"Said the motherfucker who tried to sell his step-daughter," Nina growled, her teeth clenched.

"So a passive-aggressive effort to poke him for making you feel so helpless. Sort of a take-back-control move, however small?" Marty asked with a tilt of her head.

"Yes," she whispered as tears of frustration mingled with relief rushed down her face. Yes. That was exactly why. "How did you all know?"

Nina pulled Prim's hand to her cheek. "Because I've been there. Because I know who you are, Primrose Dunham, and you're not any of the things that fucking monster told you that you were. You're good. You love animals. You're smart. Your heart is pure and you've spent far too fucking long keeping that shit to yourself. Now it's time to redirect that rage and use it for good. Fix that. Let's fix it. Okay?"

Her disbelief, her shock turned to realization—to understanding. "Is that why you do this? Why you help people like me?"

She nodded, her silky curtain of hair falling around her shoulders. "Yeah. Yeah, it is. But I don't swear to get back at anyone. I swear because I fucking like it and it makes people uncomfortable."

They all chuckled at that.

"So let us help you, Prim. When this is all over and we figure out what comes next, let us help, okay?" Wanda asked.

Prim's shoulders shook, her body boneless with relief. "Okay..."

"*Good girl*," Wanda whispered, gathering her in a warm hug. "Good girl."

Marty joined Wanda, wrapping her arms around them both. "Get in here, Vampire. Mandatory group hug."

Nina enveloped them all with a reluctant grunt, but she hugged them all hard.

Prim scrunched her eyes tight, exhausted but lighter, so much lighter.

Maybe this was what the beginning of peace felt like.

"Boss?" she heard Darnell call from the doorway.

As they dismantled their tangled arms and wiped tears from their eyes, Wanda answered, "What's up, big guy?"

Darnell's face was grim. "Got some news fo' ya. We need to git."

"To?" Nina asked.

"A nunnery."

Oh. Fuck.

Then she winced.

Sorry, Sister Felicia Margaret Cabrini.

TWENTY-ONE

As they stole through the woods and approached the stone structure of the nunnery, Prim frowned. Somehow, she hadn't expected it to be life-size. But it was, gray and looming deep into the night sky like a beast of stone and mortar.

"So we're fucking sure this nun's got some info for us, Farrah? Because listen, I'm Catholic. Er, mostly. I mean, it's been a hundred fucking years since I took confession, but whatever. I don't want to have to beat the shit out of a damn nun. You understand me?"

Farrah flitted about in the deep velvet night, her wings buzzing, lighting up Nina's skeptical face. "I'm sure my source is always accurate, and he said to talk to Sister Rosalyn. He knows for a fact she was there the night a baby was born and taken to a human family."

"But that could have been any baby," Wanda

reminded them. "Surely, there've more than just one fairy baby swapped. How do we know this has anything to do with Prim?"

Farrah twittered, her wings buzzing madly. "We don't, but how can we not investigate it on the off chance it was Prim?"

Prim shivered as Raff gripped her hand tighter. "Why doesn't he just ask her what Sister Rosalyn knows and get back to us?"

Farrah rolled her eyes. "That's not how an informant works. Surely you know that, Prim. Don't you watch *Law and Order*?"

"You have *Law and Order* in the Hollow?" she retorted.

Farrah booped her nose. "We have it all, goose. Listen, he can't afford to get caught snooping around and asking questions. He works for some very bad henchman, much like the ones who tried to harm you, Prim."

"How do we know he can be trusted?" Sten asked, looking tall and rugged next to the brightly colored trees.

Farrah bit her lip. "We don't, but that's the best I've got. It's *all* I've got."

Prim shook her head. "Of course. I'm sorry. I didn't mean to sound ungrateful."

"So let me get this straight," Raff said. "Your friend told you that this sister Rosalyn knows who might be Prim's mother and can take us to someone who can keep her from being killed?"

Farrah nodded. "That's what he said. Now, he said the sister walks to the chapel every night for vespers. If we can catch her before she goes inside, maybe we can figure this out."

But did she want to figure this out? Did she want to know who her homicidal mother was? Did she care?

Raff tugged her firmly to his side. "I know this is scary. I know you're wondering 'who cares who my mother is, she sacrificed a baby,' but if talking to this nun can get this bounty off your head, if you're really who they're looking for, we have to do this, Prim. I won't leave your side, I swear it."

"Then let's get this shit on the road," Nina urged. "You do realize it's Christmas Eve, right? If we wrap this shit up before midnight, we can all be home in time for presents and hot chocolate with the family."

Prim had no idea what day it was, but she hadn't given any thought to it already being Christmas Eve.

"Wait," she whispered. She couldn't let them do this. There was asking for help and then there was asking for help. "You guys go home. Please. All of you. This is my problem. I can talk to the nun. I'll take Farrah and Gary, but you all have families who need you. This isn't fair to them if you miss Christmas."

"The fuck you say," Nina scoffed and frowned. "I'm not leaving your hothead here without my hothead to keep your shit together. No."

Wanda and Marty both shook their heads, tucked

inside warm parkas with fur-trimmed hoods. "That's affirmative. Not a chance on earth or anywhere else we'd let you do this without us. Deal with it."

Darnell smiled in the night. "Told you they were good."

Sten waved a hand. "We need to move if we're going to catch this the sister. Let's go, and everyone stay close."

As they pushed their way through the brush of sparkling greenery, she shivered and wondered where Smitty had gotten to.

Farrah had theorized that the people looking for her had somehow gotten a hold of Smitty and, because Smitty was all about a good bribe, talked him into coming to the Hollow to trick her into going with him.

Which sacred the living fuck out of her. Was there nowhere safe from that animal? Not even in another realm?

A long walkway lined with torches and cobblestone wound its way to another stone structure, separate from the nunnery. A beaming cross on the rooftop told her they'd found the chapel.

"Stay in the shadows," Sten whispered the order.

Crouching low, they stayed hunched and alert until they heard the stirring of wings.

"That's her!" Farrah buzzed, dimming the glow of her wings to stay hidden.

A tiny woman covered in a long brown habit, with

266

gorgeous gold wings, flew toward the chapel door, skimming the snow on the ground along the way.

"I'll go long. You get her from the other side," she whispered to Marty. Nina pointed to a large statue beside the door before she cut between the snow-covered hedges and made a break to the stone statue of a fairy, her long legs a blur of motion.

Just as Sister Rosalyn was about to start up the steps, Nina hopped out in front of her. "Sister Rosalyn?"

Even as tiny as she was, Prim saw Sister Rosalyn open her mouth to scream, obviously startled by this enormous woman in her village of tiny people, but Marty snatched her up, cupping her hands over the frantic light the nun's wings gave off.

"It's okay, Sister Rosalyn, we come in peace," Marty whispered. "We need your help."

Sten directed them to a small courtyard, where the stone benches were covered in snow and monuments of what she guessed were famous religious fairies stood. "This way."

As everyone followed, Prim couldn't help but look over her shoulder, waiting for Smitty to pop out at any moment, but Raff held firm to her hand, just like he'd promised.

Marty held up her cupped hands and said, "Sister Rosalyn, if I let you go, will you promise not to scream? *Please* don't make me hurt a nun."

"Yes! I promise!" the tiny voice assured.

Marty opened her hands a bit and peered into them. "My name is Marty Flaherty, Sister Rosalyn, and I know you don't know me, but I'm here to beg you to help us. We're from another...er, realm, and we understand you might have some information that could help our friend. I promise we would *never* hurt you, if you'll just listen."

Farrah flew toward Marty's hands. "Sister Rosalyn, these people need to talk to you about the night a baby was born, a baby given up to the human world. Do you know anything about that?"

When Sister Rosalyn answered, Prim could barely hear her, but Farrah gave Marty a thumb's up and, in seconds, the nun had turned into a tiny woman who only reached Prim's ribcage.

She gripped Raff's hand harder. Would she ever get used to this?

Swallowing nervously, she approached the wide-eyed nun with caution. "My name is Primrose Dunham, and I'm told you were there the night I was born, along with another nun. If you'll just listen to what we have to say, I'd so appreciate it because I'm in a real pickle."

Sister Rosalyn tilted her head, her gray eyes understanding and warm. "Of course, child. Tell me. How can I help?"

"About a week ago, give or take, I don't know, time is just a construct, right? Anyway, about a week ago, someone snatched me from my bed in upstate New

York and, long story short, they put me in a jar. At least that's where I was when I woke up. I mean, look at me. I'm almost six feet tall. You can't stuff all this inside a jar unless you do something weird with it, right? Then I escaped. That's kind of a blur, but I flew as fast as I could to these people. Not sure why I landed in their path, but it was random. I just flew. That's all I know. Then two fairies showed up and tried to kill me with colored balls. I don't know what you call it. I'm sure there's some fairy name for it, but either way, it didn't affect me—"

"The point," Nina demanded with a hiss, as sparkly snowflakes began to fall and the wind picked up. "Get to it."

"Right. They said they'd made a mistake and they needed to fix it before *he* found out. Then, get a load of this, my friend Sten, the *troll*—I can't believe I'm even saying that—got some information about how I was switched at birth for a human baby. But worse? There's some scrit, you know, like an ancient scroll no one can figure out but a few words? And—"

"And the scrit said if this baby wasn't killed, it was going to end the dark and the light forever. The end," Nina said with impatience.

Sister Rosalyn eyed them all as they waited, their breathing making puffy clouds of condensation. "Child," she said on a hushed whisper, reaching out a hand to grasp Prim's. "I know nothing of a baby being switched. I do remember quite well the night the

269

infant was born—it's the only infant who was ever born here. But I never saw the child. I wasn't allowed in the room when the mother gave birth, nor do I know who the mother was. Sister Ophelia had me guard the door. Nothing more."

Well, fuck. Prim wanted to scream.

"But..." Sister Rosalyn paused and looked thoughtful.

"But?" Wanda inquired, her eyes wide.

She took both Prim's hands in her small warm ones. "But you, my dear, simply can't be the baby born on that night."

She frowned. "I can't?"

"No." She firmly shook her head. "The fairy who gave birth to a child that night with Sister Ophelia's help wasn't a girl—it was a boy."

No sooner had the words left her lips than someone shouted, "Get them!"

Some of the last words Prim heard were from Farrah. "You son of a ground hog! You ratted us out!"

Don't you watch Law and Order? Prim mimicked Farrah in her head, before everything went black.

TWENTY-TWO

P rim groaned, her whole body one big ache.

"Prim!" Raff whispered. "Prim! Wake up!"

The rattle of chains disturbed a very sound sleep she was enjoying, thank you very much.

Chains?

She sat bolt upright.

"Prim!"

Trying to open her eyes, it felt like she'd been on a week-long bender. Jesus.

"Prim! Open your damn eyes!" Raff insisted.

"I'm trying," she muttered as she noted a hard wall behind her back. "But tell me, can you open your eyes after you've consumed an entire bottle of Jack?"

"What?"

"That's what it feels like. It feels like I drank for a week. My head's spinning."

She felt a rustling beside her before Raff repeated,

"You *have* to open your eyes, Prim. We have to get the hell out of here."

She tried once more to push an eye open. "Where is here, anyway?"

"I don't know the exact location, but I think it's a dungeon."

"Like a sex dungeon?"

"Okay, I deserved that. No. Like the one you described when you were telling me you were turned into a fairy."

"How did we get here?" she asked, finally managing to get one eye open.

"I have no idea. One minute we were talking to the sister, the next, lights out."

She tried to sit up, but she was anchored to the wall by handcuffs around her wrists. Her other eye popped open and she got her first blurry view of their landscape, and it looked exactly like the dungeon she'd been in when she'd been snatched from her bed.

Looking around, she saw it was only her and Raff and two shadowy figures in a dark corner, their heads hanging limply.

Her throat was so dry, and her head felt like it was full of stuffing. "Where is everyone else?"

Raff shook his head, the chains around his feet clanking. "I don't know. I only know we have to get the hell out of here. I heard them talking…"

"And?"

He gave her a puzzled look. "Can't you hear them too? They're talking about us right now."

"Has this fairy thing broken you, Raff? I can't hear a damn thing but the buzz in my aching head."

"No. Listen. Listen *closely*," he demanded in an almost frantic tone.

Prim closed her eyes again because, well, it felt good, but she didn't hear a single thing. In fact, it was so quiet, it felt like they were in a tomb.

Shaking her head, which was uncomfortable at best, she winced and said, "Nope. Not a peep. What are you hearing?"

"They're talking about us," he hissed. "Someone keeps saying they have to fix this mistake before *he* finds out."

Prim sighed, leaning her head back against the cold stone. "Yeah. That's what they said to me at my house. It's not new information. I think whatever they hit us with must've hit you harder."

"Shhh," he hissed before he cocked his ear.

While he listened, Prim tried to focus on the room itself. It was almost exactly like the one she'd woken up in when she'd been inside the jar.

A heavy wooden door was the only exit. The metal torch holders on the wall held unlit candles. Chains and all sorts of contraptions that looked like some kind of medieval torture devices sat along the stone walls.

And it was damn damp and cold and her hump was starting to ache as a result.

"Something about exactly midnight. It has to be done *before* midnight?" Raff muttered. "*What* has to be done before midnight?"

"Midnight before your thirtieth birthday," a voice, quite regal in nature, said sleepily. "They must end your life by your thirtieth birthday to keep you from coming into your power...a power so significant, it will rule the land. They need you as proof I'm a traitor to our kind, and to prevent the end of the dark and the light. *You* are that proof."

Prim's eyes popped open. Licking her parched lips, she meekly asked, "Who are you?"

The voice cleared its throat. "Pria. I'm Queen Pria of the Hollow."

Clearly, they were both stunned speechless. Even though there was no light in the room but the tiny shaft from under the door, Prim saw Raff's jaw unhinge.

But hold on. They need her to prove the voice in the corner was a traitor to her kind?

Did that mean...?

"*You're my mother*? The homicidal maniac?"

Pria gasped. "What is it you speak?"

Prim strained against the chains keeping her hostage. "I'll tell you what I speak, lady! You swapped me out for a human baby so you could have a sacrifice to give to the devil. That makes you a homicidal maniac!"

"Prim! How hard did they hit you when they knocked you out? The baby born that night was a boy," Raff said. "Not a girl. It wasn't you."

Relief flooded her every cell, but confusion took relief's place. I don't understand..."

The queen's tinkle of dry, obviously ironic laughter shook Prim to her core. "That's not what happened at all. I would never commit such an insidious act. I gave birth to a child in secret and left him with a human family whose child died at almost the exact moment mine was born. I did it for his safekeeping from the Unseelie. If they had known of his existence, if they had known I was pregnant with an Unseelie child, they would have destroyed him."

"What the hell is going on?" Raff whispered as he used the heels of his feet to sit up straight.

Prim sat up straighter beside him, her hump scraping the wall as she did. "*Him.* You keep saying him. Who is him?."

"*He* is," the queen said, her voice cracking

Mic officially dropped.

"Me?" Raff squealed. *"Me?"*

"*You* are my son, born half-light, half-dark at exactly midnight, December the twenty-sixth."

Prim closed her eyes. All this time they thought it was a bounty on her head, but they'd been after *Raff?*

And poor Raff. His silence told her exactly how he

felt to find out the woman who'd raised him, who'd loved and cherished him, wasn't his biological mother.

"Raff," she whispered, trying to scoot closer to him and offer some comfort.

But he was stiff as a board, his body rigid. "So what you're telling me is the child my mother gave birth to died, and you replaced him with me?"

"Yes," she said, her voice once more cracking. "I would never hurt another child. *Never.* Your mother, that wonderful woman who was so happy to have you, was the perfect choice to raise you. To care for you, nurture you, Rafferty. She did such a wonderful job. I made the right decision, one that would protect you, and I promise you that I would have done *anything* to protect you from the Unseelie."

"This Unseelie bunch..." Prim said. "You had an affair with one. Are they really all that bad? If you're so good, why were you walkin' on the dark side?"

There was another ironic laugh. "Not all of them are bad, most especially not your birth father, Rafferty. But his family...his father in particular...he was evil. Evil, ugly people who would have killed me and taken their revenge on you, had they found out about us."

Prim knew Raff was fighting to speak, and because they knew each other so well, she stepped in. "So a Romeo and Juliet, Montague, Capulet thing?"

"What?" Pria asked.

"Forget I said that. Who's Raff's father? Who's the man of this unholy union and where the hell is he?"

There was a pause and a soft inhale before Pria said, "He knows nothing of Rafferty. *Nothing.* The only fairy who knew of Rafferty's birth and origins was Sister Ophelia, but on her deathbed, knowing after she was gone, the time would soon come for Rafferty's thirtieth birthday, afraid to take such a secret to her grave, she confessed what she'd done to my oracle."

There was that damn word again. Oracle. "So this leads back to your advisor? Isn't that what you winged people call oracles?"

Now Pria's laugh was bitter. "Elrond, that weak, sniveling coward," she sneered. "More than once I caught him in a lie. Thus, I took his powers and banished him from the kingdom to roam the outlying woods forevermore."

Interesting. Banishment was a thing. "You folks really know how to flex, huh?" Prim commented.

"Okay, so you banished him," Raff finally spoke up, his voice husky in the dark. "What then?"

"Elrond found out about you from Sister Ophelia, when he gave her last rites. My deepest regret is that I didn't lock him up and throw away the key. I should have forever revoked his privileges, Rafferty. None of this would have come to pass had I listened to my instincts."

As she spoke, Prim worked the details in her mind. "So lemme guess, Elrond decided to exact some revenge because he was mad you took away his shot at employee of the month, and he went to the evil, ugly people and told them about the baby."

"Yes. I just heard stirrings of it this very day from a *trusted* advisor. One who would never betray me."

Prim clucked her tongue. "You sure 'bout that? I think it's fair to say, your gut's been kinda screwed before."

"Are there not henchmen trying at this very moment to kill you, Prim?" she asked.

Right. Good point. "Okay, so how did I get mixed up in this? Why did they kidnap me and not Raff, and why did they give me these powers that are, if you ask me, a little on the unreliable side. If you could see the deformed hump on my back, lady, you'd understand."

There was a shuffle of chains and a deep breath before she said, "Oh, Primrose, I'm so sorry you were put in the middle of this," she whispered, her words hitching. "It is my belief that Sister Ophelia lied in an attempt to keep Rafferty safe, while still relieving herself of her guilt, confessing to Elrond I'd given birth to a girl."

Holy birthday. "And because we were born in the same hospital, only minutes apart, he snatched the first person he assumed fit the bill."

Pria sighed. "Elrond isn't known for his precision. I think that's quite obvious because when he captured you, his intent was to bring you to the king of the dark and expunge you. But he instead bestowed untold powers upon you—which you, by proxy, awakened with Rafferty."

We have to get her back before he finds out we made a mistake.

Her surprise didn't turn into anger. Instead, after last night, after all they'd been through, Prim found herself grateful. But she couldn't help relaying her disbelief. "So none of this was ever supposed to happen to me?"

"No. No, Primrose. I'm so sorry. I wish with all my heart I could take it back."

Raff had found his voice again, though it was scratchy, and she knew he was likely still trying to absorb this mess. "And this scrit? This prophecy that says I'm going to destroy the dark and the light if I come into my powers?"

Prim heard the queen swallow, heard her sigh, long and breathy. "You are the only one of your kind. Half-dark, half-light fae. There is no other like you. This scrit you've heard of has been around for hundreds of years, but no one was able to decipher its ancient language. No one gave it much thought other than the rumor it was about a child. There are many undecipherable prophecies from our kind. But Elrond, crafty and sinister, found someone he claims could read it. And I have to assume he brought it to the King of the Unseelie."

"You bet he did," another voice piped up. "And

you're all toast. There's nothing like a good game of cat and mouse, is there?"

The other shadow in the corner...

It was Smitty.

"What the fuck are you doing here?" Prim whisper-yelled. "Christ, you're like a piece of shit I can't scrape off my shoe. So what happened, Smitty, after I beat your face in? Did you get in trouble with your little buddies for fucking up the way you always do? Did you get conned—*again*?"

He growled like a feral animal. "Shut up, you nasty tramp! I'll kill you!"

"Not if I get to you first, you piece of shit!" Raff yelled, struggling against his chains.

Smitty scoffed. "Really, fairy boy? How're you gonna do that, all tied up over there?"

"Raff!" Prim called. "It's okay. Let him stew in his own shit. He's a pig who got taken for a ride by some fairies. The douche wouldn't know his ass from his elbow if he wasn't falling for some twit toad's promise to make some cash."

Prim couldn't see much but a shadow, but she heard Smitty scramble in an attempt to get to his feet. "Shut your tramp mouth, Primmy! Leave the do-gooder bullshit to your boyfriend. Just like your mother, *Sandy*, aren't you?"

Prim didn't just hear Raff's anger, she felt it beside her in the way his long body stiffened. "What do you know about my mother?" he seethed.

Smitty barked his greasy, gurgling laugh. "I know she didn't know how to keep her do-gooder mouth shut, so I shut it for her."

Prim almost fell over in shock. Oh, dear God, had Smitty...

She felt Raff squirm beside her, straining against his chains. "Shut up, Smitty!" she yelled. "Shut up, or I'll knock your fucking prick-ass to kingdom come!"

But Raff was beyond her ability to calm him down. "It was you... *You* killed her?"

Smitty snickered. "Bet your ass I did, fairy boy. Somebody had to shut her up."

TWENTY-THREE

Raff howled his anguish, screamed his rage so loud, it echoed throughout the space as Prim sat completely stunned.

Smitty had killed Mrs. Monroe. His words sliced through her heart. If she'd just said something about what Smitty was like, done something, it never would have happened.

Why? Why would he kill someone so kind?

Before she could stop herself, Prim whispered, "*Why?*"

Smitty stirred, his pained groan loud and long, but that didn't stop him from boasting. "Because she was gonna snitch on me to your mother about some high school kid she caught me talking to. We were just talking, Primmy. Imagine, making up lies about a nice guy like me when all I was doing was trying to be friendly with the girl."

Now *Prim* screamed, wishing her ability to manipulate sound would return because she's blow his ass into the next lifetime. But all that came out was a raw sound that hurt her throat.

Try as she might, she couldn't break the handcuffs, but it wasn't for lack of trying as she reared upward until she felt her skin break and blood begin to drip down her arm. "When I get loose, you'll wish I killed you the other night, you stupid, stupid fuck!"

"Primrose," Queen Pria yelled with authority. "Stop. Stop struggling and look away from this filth and listen to me. You'll only hurt yourself. The chains are bound with powerful fairy magic. Please. Please stop!"

"Listen to the fairy lady, Primmy," Smitty cooed sarcastically. "She knows what she's talking about, don't ya, hottie?"

Prim wasn't sure which was the final nail in the coffin. The fact that Smitty had killed the only mother Raff had ever known, or the fact that he called his biological mother a hottie.

Either way, Raff plum lost his mind.

He rose up until the chains strained so hard, they creaked. Leaning forward, he whisper-yelled, "You will *die*! And I'm going to make you ache for every second you've been breathing. For every time you hurt Prim. For killing my mother. I'm going to make you *suffer*!"

The room began to shake at Raff's words, a low rumbling that began behind her back and rapidly worked its way upward. A vibration so strong, Prim felt it in her bones.

Then the rocks of the dungeon began falling, slowly at first, one stone at a time, until they all began to come loose.

Suddenly Raff broke his chains and fell forward—and a light, so bright, so blinding all Prim saw was white, scorched the room.

A loud whir of noise surrounded them. "Raff?" she cried out, unable to see the rocks falling around her head well enough to duck as one glanced off her skull.

"Prim!" he roared over the mighty sound of the dungeon collapsing. "I'm coming!"

Suddenly, she was lifted off the ground, the cuffs around her wrists and ankles melting away.

And that blinding light?

That was Raff's wings, pumping madly, spanning the entire dungeon with their glowing width.

As he hoisted her into his arms, she yelled to him, "Pria! We have to get Pria!"

"No! Run, Rafferty, run! You must get out!"

Rafferty dodged the falling rocks like he was dodging snowballs, running the length of the dungeon to find the most beautiful blonde woman in a long, torn white gown, her gamine face covered in dirt, her hands nicked and bloody.

"Go, Rafferty! You don't have time! Save yourself and your beloved!" she bellowed as rocks and dirt pelted her.

"The fuck we don't!"

Nina! Oh, Jesus Christ and a combat boot, Nina had arrived!

"Go! Go up the stairs to the landing and jump over the balcony, it's the only exit!" she ordered over the crash of stones. "Get the fuck out! Find the others! I'll get her!"

Raff set Prim on the ground and they both began to run as walls crumbled and the sound of people screaming rang all around them.

He saw an exit with some light at the same time Prim did. "There! Maybe there are stairs on the landing!" she cried, dodging and ducking the crumbling structure.

As they headed for the exit on a landing high above this monstrosity of brick, one she could only assume was a castle, they ran directly into a group of men who looked pretty angry.

Raff shoved her behind his enormous wings and demanded, "Let us go!"

But they held their ground, all five of them dressed in clothes that looked like they came from a Middle Earth Goodwill. But their knives and shiny weapons? Those were universal.

She didn't know exactly where they were. If they were in a castle or still at the nunnery. One thing she did know, they were on a balcony that was also beginning to crumble.

"We got 'em!" one shouted out.

Raff tugged her close and whispered, "On three."

She blinked, spitting a piece of his wing from her mouth. "What?"

But she didn't have time to question him further before she heard Raff yell, "Three!"

And the next thing she knew, he'd scooped her back up and leapt from the balcony.

Her scream could be heard the entire way down, but somehow, with zero wing practice under his belt, they managed to land safely, if not a little rough.

They fell to the ground, rolling together as Raff's wings slapped her about...only to find themselves at someone's feet. Someone with a big ol' magic wand.

A small, wrinkled man in drab, monk-like garb looked down at them, holding them at wand point.

Hah! *Wand point.* Like gun point, but probably a lot different.

The small man narrowed his beady eyes, his bowl-cut hair pressed tightly to his skull. "If it isn't the prodigal son—returned home to die."

Elrond the oracle, she presumed.

Raff scurried to his feet as best he could with his gigantic wings. Seeing him here, out in the open, gave Prim a perspective of them she hadn't seen in the dungeon or even at her house. They somehow looked bigger, far more imposing than they had when they'd first sprouted.

They were regal, stately, wide and strong, in all the colors of the rainbow.

"Elrond?" Raff said, hauling her upward and tucking her back behind him.

But she wasn't having it. This man had turned her life upside down. Stepping in front of Raff, she shook her finger at him. Screw his wand of mass destruction, if she was going to die, she wasn't doing it until he had a new asshole.

"You did this to me, you stupid, bumbling fool! You screwed up so royally, pun intended, you couldn't even kidnap the right baby, dumbass!" Prim turned around, her anger spiking along her spine as she pointed to her back. "Look at this, moron! You left me with a damn hump on my back! You made me use vacation days I'm never going to get back because Jesus knows Darleen in HR'll see to that, and you fucked with the holidays for the people who are trying to help me, and you *still* managed to get it wrong, imbecile!"

"Prim!" Raff tugged at her arm in warning.

Elrond waved the wand like a light saber, zapping an electric spark at her feet that snapped hot, setting little fires on top of the snow before he grabbed her around the neck. "You foolish girl! I'll slice your head off!"

He pointed the wand into the darkness, stabbing it toward the woods, then ordered Raff, "You will come with me to the King of the Unseelie, and he will see you dead for your mother's unholy union! Now, if you want your beloved to live, you'll walk!"

Prim was about to open her big mouth again, but Raff silenced her with one hard glance.

"Walk!" the oracle bellowed, leaving an echo of his words swirling in the frigid air.

As they began to trudge through the snow, blood dripping from her forehead where she'd been pegged with rocks from the dungeon, her heart pounding, and a hot wand in her back, she tried to think of a way to get the damn thing from Elrond.

He wasn't exactly bright, Just look at how he'd fucked up so far. There had to be a way.

As she moved past strange-looking bushes and picked her way through the forest debris, she caught a quick glimpse of something moving.

"Prim?" she heard someone call, but when she looked around, there was no one. Nothing but snow and more snow, falling from the sky in buckets, and them walking to their death.

"It's me, Prim. Raff."

She snuck a glance over her shoulder and Raff smiled. Her glance was questioning.

What the hell was happening now? How was Raff in her head?

"Shhh. Listen to me and I'll tell *you how I'm in your head. Don't talk. I guess I can communicate telepathically. I first noticed it when we were in the dungeon with Queen Pria, and she communicated with me."*

Was there no end to the wonders of being the king of

fairies? she wondered as her feet crunched over the snow.

"I'm not the king of fairies. Forget that and listen carefully. Wanda, Marty and the gang are out here. They tell me up ahead there are more henchmen from the Unseelie, waiting for Elrond to bring me to them. We're going to ambush them. As soon as you see the women, duck and stay hidden!"

"I'm not going to stay hidden like some chickenshit," she mentally replied. *"I'm in."*

"Prim, you could get hurt," Raff pleaded. *"These people have fully formed powers to really hurt you. You need to stay hidden."*

"Look at you, superhero. Suddenly you're Batman because you have some wings you used once? Your powers aren't fully formed any more than mine are, egomaniac. I'm not going to hide."

"Move faster!" Elrond bellowed, interrupting their mental conversation with the crunch of his feet on the snow.

As they approached a clearing and the moon shined down on the spot where toadstools sprouted from the ground and small woodland creatures scattered, she heard a rustle in the trees before she saw the henchman the OOPS gang must've been talking about.

There were way more bad guys then there were of them. Suddenly, she felt quite small.

But that didn't last long before an eruption of

sound burst from the surrounding woods, and she heard Elrond call out and order, "Get him to the king!"

Then Raff yelled, "Prim, duck!"

Instead of rebelling, she did what she was told.

And when she looked up, quite suddenly, everybody was Kung-Fu fighting.

With wings.

CHAPTER

TWENTY-FOUR

M ass chaos erupted as men charged the group with wands similar to Elron's, slicing the air and leaving flames in their wake, knocking the falling snow off trees and turning it to ashes.

Limbs flailed, people flew through the air, fists swung as the wind howled.

Darnell took fairies out with a swipe of his big hand, swatting them all like flies. Sten used a sword (trolls had swords?), dueling with two men at once, sweat glistening from his brow.

Most surprising of all was Raff. He flapped his wings with a fury, scooping up one henchman after another and clobbering them between his two colorful appendages.

Prim stood in awe for only seconds before she heard a loud roar.

"Wanda! Look out!" Marty screamed as a flaming purple ball headed straight for her head.

Wanda ducked in time to take cover in a bush but there was someone else rushing up from behind her, and no one around to help.

Prim didn't even bother to scream to her—she dove for the henchman, managing to successfully knock his wand from his hand.

As she tucked and rolled, he grabbed her ankle and hauled her toward him with a howl of rage.

Prim clawed the earth beneath her, the snow seeping through her jacket, her fingers raw from clinging to anything she could get a hold of.

And where was all that invisibility now when she could really use it?

She tried to kick out, twisting in his hold until she could see his angry face and his bulging muscles. Using her free leg, she slammed the heel of her foot into his face, knocking his chin upward just before Nina grabbed him by his silver wings and launched him high in the sky.

"Get the fuck off her!" she thundered.

Pushing herself off the ground, Prim mouthed a thank you before Nina was off again, hurling herself into the clouds of snow and the scream of war cries.

Elrond stood in the middle of the melee in the clearing, his wand high in the air as he called out, "The hour is upon us! We must kill him now or suffer our deaths!"

He charged Raff, running at him with the speed of a gazelle, his wand pointed straight at Raff's unsuspecting back as he used his wings to take flight. A hot glow spring from the tip of the wand, burning fiery red as it zigzagged toward Raff.

No. No, no, no!

Not today.

Instead of screaming Raff's name, instead of thinking before she reacted, Prim ran to cut Elrond off at the pass and without warning, without so much as a blink of any eye, she took *flight.*

She was flying? Sweet baby Jesus, she was flying.

Bouncing and skidding, her hump became a single flapping wing, buzzing in her ear like that of a small motor.

Her flight was reckless, precarious at best, skidding and sliding as she went, her feet scraping the snow covered ground, but it lifted her enough to launch herself in front of the wand to keep its magic from piercing Raff's back. "Nooo!" she screamed.

Instead of hitting Raff, it slashed her, the wand singeing her ribcage with a heat so agonizing, she felt like she was on fire, knocking her to the ground and to her knees.

Tears stung her eyes as she tried to get to her feet, but the pain was so fierce it took her breath away. Prim fell forward, seeing a flash of light from the corner of her eye, aimed at her head, but she couldn't seem to move herself to avoid it—and she knew then, this was it.

It was over. She didn't have the kind of skills everyone else did, including Raff, it appeared.

Raff thundered her name. "Prim! No!"

"*Elrond!* What have you done?" a loud voice from above boomed.

As quickly as it had begun, everything stopped—and the silence that ensued in the clearing was deafening. Even the snow felt as though it stood still.

Prim fell to the ground, no longer able to hold herself up, but Raff was instantly beside her, on his knees, his hair soaked from the snow, his eyes fearful. "Prim, Jesus Christ, are you okay?"

Nina, Marty, and Wanda raced to his side, their hair plastered to their skulls, their chests heaving from battle.

"Get her the fuck off the ground!" Nina ordered.

Raff hauled her upward into the safety of his arms, tucking her next to his warmth.

Marty and Wanda hovered over her, nestled in Raff's arms, with Darnell and Sten in the background.

"Prim!" Marty said, pushing her wet hair from her eyes. "Where are you hurt?"

She didn't have time to answer before they heard footsteps stomping toward them, loud and sure. "Elrond!"

Immediately, Elrond fell to his knees, dropping his wand. "Your majesty."

A very large, very fit man with chocolate-brown hair and gold wings, dressed like Prince Charming in red and white, regally stood before a quivering Elrond, hands on his lean hips.

An army of winged men in battle gear stood behind him, their wands drawn, standing at attention.

He toed Elrond, forcing the small man to look up. "Rise! I demand an answer! Why have you attacked these people without my permission? How dare you!"

"Soren!" another voice called out. "Stop! You must listen. He must be killed!"

The group, stunned once more to silence, protectively gathered around Raff and Prim.

Soren turned toward the voice. Yet another man, much older yet equally regal, who looked a great deal like Soren aside from the gray hair and a few wrinkles around his eyes, rushed toward them while everyone else remained silent.

"Father?" Soren demanded, his deep voice resonating throughout the forest. "What have I told you about interfering in official matters of the Unseelie? You are retired from running the kingdom. *I* am the king."

Ignoring the pain in her ribs, ignoring her rapidly beating heart, Prim gasped, "Unseelie..."

Oh, this was bad, right? So bad. The Unseelie were bad guys.

If you'll recall, not all of them are bad, Prim.

295

Yeah, but the way her luck had been going, a girl could never be too careful.

The group tightened their protective stance, Sten with a hand on his sword, but the king held up his hand as if to tell them they were safe from him.

Soren bowed before her, his dark eyes apologetic. "Primrose Dunham, is it?"

She fought not to stutter as she straightened in Raff's arms and with her eyes, dared this fancy pants to lay a finger on him. Clinging to his arm, she narrowed her eyes. "You leave him alone!"

He chuckled, a deep, pleasant sound. "I am Soren, King of the Unseelie. I mean you no harm. However, it's my understanding this little toad has, with the help of my interfering father, created a *situation*."

"Is that what you nuts with wings call this shit?" Nina crowed, pointing to the single wing on Prim's back as she glared at the man

Prim slid from Raff's arms and hobbled on one foot to face the handsome king, and he was, indeed, handsome.

Wiping the falling snow from her eyes, she waved a finger under his nose. "If that's what you call trying to kill me and Raff, then yeah. It's a *situation*."

He pressed a wide hand to his heart. "My deepest apologies, Primrose, and to your friend, as well. We seem to have a mix-up, one that could have been completely avoided if my father had simply let me run the kingdom instead of listening to an old fool who enjoys a bit of gossip...and who entertains the idea he might have the prestige of advising the king one day."

From out of nowhere, Farrah appeared and flit to Prim, her wings beating out a pulsating sound, smiling a cheerful smile as she pressed her deliciously warm hands to Prim's cold cheeks. "That's a big deal, by the way. Oracle to the king. That means Elrond is a suck up." Then she brushed her hands together. "Do your ribs feel better?"

Prim looked down at her stomach, where her bulky jacket had been torn by the fiery wand, only to find the stinging wound gone. Holy shit. It *did* feel better.

"It...it does..." she said in wonder. "Thank you."

"It does, indeed, mean Elrond is a suck up, and he shall pay for his transgressions!" Soren thundered the threat, his dark eyes flashing.

Elrond quivered, clasping his hands together. "Sire, I beg of you, please spare me your wrath!"

"Quiet!" Soren shouted. "I'll deal with you later. Guards, contain him."

The guards instantly sprang into action, seizing Elrond and shackling him.

Soren turned back to the group. "And this man, is he one of yours?" He snapped his fingers and a guard brought forth a sniveling, bloodied Smitty, who'd somehow survived the collapse of the dungeon.

"Please let me go! Please," he begged. "I don't know what's going on, but I'll never tell a soul what I saw. I swear it!"

Nina snatched him from the guard, ripping him right from the man's hands. "You cowardly piece of shit—shut the fuck up! Remember when I told you to pick the way you wanted to die? It's time to choose, fucknob!"

"Nina!" Wanda grabbed her arm and pulled her away. "Why don't we let Soren handle this. No one ever has to know what happened to Smitty back in our realm, now do they?"

Nia grinned and tweaked Wanda's cheek. "You crafty bitch. I like the way you think." She virtually lobbed him back at the guard, then looked to Soren. "Nah. He's not one of ours, but he did help your little pecker of an oracle try to kill Prim."

Soren glared at Smitty, his eyes terrifying. "Away to the dungeon!" he yelled, snapping his fingers as Smitty begged for mercy and the guard dragged him away.

As Prim watched him being carried off, kicking and screaming, she looked upward. *That one's for you, Mom.*

Then Soren looked to the crowd of men behind him. "Draco, come. Show my father what you hold in your hand."

A man of medium height, dressed in a long red robe with a similar bowl cut to Elrond's, let a roll of paper unfurl. "Sire? Shall I proceed?"

Soren gave him a curt nod, rocking back on his heels. "Please do. Let us settle this once and for all."

Draco cleared his throat. "As it is written, unto the

world a child will be born. The only one of its kind. Half-light, half-dark. It will *unite* the two worlds and there shall be peace for all."

Oh, boy. Someone was in deep shit.

Soren grabbed the scroll from Draco and held it up to his father's worried face. "Did you hear that, Father? *Unite*. The prophecy claims the child will *unite* the dark and the light. Not destroy it! In future, rather than entrust ancient writings to an oracle, might I suggest you use an expert in the field?"

There was an incredibly awkward silence before Elrond began to sob as the snow fell on his head and the wind howled. "Please, sire. I beg of you, I did not know!"

Soren lifted his chin as he gazed at the sniveling oracle. "I do not believe a word you speak! You sought hierarchy for your own gain. You aren't a selfless guide to the royals—you are a fraud! Take him away! I will not look upon this imposter any longer."

Soren's father's face fell, his eyes downcast, his gray head hanging between his shoulder blades. "Oh, Soren. I am so deeply remorseful for all that I have caused."

"Tell that to them." Soren pointed to the group. "Tell that to Primrose and..." He looked to Raff, waiting.

He lifted a hand and wiggled his fingers. "Oh. Um, Rafferty. The dark and light guy."

The corner of Soren's lip lifted into an almost smile

before he shut it down and once more, grew stoic. "Rafferty. Of course. Look what you have done, Father! You have ruined two lives with your interference. Had you left well enough alone, this young couple's lives wouldn't be in such upset. For that, I do apologize to you—to both of you. Father, apologize this instant!"

Soren's father looked at both Raff and Prim as he bowed. "My deepest apologies. I shall find a way to make amends."

What did you say to a guy when one of his people had turned your life upside down? Not a problem? We cool?

But apparently, that wasn't good enough for Soren. His wings flapped wildly. "Father! how can you *amend* changing the trajectory of a man's entire life? For stealing his beloved past from him with truths you had no right to reveal? You must stop this nonsense of declaring strife between the dark and the light, or I promise you, I shall have you locked in your wing with nothing more than a visit from a guard with a plate of food three times a day!"

"Soren?" a quiet voice spoke up from the crowd.

He whipped around, his dark eyes going from hard as nails to soft as butter when he recognized who'd spoken. "Pria?"

"Soren!" she cried, pushing her way through the guards and giving Prim a good look at just how much Raff resembled her.

She hadn't been able to see her very well in the

dungeon, but if she hadn't confessed to giving birth to Raff, there would have been no hiding it when they were side by side.

She was as beautiful as Raff was handsome, her glistening blonde hair, long and shiny even in the snow, falling well past her waist. Her eyes were round and bluer than blue, just like Raff's

The pair eyed one another with longing so obvious, Prim's heart hurt.

And then the light bulb over her head went off.

Romeo and Juliet.

Soren was Pria's dark fairy lover—and that made him Raff's father.

This felt too much like an episode of *Days of Our Lives*.

Pria fisted her hands, her eyes on fire. "Tell me you're not here to bring harm to my son! I will fight you with everything I have in me to prevent his death!"

"Harm him? Pria, no. *No!*" Then Soren gasped. "*You* are the fairy who gave birth to this boy?"

She stood tall, grabbing Raff's hand, lifting her chin in regal fashion. "I am and I will protect him at all costs."

"Is he...?"

"Yes," she sobbed.

He looked at Raff in disbelief. "Why didn't you tell me I had a son?"

"Because look what would have happened had I

confided in you!" she spread her arms wide at the fallen men and the OOPS gang, their hair a mess, their clothes torn, streaks of dirt covering their faces. "This is what your father would have done. We were forbidden, and I would not allow your family, your *father*, to take my child! I gave him to a wonderful family who were never the wiser, and he was well loved. Had your father known of our unholy union, he would have killed my son!"

Soren glared at his father, his jaw clenched. "Guards, take him back to the castle and keep a close eye on him. We shall revisit this conversation upon my return, *Father*."

As the guards escorted Soren's father away, he turned back to Pria, his features softer as he held out a hand to her. "Pria. My one and only beloved. I would have protected you, had you come to me. The dark is different now under my rule. I promise you, things have changed. Let us talk, shall we? All of us—Primrose, Rafferty—together we shall find our way through this."

Pria let out a small sob, taking his hand and going to his side, her smile tremulous, hopeful. If nothing else was certain, their love for one another was crystal clear.

"I think your fairy mommy and daddy just made up," Nina cackled in Raff's ear.

Marty and Wanda, enraptured by the star-crossed lovers based on the expressions on their faces, scowled at Nina. "Hush, Vampire! Something beautiful is happening."

Raff, who in the span of an hour had met not only his biological mother, but his father, too, stood in the middle of them all, frozen in place.

She reached for his hand and squeezed it. "Are you okay?"

He looked shell-shocked as everyone anticipated his answer. "I don't know. I feel numb."

And how could she blame him? His whole world had just been tipped on its axis. What did you say to someone when that happened.

Pria held out her hand to Raff, her eyes warm and welcoming. "Will you talk with us, Rafferty? Will you let us at least explain? Let us to show you how to use your abilities properly and help Prim with her wing?"

Prim stood in front of him and cupped his cheeks with her freezing hands. "Listen to me. You don't have to do anything you don't want to do, Raff. It's up to you...but if you decide to do this, Mr. King of the Light and Dark, I'll be your paper towel."

Raff smiled down at her, focusing only on her face. "I dunno. This is a pretty big spill, Prim."

Prim nodded. "Not a lie. But! I'm the super self-absorbent kind of paper towel. Two-ply, select-a-size," she joked, her gaze tentative.

"Two-ply? Isn't that toilet paper?"

Prim waved her hand in a dismissive gesture. "It does the same thing. It cleans stuff up, doesn't it?"

He dropped a kiss on the tip of her nose. "Well, in that case, how can I resist?"

"You sure, buddy?" Darnell asked, clamping a hand on Raff's broad shoulder. "Say the word and we get Gary to take us back. We got you two."

Sten nodded and held up his phone, his green hair beautiful under the moonlight. "All it takes is one text."

Raff patted Darnell's hand. "Listen, you guys, I just want to say thank you. For everything. But I'm okay."

"And look the fuck at you," Nina crowed with a grin, giving Prim's wing a tug. "Who has a big girl wing?"

Prim curtsied and somehow managed to make her wing wiggle with a beaming smile. "Well, it's only one and I don't even know how it happened. It didn't hurt or anything, but I thought you'd never notice."

Wanda chuckled, smoothing her hair from her face before she ran her finger down the line of Prim's nose. "And a what a beaut that one wing is, all purple and green," she praised.

Marty hurled herself at Raff and Prim and hollered, "Group hug!"

As everyone piled on, clapping each other on the back, Prim savored the moment, savored the feeling of belonging, relishing the luck she felt in finding these people.

Raff broke away first, taking Pria's hand and

tucking Prim to his side. "C'mon, Two-Ply. We have a spill in aisle seven."

Prim tipped her head back and laughed. They had a pretty big spill. The biggest spill ever.

But as they left the clearing, following Pria and Soren, leaving behind the debris of a battle hard won, she was pretty sure if the two-ply didn't clean it up, the select-a-size definitely would.

EPILOGUE

Five months later...

One not nearly as grumpy, angry, or foul-mouthed accidental fairy who's discovering what it is to be part of a framily; a handsome, newly crowned King of the Realm of Fairies, who finally got his much-desired magic wand and is getting to know his biological Seelie mother and Unseelie father; a crabby AF vampire who, without fail, chauffeurs her sister-from-another-mister to biweekly therapy; a sweet, pale green zombie who reads *War and Peace* and actually likes it; a blonde werewolf who's green with envy about her new fairy friends' beautiful wings; an elegantly refined halfsie who never tires of babysitting a particular fairy's dog and cat while she's at therapy; a happy-go-lucky demon who's been helping his new friend, the King of Fairies, discover the joys of a bandsaw and home improvement; and a short of stature but big on personality blue British troll who knows the distinct art of making a superior PB and J...all gathered together on a beautiful spring day in the Realm of the Hollow for an auspicious wand graduation ceremony...

"Ooooh, ain't you fancy?" Nina cooed in Prim's ear. "Look at those big ol' wings ya got, they match your big ol' ears."

She did have both wings now. Pria had fixed that, and every day she got better at flying with them— well, except when she'd crashed into the castle's bridge. But listen, it wasn't like driving.

She whirled around and threw her arms around Nina's neck. "You came!"

"I'm your sister-from-another-mister. Of course, I fucking came, dipshit!" She gathered Prim in her arms and gave her a tight hug before setting her back from her. "Wow, this is some big fucking deal, huh?"

Prim looked around the clearing where not long ago they'd fought a battle, and smiled at how different it was today. "I guess so."

The fairies in the village had come out in full force, decorating every inch of the clearing with twinkling lights and bouquets of flowers, spilling over tables set out for the after-party buffet Arch had organized.

Fairies flit from place to place, buzzing their

colorful wings and leaving a trail of bright vapors in their wake.

She loved the time she spent here with Raff, Pria and Soren, and she'd come to love the people of the village almost as much.

"You *guess* so?" Marty squealed, gathering her in a hug before she reached up to straighten the flowered wreath on her head. "Excuse me, Miss Ma'am. You're getting a wand today. A wand! I mean, does it get any better than that? That's a big deal!"

If they only knew how long it had taken to master that colorful wand of death. Last count, it was nine trees, seven cars, and fourteen lampposts. But she was getting better...

Wanda snuck up behind her and tugged at her hair, longer now, since she had so little time to get it trimmed.

When she turned around, she threw her arms around Wanda's neck, admiring her silky, green dress.

"Thank you! And you look so pretty, honey! That tutu is everything."

Prim curtsied, spreading the pink tulle outward with a smile and holding up a foot. "Ya think it works with my work boots?"

"Everything works with work boots," Nina teased. "Every fucking thing."

Carl and Darnell tapped her on the shoulders, enveloping her in a warm hug. "How's the student?"

Prim giggled. She'd left her job and the wretched

Darleen behind to get her mental health in order. Two days a week she saw Dr. January, and they'd made amazing progress.

Prim was getting better at sharing her fear, at holding her tongue, but mostly she was getting better at letting people in.

And one night, after a game of old school Zelda, she'd told Raff what Smitty had done to her the night of her graduation.

They'd sat together for a long time, holding each other, soothing each other.

As she talked through all that had happened with Smitty when she was a kid—as Dr. January reminded her, she had been, in fact, a kid—she'd begun to accept what she couldn't be changed.

And that had brought an enormous sense of peace to her life.

She tweaked Darnell's round cheeks before running a hand over his sharp tie, smoothing it out. "I start classes on Monday. I've got my pencils and my notepad ready."

"Man, are we ever proud of you, Miss Primrose. Or is that Dr. Dunham? You're going to be the best therapist ever," Marty assured her.

Prim had made a big life decision as she sifted through her mental health and learned how to be a fairy. Because Nina and the girls had encouraged her to seek counseling, and because they were so committed to her well-being, they'd inspired her to go back to school.

She hoped that one day, she'd be able to help others who'd been through similar traumatic experiences navigate those murky waters.

She crossed her fingers. "Here's hoping I can keep up with all those kids," she joked.

Nina leaned toward her. "Hey, remember I told you I'd take care of that fucking problem?"

Her wings pulsed, intuitively responding to the conversation she and Nina had not so long ago about the dick who'd dumped Freddy. She'd run into him one day on her way to counseling with Nina.

He'd brazenly gawked at her and had the nerve to ask how her "stolen" dog was doing. When she'd told Nina who he was, she hadn't said much other than he deserved to have *his* ass dumped somewhere. Then he'd know exactly how Freddy felt.

Prim winced and prayed a homicide bloodletting hadn't been committed in Freddy's honor. "Uh-huh. I remember."

Nina brushed her hands together and grinned. "Done and done."

Prim gasped, even if she was secretly pleased. "You didn't!"

"The fuck I didn't. Dropped his ass off somewhere it'd take him a long damn time to find his way back home from."

Marty pinched Nina's arm. "Nina! You didn't."

"Oh, shut the fuck up, Ass-Sniffer. I made sure he got back to his swanky house safe. I mean, I'm sure he was hungry and thirsty when he fucking got there, but he's fine, and he won't be adopting any dogs anytime soon. I made sure he's on a list."

"You are incorrigible," Wanda said, but she smiled and tweaked Nina's cheeks as a soft breeze, scented with roses, wafted by. "But I like the way you think, Vampire."

"Ladies? How've you been?" Sten strode up to them with his gorgeous wife Murphy on his arm, who Prim had met a few weeks ago at a fairy-hosted framily dinner.

"I'm great. Like, so great I could bust, buddy."

Sten dropped a kiss on her cheek, his orange eyes smiling. "I think everyone's getting ready to sit down. We'd better grab a seat. The turnout was pretty great."

As Prim looked over the many, many faces of the fairies she'd fallen in love with, she waved to Pria and Soren, sitting in the front row, now happily planning their wedding.

They, too, had worked through years' worth of separation, and as they planned their wedding and got to know their son, they looked happier than ever. Serena was there, too, better now since Pria had wiped away the magic keeping her in a coma.

Gary sat in the back of the crowd, his enormous green frame covering a good deal of the clearing, but Farrah was with him, and they were still going strong.

The dark and the light had definitely united—for better or worse. But it was Raff she was most proud of.

He'd stepped into his role as the King of Fairies the way he did everything else. With thought, with intention, with his genuine wish to learn and grow with the people he now called family.

He'd begin counseling with Dr. January, too. To help him through the guilt of surviving Amal's death, but also to help him come to terms with what happened to Sandy, and he was doing pretty great.

He'd found his calling in ruling the dark and the light, in coalition with his biological parents, who loved him to bits.

And who Raff was coming to love in return.

He'd talked long and in detail with Prim and Doc January about when to tell his adopted father about his switched at birth story.

Raff still wasn't sure if he was going to tell his dad about all that had passed, but Doc January assured him, whatever decision he eventually made, she knew it would be done with love and care, and none of the warm feelings he was experiencing for his biological parents changed how he felt about his adopted father.

Not one iota. Mr. Monroe was the man who'd helped raised an amazing man and nothing would ever change that.

Smitty, on the other hand, was living a life of servitude in a dungeon far, far away from the Hollow, safe from hurting anyone else.

Though, they *had* finally found out what he wanted from Prim. He'd left behind a stash of drugs in the floor under her bathtub. She and Raff had found it quite by accident when they were renovating together.

Nina had immediately confiscated and disposed of it, but not before sending word to Soren that more punishment was in order.

"Prim?"

She heard Raff's deep voice, a voice filled with their newfound love.

They'd spent what felt like a million nights just getting to know one another again. Slowly at first, seeing each other a couple of times a week for a movie or dinner with the OOPS gang.

Playing Zelda, watching TV, learning how to use their wings to fly with Farrah, how to control their invisibility, her sound manipulation, his telepathy, how to straddle both worlds successfully.

And in the process, as they'd set out to strengthen and rekindle a friendship, they'd fallen deeply and irrevocably in love.

But at Dr. January's suggestion, they'd decided to wait to become intimate. To wait until all these new changes in their lives had gelled. Until their mental health was stable and they knew how to love themselves first.

Just last week, Dr. January had given them a mischievous thumbs up to explore their deep feelings with the knowledge that they were healthier, happier people.

Raff wrapped his arms around her and pressed a warm kiss to her eager lips. "Are you ready?"

She draped her arms around his neck, admiring how handsome he looked in his white suit, his wings pulsing behind him. "Ready for what, Mr. Dark and Light?" she whispered, pressing her frame tightly to his taller one.

He groaned, kissing her deeply. "Can we just split and I'll give you the wand when we get to your place? Or mine. I don't care where it happens. Just that *it* happens."

She swatted his shoulder. "We cannot. We have a zillion and two guests here, and I'm getting my wand, buddy. I did some intensive fairy boot-camp-like stuff to learn how not to send a car into the next state with my big mouth. I earned this wand, big buy."

He grinned at her, giving her another deep kiss. "Yeah, you did. Fine. Wand it is. Then we go back to your place and seal the deal?"

She giggled, the anticipation tingling through her body setting her nerve endings on fire. "Yes. Then we can seal the deal. But only if you wear your wings."

"Ahhh, my girl likes it kinky, eh?"

Prim rolled her eyes. "Your girl likes *you*."

"And your guy *loves* you," he whispered, holding her tighter.

She'd waited a long time to hear those words,

maybe even longer than since the moment she'd said them herself in the turret.

She cupped his chin, running her thumb over his flesh. "I love you, too, Raff. I love you, too."

This time when she said the words, they didn't just bring her excitement for their future, anticipation for their future *nights* together.

They brought her peace.

So much peace.

The End

I hope you'll join me next year for *The Accidental Witch* and *The Accidental Ghost*! Until then, have a wonderful holiday season!

STAGE FRIGHT

Stage Fright

Book 1

"Know what this room needs, Fab?"

My best friend since first grade, Fabiola Fabrizio, lifted a meticulously manicured eyebrow in question. She stared down at me while I lie on the floor of the house I'd just finished staging for her, hoping it would help stretch my leg and hip.

According to what I'd read on the Internet, it aided in easing the stabbing pain of my most recent affliction—bursitis.

Toad's spit, bursitis hurts. The doctor who gave me a cortisone shot with a syringe the size of the Space Needle says it often happens to people who sit at a computer all day. While those days are now officially gone for me, the suck of my soul from my very core as an HR manager who sat at a computer all day is apparently on an extended stay and continues to haunt me.

"I don't know what the room needs, but I know what *you* need. You need a physical therapist. I know a super cute one, by the way. Cute in a seventy-year-old way, if you don't mind dentures and some liver spots. But everyone says he looks sixty," Fab assured me with a wink, her thick lashes sweeping her cheek. "Sold him a house down on Old Bluff Road—twelve hundred square feet of oceanfront cottage. Beyond cute."

I looked up into her midnight-dark eyes set in an olive complexion that never appeared to age. "When you say *cottage*, Fabiola Fabrizio, that's code amongst you real estate agents for fixer-upper shack, right? Meaning, the price is outrageous for a house with dirt floors and the only real bennie is the ocean view?"

Fab curtsied, lifting her unlined red lips in a coy smile. "Sure, it needs a little work, maybe some updates, but Gerard knew what he was getting into when I sold it to him. I was Honest Abe about it. Plus, he has plenty of money to spare. What else does he have to do but put it to good use for renovations?"

I sat up on my elbows and shook my head at how disappointing the housing market was here. "Buying a house here in Massachusetts means you either have to be a millionaire or willing to roll up your sleeves and put in some elbow grease. So by updates, you mean the poor man's cooking over an open fire in the backyard because the kitchen is nothing but two by fours and some studs?"

Fab put her hands on her hips. "If you must know, it's a Bunsen burner in the guest bedroom, Smart Girl, but you'd be amazed what you can cook on a Bunsen burner if you're hungry and motivated. Just ask Gerard."

She wrinkled her nose at me, but she was still smiling like the cat who ate the canary as she checked her glossy dark hair in the gold oblong mirror in the entryway.

I laughed out loud with a snort and a shake of my head. Honestly, my BFF could sell breast implants at a dental convention. She was an amazingly good real estate agent and an even better house flipper. Both of which she'd turned into a profitable business all on her own.

In fact, she's who'd convinced me to come back to our hometown of Buttermilk Bay. Not far from Salem, for those who are curious.

Anyway, if she'd conned someone into buying the "cottage" on Old Bluff, she'd done it using all the tools in her arsenal and her intense charm, because it was the very definition of a dive. An expensive dive, because everything on the ocean here in BB was over-priced, but still a dive.

"It's beachfront, Evan. It wouldn't matter if it was a pup tent. It's *on the beach*. That's real estate one-o-one. Have I taught you nothing?"

Since I'd moved back to Buttermilk Bay from Boston at the behest of my dearest friend, in order to start the next chapter of my life staging houses, I'd learned a lot about the whys and wherefores of real estate and house flipping.

One—beachfront property could have a house made of sticks on it with pine needles for a roof and someone would buy it.

Two: location, location, location.

I ran my hand over the faux vintage-inspired area rug, smoothing out the wrinkles, repeating the very words I'd just thought.

"You've taught me that you could sell dentures at a breast implant convention and that every night when I get into bed, I'm beyond grateful you've included me in your selling spree. I'm happy just to ride your coattails."

Fab had always been the more adventurous of the two of us, so when she'd taken on the project of revitalizing Buttermilk Bay, our small, maybe even antiquated town, to bring in more commerce and young families, she'd gleefully accepted the challenge and invited me along for the ride with this whacky scheme of staging houses.

Of course, I was sort of at loose ends when she asked, for reasons I'm not sure I'm quite yet ready to reflect upon out loud.

Let's just say, I lost my HR job of twenty-two years,

two months and eight days and leave it at that for now, shall we?

Anyway, Fab had always loved Buttermilk Bay, and she'd proven that by coming home after college and planting roots, while I left and stayed left.

Er, stayed *gone*—in Boston, that is, until only last year. Which I suppose should make me the more adventurous one, seeing as I left home and went to a strange new city to live.

But the difference is, I'd chosen a safe HR position, eventually becoming a director while still sucking the soul from my very core, and Fab had struck out on her own, doing what she loved. First selling houses and starting her own real estate business, and then ten years ago, flipping houses.

As far as I was concerned, being self-employed was scary AF, as the kids say these days, and far more adventurous than I'd ever been, but Fab had excelled.

And I hoped to follow in her footsteps, now that I'd started Stage Right.

Which, by the by, was the very definition of scary AF.

"Hey," she said on a tinkly giggle, settling on her haunches in front of me in heels, no less—a position I fervently envied, mind you. "You're not riding anything. You're starting a new chapter in your life with a little help from your best friend. You're writing a new beginning. It's called *Over Fifty and Stinkin'*

Amazing, by Evanora Lavinia Dark: A Guide to Living Life Your Own Way After Almost Dying."

It's true. At fifty, I'd almost died.

Chuckling, I responded, "That's a pretty long title. Don't they say titles shouldn't be longer than five words?"

She shook her dark head at me, the curtain of her thick black hair swishing against her official navy-blue real estate blazer as she rose on graceful legs. "Not when you're over fifty. When you're over fifty, you can have whatever-length title you want. It says so in the *Over Fifty Guide to Living Your Life Free of the Chains that Bind.*"

"I think you'd better not apply for any publishing jobs," I teased, holding my hand out to her.

She grabbed it and helped yank me upward, pulling me into a hug. "Have I told you how happy I am you're here and that I no longer have to have girls' night margaritas over Skype while I'm in my sweats and a baggy T-shirt?"

I hugged her back, just as happy to be here, believe you me. "I've been back for almost a year, Fab. You've told me that often."

She gripped my shoulders with her perfectly manicured hands and squeezed. "I think we've both learned, we can never say it enough because you just never know." Then she pulled me into another tight hug. "Don't ever do that to me again, Evan," she whispered, her tone fierce. "Not ever."

I leaned back in her hug and shot her a teasing smile. "You mean have a stroke followed by a heart attack, a quadruple bypass and a carotid artery clean out just before boarding a plane to my dream vacation in Hawaii?"

Her lips thinned and her velvety dark eyes narrowed. "Still too soon, BFF. You almost died, Evan. *Died*. You almost kicked the bucket and left me here all alone with nothing but the wolves at the door."

I threw the back of my hand up over my forehead, my tone light and teasing when I said, "The wolves? Drama be thy middle name." Then I sobered. "Listen, if I can laugh about it, why can't you?"

Her eyes grew watery. "Because you didn't see you hooked up to more machines than a machinist's shop holds, while tubes came out of every orifice on your person and you were a lovely shade of chalk white. That's why. It was three weeks of sheer terror I choose to take very seriously, even if you won't."

I hated that I'd frightened everyone. Hated that they'd been inconvenienced because I'd worked myself almost to death. It was my fault.

Back then, I hardly ever ate more than one meal a day and that had usually been on the fly. I fueled myself with not much more than coffee and Twizzlers. I worked long hours and hadn't had a vacation since my son left the nest—which was why I was going to Hawaii. Because I needed a break.

I dabbed at her eye with my thumb. "Stop or you'll

323

ruin your perfect makeup. I'm sorry, okay? I know it was a scary time for everyone who wasn't flat on their backs, higher than a kite on pain meds. I'm sorry I put you all through that, but it's been almost three years, Fab. Time to let go."

I can't tell you how grateful I was for the people in my life. My father, Fab and her mother, Mama Fab, my son Callum. They'd all sat vigil after my surgery while I healed, and I was grateful, but I was also about moving forward.

She pointed to the jagged scar between my not-so perky breasts, still ugly and a little pink. "Tell Mama that, would you? She hassles me every time I tell her you're staging a house for me. She thinks I work you too hard."

Fab's mother was like a mother to me, too. She'd welcomed me to the fold from the very first day my best friend had brought me home to her house for a snack (which had turned into a four-course meal, as it always does with anyone Italian) and I'd been part of the Fabrizio clan ever since.

I vehemently shook my head. "Nuh-uh. If I do that, she won't bring me any more Tagliatelle Al Ragu. No dice. I love you, but not enough to sacrifice my pasta."

Now she laughed, her giggle returning to its light, airy tone. "All I'm saying is, I'm glad you're back home where you belong and that you've decided to do what you were meant to do *and* that you're doing it with me."

324

I squeezed her hand and nodded. "I'm glad, too."

I looked around at the cute three-bedroom, two-bath house Fab had so painstakingly, beautifully flipped and I'd only just finished staging to prepare for sale, and smiled.

Decorating was my jam—it's always been my passion. Throw pillows and rugs, candles and vases, fill my soul like almost nothing else. Other than my son, Callum, that is.

I won't deny I love pretty things. I'm an aesthetics girl through and through. It doesn't have to cost the earth, but if it makes me smile, I've probably given in to it and purchased it.

Often, it was my solace when I was stressed from work. I don't have a degree in design, no formal training or fancy internships under designers. Only my love of a good bargain and the joy of making a home feel cozy and well-loved.

Now it's my livelihood, and things were going pretty darn good thanks to the work Fabiola threw my way, along with the recommendations she'd given other house flippers and fellow agents looking to spruce up a home to ready for sale.

I hoped to rent an office if things kept moving the way they were instead of working out of my renovated mobile home. I'd sort of appropriated it from my deceased father (I have two dads) and called it my own.

When I first moved back, I invested my substantial

severance and savings into Stage Right rather than buy a house—which, like I said, costs a bloody fortune here in Buttermilk Bay.

That left little to buy a stick-built home if I planned to eat and pay my bills, should things go belly up with a new business. I hoped to have a long life now that I had a patched-up heart. My savings and hush money were good, but they weren't forever good if I didn't live modestly.

So I lay claim to my deceased father's mobile home, already bought and paid for, in the sweet little mobile home park where he'd once stashed his treasures (more on that later). Completely renovated it and made it my tiny two-bedroom two-bathroom palace with a free-standing tub overlooking the ocean.

Wildflower Meadows by the Sea was an adorable little over-fifty-five park, nestled in a tree-lined burg, and nothing like what comes to mind when you think "mobile home."

There are no meth-heads or people who sell guns for the cartel, housed in rusty metal boxes smelling of cigarette smoke and stale beer. Well, unless you count Fergus McGee. I mean, he doesn't smoke meth. No-no. He does, however, smell like stale beer and that's only due to his ale choices—they all stink, mostly because he's always trying some new craft brew he made to save a buck and keep "the man" from getting his tax dollars.

But for the most part, Wildflower Meadows by the

Sea is nestled on a sweet patch of winding roads with a decent amount of space between mobile homes that feature backyards, landscaped common areas filled with flowers in the spring and summer, and lots and lots of retired folks over seventy.

Making me one of the youngest residents, but welcomed by proxy due to my father's gregarious nature.

I'd never have expected to find my cultured, well-groomed, maybe even a little snobby father had a mobile home, but if he had to have one, this cute little '90s Redman suited him.

Anyhow, that's how I started Stage Right. Saving on the purchase of a house gave me the money for an enormous storage unit and plenty of shopping finds. Gosh, that had been a blast, buying inventory for various staging projects. Lots of antique road trips with Fab, and sometimes Mama Fab, too.

"Hey," Fab said with a nudge and a look of concern. "Where are you?"

I waved her off and smiled, stretching my tired arms. "I was just thinking about how good it is to be home. Now, lemme give the place one more sweep to be sure everything's perfect for the photographer and we'll go grab some dinner, 'kay?"

Fab brushed lint from the rug off my black T-shirt. "Done."

I gave the open-concept living room and kitchen one last look, satisfied with the flow of muted colors and continuity of my European farmhouse theme. It was a personal favorite of mine to style. Lots of neutral shades of taupe, cream and some charcoal black thrown in.

I grabbed my purse, sitting on the distressed wood table beneath a whitewashed wood chandelier. I checked the thick black chain securing it to the ceiling to be sure it was sturdy.

"What do you feel like eating tonight?"

She checked her lipstick in the mirror and winked. "German?"

"Because of Jorge or because you love sauerkraut and schnitzel?"

Jorge Durchenwald had recently moved to Buttermilk Bay and opened a delightful German café called Schnitzel Haus, and it was an enormous hit. Not only with the locals, but with my gorgeous friend, Fabiola.

She giggled and slung her purse over her shoulder. "Because *muscles* and sauerkraut. Sooo many muscles." As she made her way to the black Dutch door, she peered over her shoulder at me. "Wait. We got to gabbing about everything but the original subject. Before we go indulge in sauerbraten and spätzle, what does this place need?"

I tilted my head, a little distracted for some reason. "Huh?"

"You said this place needed something."

I looked around at the serene setting, inhaling the

scent of new house. "Oh, right! Glad you reminded me. Whimsy. It needs whimsy."

"Whimsy," she repeated, deadpan, her olive skin glowing beneath the setting sun of early fall.

Fab gave me that look often. She didn't share my love of decorating. She was just as happy with nothing more than a boring beige couch and an ugly sherpa blanket to keep her warm while she binged on Netflix.

Nodding, I ran to the last big red tote left to be packed up in my old Chevy truck marked "throws" and pulled out a black and cream-colored blanket with fringed edges.

I held it up and sighed a happy sigh. "Duh. What have I always told you about staging?"

She rolled her eyes, and teased, "You want clients to imagine themselves curled up on a couch with a blanket and a book in front of a roaring fire, and that means adding whimsical items. Blah, blah, blah. I'd mock you, but apparently it sells houses and who am I to rain on this cash parade?"

"Exactly, Grasshopper." I grinned, splaying the blanket over the edge of the white slipcovered couch, letting its bottom half fall gracefully to the floor. I brushed my hands together. "Perfect. Now, let's go find Jorge and all his muscles."

"Are you Evanora Lavinia Dark?" a meek voice asked.

I fought a groan.

No. Not now. I closed my eyes and inhaled,

clenching my fists in the hope it would go away. I'd had a long day and it was a miracle I was getting out of here before midnight, let alone dinner.

I didn't want to deal with this today.

Not that I mind, let's be clear. But I'm starving.

Someone cleared their throat and repeated with a bit more authority in their tone, "I repeat, are you Evanora Lavinia Dark?"

My shoulders sagged as I turned in the direction of the voice.

And there it was. Plain as the day is long, sitting on the chunky wood mantel above the white and gray fieldstone fireplace I'd personally distressed and stained.

A ghost.

"Well?" he asked, his deep chocolate eyes piercing mine. "Are you?"

Crap.

Crap, crap, crappity, crap.

Okay, so here's the scoop. My name is Evanora Lavinia Dark and I'm a witch. Not a broom-riding, cauldron-bubbling, Halloween-*Hocus-Pocus*, cast-wicked-spells witch. I'm not even really a Wiccan witch.

Alas, I'm Wimpy Witch. I'm a weak one at best. But if we have to compare, I'm more *Practical Magic* witch.

I am, however, what some old schoolers call a kitchen witch.

You know, an herbs-and-essential-oils, creates-mild-magic witch? Emphasis on *mild*.

My mom was the real-deal witch, according to my father. Spells, potions, making things disappear. She was that kind of witch.

I allegedly inherited some power from my mother's side of the family, all of whom are almost always unavailable for comment on my heritage and how exactly it affects me.

Except for my great aunt Tuppence, but we haven't heard from her since dad number one died.

Either way, my magic is—or was—mild to say the least. I could whip up home remedies, a potion, healing oils (though, I sure hadn't figured out how to help my bursitis) every now and again, etcetera.

Then all that changed. Big time.

After my open-heart surgery, I became a kitchen-slash-talk-to-ghosts-I-can-see-as-clear-as-day-and-who-need-me-to-solve-a-crime witch.

Or what some in my circles might call a hedge witch.

Again, I'm Evanora Lavinia Dark.

A witch.

A tired (though happily so), over-fifty (okay, fifty-three), house-staging, bursitis-riddled, ghost-seeing, crime-solving *witch*.

Pleasure to meet you.

Stage Fright

ABOUT THE AUTHOR

Dakota Cassidy is a USA Today bestselling author with over almost one-hundred books. She writes laugh-out-loud cozy mysteries, romantic comedy, grab-some-ice erotic romance, hot and sexy alpha males, paranormal shifters, contemporary kick-ass women, and more.

Dakota lives in Texas with her real-life hero and her dogs, and she loves hearing from readers!

Join my newsletter: **The Tiara Diaries**

https://www.dakotacassidy.com/contact.html

Facebook

https://www.facebook.com/DakotaCassidyFan Page

ALSO BY DAKOTA CASSIDY

Visit Dakota's website at http://www.
dakotacassidy.com for more information.

9. Witches Get Stitches

10. Witch it Real Good

11. Witch Perfect

12. Gettin' Witched

13. Where There's a With, There's a Way

14. A Total Witch Show

15. Just Witched

Marshmallow Hollow Cozy Christmas Mysteries

1. Jingle All the Slay

2. Have Yourself a Merry Little Witness

3. One Corpse Open Slay

4. Carnage in a Pear Tree

Bewitching Midlife Crisis Mysteries (Paranormal Women's Fiction)

1. Stage Fright

2. Bohemian Tragedy

3. Exit Stage Death

Nun of Your Business Mysteries, a Paranormal Cozy Mystery series

1. Then There Were Nun

2. Hit and Nun

3. House of the Rising Nun

4. The Smoking Nun

5. What a Nunderful World

Wolf Mates, a Paranormal Romantic Comedy series

1. An American Werewolf In Hoboken

2. What's New, Pussycat?

3. Gotta Have Faith

4. Moves Like Jagger

5. Bad Case of Loving You

A Paris, Texas Romance, a Paranormal Romantic Comedy series

1. Witched At Birth

2. What Not to Were

3. Witch Is the New Black

4. White Witchmas

Non-Series

Whose Bride Is She Anyway?

Polanski Brothers: Home of Eternal Rest

Sexy Lips 66

Accidentally Paranormal Novel, a Paranormal Romantic Comedy series (published with Berkley Sensation)

1. The Accidental Werewolf

2. Accidentally Dead

3. The Accidental Human

4. Accidentally Demonic

5. Accidentally Catty

6. Accidentally Dead, Again

7. The Accidental Genie

8. The Accidental Werewolf 2: Something About Harry

9. The Accidental Dragon

The Accidentals, a Paranormal Romantic Comedy Series (self-published)

1. Accidentally Aphrodite

2. Accidentally Ever After